THE SPANISH COVE

ALSO BY CHERRY RADFORD

The Spanish House
The Spanish Garden
The Spanish Cove

THE SPANISH COVE

Cherry Radford

An Aria Book

First published in the UK in 2022 by Head of Zeus Ltd,
part of Bloomsbury Publishing Plc

9 7 5 3 1 2 4 6 8

A catalogue record for this book is available from the British Library.

ISBN (PB): 9781803283890
ISBN (E): 9781803283883

Cover design: Leah Jacobs-Gordon

Typeset by Siliconchips Services Ltd UK

Printed and bound in Great Britain by
CPI Group (UK) Ltd, Croydon CR0 4YY

Head of Zeus Ltd
First Floor East
5–8 Hardwick Street
London EC1R 4RG

WWW.HEADOFZEUS.COM

Music Playlist

Create a free Spotify account and listen to some of the music in *The Spanish Cove*.

Chapter 1

'Aqua Marina' (from 'Stingray') – Barry Gray, Gary Miller (Barry Gray)

'Father and Daughter' – Paul Simon (Paul Simon)

'You're My Number One' – S Club 7 (Mike Rose, Nick Foster)

'Rock the Boat' – Hues Corporation (Waldo Holmes)

Chapter 5

'Me Maten' – C. Tangana, Antonio Carmona (Alizzz, Antonio Carmona, Antón Álvarez, Cristian Quirante Catalán, Víctor Martínez)

'Rebelde' – Beatriz Luengo, Omar Montes, Yotuel (Beatriz Luengo, Manuel Alvarez Beigbeder, Omar Montes, Ramón Velasco Jiménez, Yotuel Romero)

'10 Years' – Daði Freyr & Gagnamagnið (Daði Freyr)

'Leave the Door Open' – Bruno Mars, Anderson Paak, Silk Sonic (Brandon Anderson, Bruno Mars, Christopher Brody Brown, Dernst Emile II)

Chapter 6

'You'll Be in My Heart' from *Tarzan* – Phil Collins (Phil Collins)

Chapter 7

'Shining' – Steel Pulse (Alphonso Martin)
'Find Me in Your Dreams' – Estrella Morente, Santiago Lara (Enrique Morente, Pat Metheny)

Chapter 9

'Agustito' – Ketama (Antonio Carmona, Juan Carmona, Josemi Carmona)

Chapter 10

'The Water is Wide' – Eva Cassidy (folk song of Scottish origin)

Chapter 11

'Kiss Me More' – Doja Cat, SZA (Rogét Chahayed, Amala Ratna Zandile Dlamini, Carter Lang, David Sprecher, Gerard Powell, Lukasz Gottwald, Solána Imani Rowe, Stephen Kipner, Terry Shaddick)

'Mencanta' – Antonio Carmona, Juan Carmona Jr. (Antonio Carmona, Juan Carmona Jr.)

Chapter 16

'Adagio Flamenco' (Aire de la Cueva) – José María Gallardo del Rey, Miguel Ángel Cortés (José María Gallardo del Rey, Miguel Ángel Cortés)

Chapter 18

'Orange Coffee'–Rocketman (Panithan Chaiarksornwec) 'Volver' – Estrella Morente (Carlos Gardel, Alfredo Le Pera)

Chapter 20

'Duende del Sur' – Chambao (Gipsy Kings, J.A. Peña, María del Mar Rodríguez, R. Blades)

Chapter 21

'Midnight in Harlem' – Tedeschi Trucks Band (Derek Trucks, Mike Mattison)

Chapter 22

'She' – Elvis Costello, Geoffrey Alexander, London Symphony Orchestra (Charles Aznavour, Herbert Kretzmer)
'Remember Me' (from 'Coco') – Miguel, Natalia Lafourcade (Kristen Anderson-Lopez, Robert Lopez)

I

San José, Almería, Spain

There she is. Bobbing and clapping on the water, as if she can't wait to get out from between the bigger boats either side of her. As keen for an adventure as she and Daddy are. So pretty with her repainted blue stripe, blue like the colour of the water in Cala Turquesa. Would they go there today, wave to Mummy and Ted on the terrace of the house, or would they go to the beaches in the other direction?

La Mari. A short Spanish version of her own name, Marina, but with the 'The' before it, as used for special ladies, like flamenco dancers. Next time they buy a boat, Daddy said once, they will have to include her brother Ted's name in it. But that's far, far away in the future, when Teddy isn't six but grown up – and maybe even less excited about boats than he is now.

Or maybe there will never be another boat. What? That isn't possible. Boats eventually die, like people, don't they?

5

So the only way there won't be another boat is... if *they* die, first.

Oh no. Here she goes again. Why has she started getting these dark thoughts that pull her aside and make her... sort of melty, like she has to touch something solid and squeeze it to bring her back to the world? If this is what growing up is, now she's turned ten, she needs to slow it down.

She holds on to the lamp post on the dock and watches Daddy chatting to Diego the smiley port man, while Daddy carries on the fuel can, icebox, the zippy black folder thing with his boat licence in it. Of course, at work back in Eastbourne, somebody else probably puts these on the boat (but maybe they don't bring an icebox), while he's putting on his yellow lifeboat clothes so he can drive out to people in trouble in the sea and save them. Or *try* to save them. She needs to talk to Daddy about the dying. Apart from Gertie next door's cat, she doesn't know anyone who's dead – but Daddy does. Not just the poor people who drowned, but his parents. How do you live with dying?

He grins at her. 'All right, Marina-Fish? You look like maybe you had one too many of those chocolate croissants this morning!'

She smiles back at him. Marina-Fish: better than the 'Fish Face' she gets at school. Daddy has promised that she'll grow into her googly eyes and big lips, like he did – and look at him now, Spanish ladies in the boat opposite watching her goldy-handsome Dutch Daddy with their mouths open. 'No, no, I gave the second croissant to Teddy. I'm fine!'

That's it, she's fine, the happiest ever, with lots and lots more lovely holiday days here before going back to school, and lots more boat trips – with Mummy and Teddy, when they're not riding, painting or at kids' club, but also more with just Daddy.

He's talking with Diego again, something with *seis* (six), *mar* (sea) and *tiempo* (weather) in it, but she doesn't know the words that are sticking them together. She waits for a gap in the ricky-ticky-tado language she so wants to learn.

'Daddy? Did you remember the CD?'

'Well of course! And specially updated – as you'll soon find out,' he says with a wink.

'Great!' She takes off her pink cap and loosens the overtight plaited ponytail Mummy did. Why can't Mummy leave her hair just flat and straight? Or cut it messy-short, so she looks even more like Daddy.

Daddy looks over at the car park. 'Er... Mummy might still be over there and see you take that off...' He takes her backpack off and puts the cap in it. 'At least don't lose it.' He steps back onto the boat. 'All aboard then!' He grips her hand and her shoulder as she comes on, even though she's never even nearly fallen off. The world then turns orange as he puts the life jacket over her head. She groans as he ties it tightly.

'Marinita! You want to sit on *La Mari*'s nose, later?'

'Yes.'

'Well then.'

She bustles down into the cabin, which Mummy says is much too small but she's wrong, it's just perfect. She gets a blue hand-wash bottle out of the tiny cupboard above the loo and puts it in the ring next to the teensy basin. Opens her backpack and puts *The Island of Adventure* on the wooden bit next to the half-of-a-V bed. Gets a pillow out of the locker and puts Mog Cat on it; the sea doesn't look too wavy, so she won't fall off. All cosy and ready for her siesta after lunch.

She goes back up on deck just as Diego throws Daddy the rope and they're saying *hasta luego*. Daddy yanks the string to make the engine start, and off they go, put-put out of the harbour, past the super-awesome Guardia Civil police boat with its big green pointy nose and red-yellow-red Spanish stripe, past the stumpy red and green lighthouses on the rocks either side of the entrance, and out into the sea.

It's still early. There aren't many people on the sandy curve of the San José bay.

'Which beach?' he asks her above the engine. There was about an hour-long string of them, all different, all lovely and soft, and some you could only get to by boat.

'Um… I can't decide!'

'Okay, we'll go as far as the lighthouse and then come back and moor up in an empty one.'

'*Estupendo!*' she yells, which sounds like stupid but means fantastic.

They were coming out of the bay now, round the rocky mountain, the water a deep dark blue with a sparkly surface. He turns to her from the wheel, flicks his head towards the padded seat next to him to make her sit down. 'Ready?'

She sits down. 'Ready!'

The engine roars and they yelp with delight as they go hurtling out towards Africa at full speed. This is the point at which Mummy does a flappy hand asking him to slow down, and Teddy holds on to Mummy and closes his eyes to make it all go away. It was best to make trips with them slow, short, and with at least one boring eating and shopping stop to keep them happy, but Daddy is sometimes naughty about this.

They come back towards the shore to start looking at the beaches. Daddy puts the music on. He laughs as the 'Aqua Marina' song – about the dumb mermaid from the TV *Stingray* puppets – blasts out.

'Oh no, how come that gets on there every year?'

'I like it!' He laughs and fast-forwards to the song the father sings to the daughter in *The Wild Thornberrys*, which has also come back for yet another year. It's nice, it's soothing... and sort of about them.

She folds her arms patiently as he sings along to it.

'Okay, I'll stop teasing...' he says, and makes the machine jump to the next track, turning up the volume. The opening drums of S Club 7's 'You're My Number One' fill the air.

'*Yes!*' She's up and dancing to it, soon singing at the top of her voice. Dad joins in at the chorus with all the right words – he's heard it that many times at home. The song is about Daddy, *La Mari*, this hottest lowest edge of Spain, everything.

'I'm off to her nose,' she says, getting up and starting to go round the side.

He slows a bit and tells her to hang on to the rail.

'*Course* I am!'

She can feel his eyes on her as she sits down with her legs over the front of the boat, under the net thing added to the rail. This year, she'll not bother asking when that can be taken off. She hangs her head over and watches *La Mari* cutting through the water with a hiss, the wind throwing a cooling spray over her. 'Heaven!' she calls back, above

S Club now singing about a *fiesta* party, as if they know they're in Spain today.

Daddy starts testing her on the names of the beaches. Genoveses, with a 'gh' sound that hurts your throat. Mónsul, with its mountainous soft sand dune and its big volcano rock that looks like a wave that turned to stone... Soon they're going past the smaller beaches, with cute names like 'Chico' (Kid) and Media Luna (Half-Moon), with Marina shouting 'ooh, *that* one!' nearly every time.

She waves to the lighthouse sitting on top of the mountain, as Daddy turns *La Mari* round... and then she waves again, because the super-awesome Guardia Civil boat is slicing its way towards them, and then passing them, the matching green policemen on board waving to Daddy, because maybe they know he also saves people on the sea.

La Mari rocks and bumps excitedly over the waves the big boy boat makes.

'He-he, I think *La Mari* has a crush on him, don't you?' she calls back to Daddy.

'Oh yes, definitely!'

On comes the 'Rock the Boat' song, which is a really, really old song, even for Daddy, but they both love it and join in.

Then Daddy moves the boat nearer to the coast, turns off the music and reduces speed – so they can hear the quietness of the coves, the birds sighing with the heat, the tumble of little waves on the sand. They come to a deserted beach they've sat on before. Marina turns, they exchange a nod, and Daddy turns off the engine and throws the anchor.

They take their T-shirts off and go down the ladder, swim to the shore. It's a tiny cove of a few baby palms, soft sand,

and pretty grey, white, yellow and orange stones. Above them, tall grey cliffs seem to have provided a village for birds.

She picks out some special stones for her collection and sits down on the sand to watch Daddy dive off some rocks at the edge. He comes up with his hair the colour of the wet sand. He says he was a fish in his last life. Maybe she was too – it would certainly explain her eyes. She runs into the water again, swims with him like a baby dolphin, then gets him to let her jump off his shoulders, asking him to fling her higher and higher into the air.

Then they both start thinking about what's in the icebox, and clamber back on board for the Coca-Cola and crisps Mummy doesn't usually allow; the mixed-up jam and cheese sandwiches (Daddy is 'chaos in the kitchen', Mummy says); juicy tomatoes that always explode; and *bizcocho*, which is Spanish for cake without icing, but it's too hot here for icing, so it doesn't matter.

'Okay, siesta time for you,' Daddy says.

She groans.

'We promised Mummy.'

'She won't know.'

'She will if you're grumpy at tonight's special restaurant. Come on.'

They go down into the cabin. Marina changes out of her wet bikini, puts on knickers and the soft thin turquoise dress from the market, and lies down with Mog under her arm.

She sighs. 'Why can't we just *live* in Spain? I don't want to go back, ever.'

He smiles. 'Well, who knows? Maybe when Mummy and

I are old. But meanwhile, what about your piano lessons? That's something to look forward to, isn't it? All those new Grade Three pieces!'

'I s'pose.'

'You've caught up with as far as I got. Maybe I'll ask Mrs Haynes if she'd take on a rusty adult.'

'Ooh, I'm sure she would!'

'Tell you what, there'll be a music shop in Almería that sells little electric pianos. Maybe we should get one for the house here, so you and I can practise when we're here in summer and at Easter. How does that sound?'

'Completely *estupendo!*' Marina says, kicking her legs. 'Can we go tomorrow?'

'We'll see. Anyway, time for your siesta now.' He picks up the book, lies down next to her.

She puts her head on his chest, which goes up and down like the swell of the sea.

'I'll read a few pages of this... ooh look, they've got a boat.'

'Of course. They always do. And a tent. All on their own.'

'A-ha.' He reads until the end of the chapter, the sound of the sea gently slapping against the boat being just right for the story. Daddy will probably take *La Mari* further out and do a bit of snorkelling where the bottom of the sea has grass like an underground field. Sure enough, he goes up the steps, pulls up the anchor and sets off, knowing the chug-chug of the engine will send her off...

She dreams they're sailing right round the edge of Spain, even though, when she wakes, she remembers Spain is stuck to France on one side. She opens her eyes. Mummy was right about the Coca-Cola, or the peeing part anyway. She gets up and uses the loo and the blue hand wash.

Even putting her head from side to side, she can't spot Daddy through the slats of the doors. Maybe he's snorkelling. It's very hot in here; there's no way she can go back to sleep. She goes up and opens the doors, enjoys the refreshing breeze, looks at the shore, which looks a slightly scary long way away. Daddy's not snorkelling here, he must be round the other…

'Oh!' she gasps. Another boat, right next to *La Mari*. About the same size, but all deck with just a little hut in the middle. Like a fishing boat.

There are voices.

'Daddy?' she croaks. 'Daddy!' Where is he?

Daddy appears out of the other boat's hut, with someone behind him. 'Marina,' he says, smiling but looking sort of… surprised.

'I woke up,' she says.

Now she can see that the other person has a plaited ponytail like hers – and is smiling at her, even if rather sadly. The woman says, '*Hola, guapita*,' which means something like 'Hello, sweetie'.

She smiles back in relief. Not a pirate then. But why are the boats tied together?

'Try and get a little more sleep, darling,' Daddy says. 'I'll come and start the boat in a minute, and you'll soon nod off again.'

She looks from one to the other. 'Okay.'

She goes back down into the cabin and lies down, pulling Mog to her. Who was the woman? She looked a bit familiar.

Maybe that's why Daddy didn't say who she was. Anyway, she hopes she'll go soon; they've obviously spotted each other and said hello, maybe she was showing him something on her boat, but now it's time for the woman to leave and let her and Daddy enjoy the rest of their afternoon together. Well, once she's got a bit more sleep done. She closes her eyes, puts the tip of her thumb in her mouth, even though she's supposed to have grown out of that.

Then the woman screams.

Marina jumps up and rushes up to the deck. Did the boats hit? She thought she heard something. But the boats have those padded things that—

Daddy's in the sea. In the gap.

'Daddy!'

The woman is leaning over the side of her boat, shouting madly.

'Daddy! Are you—'

'I'm fine, *no pasa nada!*' he says to them both with a wave and a smile, after touching his head like he can't believe he's done this.

He comes up the ladder and back on board, but not with his usual fish-jumping-out-of-the-water movement. He pats the pocket in his swim shorts, takes out his phone, looks at it and says a bad word. His T-shirt is wet and stuck on him. He didn't jump into the water, he *fell*. *Daddy fell into the water*. Like he's always worried *she* will. She looks over at the woman, who is jabbering away with her hand on her heart.

Daddy says he's fine, again, and a third time. 'You see how careful you... have to be?' he says to Marina.

She nods uncertainly. It looks like he also lost his

sunglasses, and one of his eyes seems to have gone all dark to make up for it. And he might be fine, but… he's sat down heavily on the seat that's *her* seat and knocked her special stones off it.

He and the woman are saying goodbye. The woman looks like she wants to stay but has to go. Or maybe Daddy told her to go. She starts her engine, waves and leaves, *La Mari* rocking in her wake.

Now Daddy's forehead is crinkled like he's hurting, and he puts a hand to his head again. There's a big lump above his ear, she now sees.

'You bumped your head! Poor Daddy! What can I do for it? Shall I get the red medicine box?'

He squeezes his eyes shut, then opens them and looks out to sea. 'No. But we have to get back.'

'Oh. Okay.'

He hauls himself up, stumbles towards the engine and pulls the string. But his strong arm isn't strong anymore; it doesn't seem to want to pull or do anything. He tries with the other, but it's not working.

'Is it broken?' she asks.

He doesn't answer. He's holding on to a rail, fiddling with the radio and shouting Spanish at it as if he's cross with it.

'Will someone come and mend it?'

He nods. 'S'okay, my Aqua Marina.' Then he tries to sit down in his seat, but misses it and stumbles to the deck, managing to lean against the cabin. 'Come here,' he says, waving a hand towards himself. Then he smiles for a moment, looking more like Daddy.

She crouches down next to him. 'What shall I do?'

'You can promise. You don' tell anyone…' He's sounding

out of breath. 'Specially Mummy... about the lady, or the other boat. So they don't blame her. She's good person. Un'stand?'

'Yes.'

'Promise?'

'Yes, I promise.'

'S'important to me, baby.' He takes her arm. 'And listen. If I'm... sleeping, and nobody's come, you do Mayday... radio. Like I've shown you. Channel sixteen.'

'Okay, but...' Isn't that for sinking boats? Maybe also for those without a captain. 'But wait, the lady...'

She jumps up and over to the side, shouting at the woman's boat to come back and help them, but the woman is too far away to hear, and the shouting makes Daddy groan.

When she comes back, he's disappeared... down onto the deck. But not lying like when they lie down flat on the deck to watch the stars together. More like a broken doll, one arm strangely squished underneath him. She rushes over and kneels next to him, puts her face near his. His eyes are nearly closed. 'Poor Daddy. But the Guardia will be here soon, whizz you to the hospital and make you better. Does it hurt a lot?'

His lips move but nothing comes out. He lifts his hand. She puts hers in it. Daddy's big warm strong hand. But not so strong now. It drops to his chest but keeps hold of hers. Then his hand gently squeezes. Twice, and then three times. Somehow it says 'A-qua Ma-ri-na' to her, like the dumb song. Like he's trying to tell her she can do it.

'Okay, I'll do it now.'

She goes over to the radio, but as soon as she's there, she

can't think what to do, not with Daddy all like this, her breath starting to catch... She looks at the engine. He let her do it once, just so she could prove she could. She goes over and pulls the string once. Twice. She *has* to do it. She takes a big breath and yanks with all her might, a knife of pain going through her shoulder that makes her see blue and black bits, but yes! *La Mari* is puttering into life, ready to save Daddy.

Before dealing with the gears and setting off, she goes to Daddy and puts her arms round him. 'It's okay, I'll take you back towards the port. I can do it. Even though we both now have only one arm.' A last squeeze, and she'll set off. She puts her head on his chest – but it's no longer going up and down like the swell of the sea.

2

Richmond and Brighton, England

Marina looked out of the window at the almost Mediterranean blue sky above the treetops and the art deco block of flats opposite. This glorious weather was promised for the whole weekend, so it was going to be a lovely day to drive down to Mum and Guido's in Brighton and perfect for tea in Kew Gardens with her friend Polly tomorrow.

She realised she'd not really been listening to the description of her sister-in-law's recent holiday, which was still coming through the phone into her ear. With her other hand, she picked up her hairbrush and vaguely ran it through her long flat hair, then put her car keys by her handbag. She'd sort of switched off when Hannah had started saying how much she and Ted had enjoyed hiring a *boat* to get about on this Greek island.

Once again, she marvelled at how Teddy, for whom she'd

been a second parent for so many years, had somehow sort of overtaken her, in every way: he continued to dazzle academically, now starting his ophthalmology training at apparently the best eye hospital in the world; he was already married, to one of the consultants; co-owned a delightful garden flat in Islington; and was expecting a baby. Now, it appeared, while she hadn't been able to set foot in a boat after what happened, Teddy had moved on, happy to holiday in one and let his wife go on about it to his sister.

Marina had also had a holiday planned – a long weekend in a pretty hotel surrounded by ponies in the New Forest – but that had been cancelled when she'd broken up with Will a couple of months ago. He too had overtaken her; she'd nursed his gentle out-of-work actor depression and anxiety for months, only for him to blossom, get a theatre job and gain the confidence to ask out the girl of his dreams – who also happened to be one of her flatmates.

'That sounds amazing. And how are you feeling now?' Marina asked, to change the subject.

'Oh fine, fine. The nausea's over, thank God.'

'Oh good. Shame you can't come to Mum and Guido's today – I gather Ted's on call. Hannah, I need to go. I've got a piano pupil soon.'

'In the flat, or are they all still on Zoom or whatever?'

'Zoom. I offered the mask option this term, but they've all got used to not having to sit in traffic and find a parking space.'

'They're adults?'

Jesus, how come Hannah could never remember anything she told her about her piano teaching? 'Mostly. This morning, for example, I have a thirteen-year-old from when I used to teach at Oakfield House, a retired nurse in Scotland, and two accountants from the same company in Putney – apparently with a third wanting to start.'

Hannah groaned.

Was that how Hannah felt about her patients? Why was getting up close and examining an oozing eye preferable to helping someone discover the excitement and the healing powers of music? Other than the money, of course.

'They're all *lovely*, actually,' Marina said, followed by a vague 'see you soon.'

She put the phone down and turned it to silent, opened her notebook and Izzy's piano music, sent her the Zoom email and set up the keyboard camera.

They said hello and beamed at each other.

'Hi there, how did the school play go? I'm not expecting masses of practice to have happened!'

'It was great, but...' Her little face fell. 'Grammy died.'

The fun-loving grandmother Izzy clearly adored; Marina's throat tightened as she imagined poor little Izzy's shock and despair. 'Oh, Izzy, I'm so sorry. I know how special she was.'

She nodded, watery-eyed. 'So I didn't really do much. But I was wondering, could we practise the aural tests for the exam next term?'

Marina nodded and made herself smile. 'Just what I was going to suggest. And there's a lovely one for which you'll just be listening to lots of gorgeous little bits of music today. We'll practise telling the difference between major and minor.'

'Oh yes. The happy pieces are in a major key and the sad ones in a minor key?'

'It's not quite as simple as that. Let me show you...' She

played minor key pieces that were dramatically sad, but others that were sprightly, almost humorous. Then pieces in a major key that, with luscious jazzy chords and a slow tempo, pulled every heartstring. 'Can you hear how that was sad, but... in a nostalgic way?'

Izzy looked puzzled. 'What's *nostalgic?*'

'Well... As if you're sad but only because you're remembering special happy times in the past that you can't go back to.'

'Or special *people*,' Izzy said, but no longer with a quiver of the lip.

Marina nodded and managed to say, 'Yes.'

Marina had finished for the morning – and for the term. No teaching for six weeks – and since she wasn't going on holiday, she'd definitely be using the time to find a new flat. Shortly after her special moment with Izzy, housemates and their boyfriends could be heard swearing, laughing, shouting downstairs to someone making breakfast and in one case, for God's sake, moaning with ecstasy. Then it began, the blaring four-square music that she could have used as an example of a piece with no emotion whatsoever. How many times did she have to talk to them about this, hear their apologies and suffer the same thing the following Saturday? There was nothing for it but to see how far out of London she would have to go to be able to rent a place of her own. Polly was wondering the same, and they were going to chat about it tomorrow.

Her phone rang.

'Mum. I'm just leaving.'

'Well, I hope you are, or you'll be late,' Mum said. 'And it's not like we'll have that much time, with the exhibition this evening. I mean, obviously you can come to that, stay the night afterwards if you like, but I don't think it's your kind of thing.'

'No, no, I've got to get back.' Mum never thought the art at their gallery was her kind of thing – or any art at all. That wasn't fair, but the problem was Marina couldn't even enjoy what she *did* like, without Mum – and Ted, if he was there – laughing at her comments on it. Fortunately, her stepfather Guido was more encouraging – perhaps remembering his earlier years in the art world, selling paintings in a scrubby market in London, rather than the smart place he now had in the Brighton Lanes.

Mum told her to drive carefully and was gone.

Marina reached up to unclip the keyboard camera and winced at the sudden pain knifing through her shoulder. Stupid – she should always use the left arm instead. There was nothing more that orthopaedics could do for her; the surgery had made little difference, so she would just have to live with it. She closed her eyes and used her other hand to push her shoulder backwards, which sometimes helped. Waiting while her heart slowed back down, she came away as quickly as she could from the memory of that moment on the boat when she'd started the engine and caused this...

She distracted herself with thoughts of a relaxing little flat on her own. Maybe in one of those villages near Haywards Heath – or further down, with coastal fresh air, but still close enough to be able to get up to London for a concert. Maybe she could take a mini holiday somewhere like Shoreham for a few days, to look around. Have some peace and quiet, but also a little adventure.

Marina looked out of the Victorian balcony windows at the Brighton sea – which was a sickly green, even on a day like this. It must be, what, two years since she'd seen a *blue* sea – in Valencia, on a long weekend with Polly. Before that, there'd been the Minorca Disaster with Ian, the English teacher at Oakfield House, whose phone had kindly flashed up a very spicy WhatsApp from the married history teacher. Before that, there'd been the GCSE Spanish trip to Barcelona, but she must have been still not quite all there because she couldn't remember anything about that. Then before that – well, there'd been the ultimate blue of the sea at Cala Turquesa...

So much for the importance of getting here on time – which she'd managed with an exhilarating hurtle down the A23; both Mum and Guido had disappeared to answer what sounded like frantic calls on their mobiles about tonight's exhibition. They'd also had no time to make the elegant flat look a little less like a dusty storage room for paintings and display materials. Heaven knew how she could have stayed the night in the spare room – basically now an art studio, the bed covered in canvases, bedside table with paints. Even using the loo was an assault course of packages. The flat was reaching another level of artistic chaos – but they seemed happy, so good for them.

'Sorry about that,' Guido said, coming in with a bowl of salad, Mum following with the lasagne. Both still managed to look glamorous in their loose trousers and tops suitable for shifting stuff about, but Mum already 'had her face on' for later, and her luscious brown wavy hair – so different to Marina's long fair strands – was swept up into one of her usual effortlessly arty topknots.

'Ooh *lovely!*' Marina said, laying the small dining table in the living room as they put the bowls down.

'Guido made you the veggie lasagne you so loved last time.'

'Brilliant!'

They put her at the head of the table, facing the sea, and all sat down.

Mum patted her arm. 'It's been *far* too long since we saw you.'

'I know. I brought The Boyfriend down last time, so it must be about two months.'

Mum gave her a big spoonful of lasagne. 'Are you eating properly? There's nothing of you, darling.'

How many times had she heard *that* over the years? There never *had* been anything of her. Being tall didn't help. She was wiry – like Daddy, except he'd had the muscle to carry it off. 'Of course I am.'

'Have you lost weight?'

'No idea.'

'It must have been such a shock about Will; you were so devoted to him.'

'Yes. Well, being too devoted, blind to someone's faults, is never a good thing,' Marina said. Jesus, where did that come from? Mum and Guido exchanged a look; they thought she blamed her adored father for risking injury by being impulsive and carelessly snorkelling right by the boat.

For years they'd tried to get her to talk to counsellors – but they didn't know the half of it.

'Anyway, I'm over Faithless Number Four now,' Marina said.

Her mother looked puzzled. 'What?'

'My fourth cheating boyfriend. Once they join the list, I no longer honour them with a name.'

Mum looked appalled, and Guido shook his head in sympathy.

'Anyway, enough of him. How are you two?' Marina asked. 'You said it was the busiest summer *ever* in the gallery?'

Guido nodded. 'It is. I'm sorry, we should have somehow made time to see you before. But here you are.' He put a hand on hers, and there was a big smile on his handsome creased face. There were moments when she regretted having refused to call him Papà – the Italian word for Dad – but although Teddy had, immediately, for her it had been too soon after Daddy had died. So he'd stayed Guido.

'Mm, this is delicious,' Marina said, weary of her own quick and hopeless cooking efforts in the mucky shared kitchen at the flat.

Mum poured champagne into each of their glasses – from a half bottle, mindful that they would all be driving later. 'So, happy birthday for last Wednesday, darling.' The three of them clinked glasses. 'The big three-o! What have you got planned for the rest of this weekend?'

'Well...' Mum still had this idea – despite any evidence – that her daughter was having an exciting and hopefully husband-producing social life in London. Or at least was restarting one, after the lifting of Covid restrictions. In reality, it consisted of a weekly aqua dance class, café cake eating and occasional karaoke with Polly, and a rare concert or ballet – on her own, or with whoever she could persuade to come with her. 'I've got Kew Gardens tomorrow, followed by... not sure yet.'

'Let me guess, just you and your Spanish friend Paulina? Sorry... *Polly*,' Guido said, with a laugh. 'What a funny little pair you are: the Hispanophile and the Anglophile!'

Marina smiled, remembering how, when they finally met in Madrid after years of being Twitter friends, they'd laughed at their mix of languages and called themselves 'the bilingual sisters'.

'We're going to chat about moving out of London so we can have our own place.'

'*Together?*' Mum asked, looking slightly concerned.

'No, separate but nearby. Polly and I need our own spaces. But hopefully we can find a lovely but affordable area where she can give yoga classes and I can do online piano lessons – without flatmates swearing and shagging in the background.'

Guido put a hand to his face.

'Marina! Can't you *say* something?' Mum asked.

'Well of course I do. But they're hopeless. Or maybe piano teaching is just something you can't expect to be able to do in shared accommodation. I don't know.'

'Where are you thinking of?' Guido asked. 'Not even further from us, I hope.'

'Oh no. Nearer. Probably West Sussex.'

'Well! That's exciting!' Mum said. 'Just don't hole up somewhere where there are no nice young men.'

Marina groaned and raised her eyes to the heavens; Mum would be starting up about dating sites again soon.

'So, what are you doing about a holiday now?' Guido asked.

'Oh, nothing planned. Maybe a minibreak somewhere in the UK, to avoid doing all those Covid tests.'

Mum looked at Guido.

'We were hoping you might use your birthday money to have a break,' he said. 'In fact, we have a suggestion – something that would be practically free.'

'Oh?' A paid-for visit to Guido's relatives in Tuscany – particularly all his unmarried nephews. She'd turned this down before.

Mum put her hands together as if in prayer. 'Marina… we want to sell the Spanish house. The agency has been saying for some time that it's become practically unrentable. We were wondering – with your time off now and your Spanish – if you could go over, clear out the locked cupboard, tidy it up a bit and put it on with an estate agent.'

'You mean… *stay* in it?' After none of them had been there for twenty years.

'Well, you don't have to do that, if you don't want to. Obviously we'd pay for everything, including a hotel if that's what you'd prefer. Maybe a couple of weeks, longer if you need.'

'Um…' It would feel like Daddy was round every corner. She wasn't sure she could handle that.

'Maybe Polly could come with you?' Guido suggested.

Yes, but she'd still have to… 'There'll be some things of Daddy's. *You* should do this, Mum, not me.'

'How can I?' she replied. 'Neither of us have the time to do it for the foreseeable future, and if the place has got problems, we really need to do something about it now.'

'And... there's something else we wanted to talk about,' Guido started, looking at Mum for approval and getting a nod. 'If you can sell the house – even though it won't be worth much now – we'd be in a position to help you with a deposit on a little flat – so you could *buy* rather than rent.'

Marina looked from one to the other in amazement. 'Really? Wow!'

'Yes,' Mum said. 'We've been wanting to help you get on to the property ladder for a while but haven't been in a position to do so. This is the only way.'

Her own place! But for that she'd have to visit the house, San José, the *port*...

Mum squeezed her hand. 'I know it will be difficult for you, bring back a lot of memories. But surely most of them will be happy ones?'

The port. Somebody was bound to remember that hysterical ten-year-old who'd driven a boat with her dead father in it. Marina shook her head. Better to wait until Mum and Guido could do this themselves.

'Talk to Polly about it tomorrow.' Mum stood up. 'Meanwhile, it's cake and cappuccino time!'

Guido went off to the kitchen, and the coffee machine could soon be heard growling away.

Mum came back with a cake iced in Marina's favourite turquoise blue – but with an image of Nemo and Dory on it. 'Sorry, no time to make one, and this was the only blue one in Waitrose. Then I went and left the blue candles in the basket!'

'Ha! Not to worry, these kids' party cakes are ridiculously yummy. When I worked at the school, we had a rule that any staff with a school-day birthday had to bring one in,' Marina said, instead of mentioning those blue birthday cakes Daddy used to make for her in Cala Turquesa.

Guido came back with a tray of cappuccinos.

'Shame Ted and Hannah aren't here to help us with it! You'll have to take some home,' Mum said. 'But at least it's been easier for us to talk about Spain, just the three of us. Please say you'll think about it, darling.'

3

Richmond and Shoreham, England

The photos were on the external hard drive and a memory stick – both blue, of course – and kept in her bottom drawer behind a tangle of unused scarves. Always there in case she felt strong enough on the anniversary of his death. This year, she was going to brave it two weeks early.

She went for the memory stick, as if its smaller size might leave less of an impact – because that's what it felt like, an impact, a blow to her heart, like an aftershock of the blow to his head that killed him.

At some point, she'd renamed the file 'DAD', removing the 'DY' at the end, but she decided to put it back. After all, their relationship would always be stuck at the one between a ten-year-old and her daddy. Even if, as the years passed, a cloud had gathered over that last hour together, constantly threatening to take away her ten-year-old's belief in her lovable, dependable, handsome hero of a daddy. Because, was there really any possible reason – other than the obvious – for her being sworn to secrecy about the woman he met up with out at sea that day? He'd said he didn't want the woman blamed for the accident, but surely he could have just left her with those words to repeat to Mum, rather than completely rubbing the woman and her boat out of the picture?

And that was the other thing: *the woman*. Twenty years later, and she was still sure he never told her the woman's name. Either because he didn't want it repeated, or because the woman was *somebody she already knew*. She'd looked slightly familiar, but maybe only because she'd looked much the same as the several dark-haired Spanish boating ladies in the port, watching and waiting to engage with the golden Dutchman as he moved around his craft with the fish-like fluidity of someone in his element...

She started with some of the older ones. Mostly blurred photos of photos. A younger Daddy looking much less himself, with clipped hair, smart shirts. Sometimes even in a suit, having just come back from work. Not in his element at all. Mum looking happy in the lawned garden of her detached Surrey house. Then, when she was nearly six, it all changed: Daddy was pictured in lifeboatman yellow, training to be a low-paid coxswain but still trying to maintain their Spanish house and its little boat. Mum grimaced on the toy-cluttered terrace of the Eastbourne Sovereign Harbour town house, missing her friends in Cobham and London.

There were still photos of the four of them, but mostly they seemed to become a family split in half, the blondes and the browns, doing their own thing. But that might be just because, from then on – apart from Christmases, Teddy's birthdays and RNLI Open Days – the photos were mainly in Spain. She flicked through, Daddy looking happier and more golden in every photo. The googly-eyed Marina gradually elongating, the blue birthday cake candles increasing, on a countdown towards the tragic ten-year-old left alone in a boat with her dead father.

She took a big breath and let it out slowly. If only that woman hadn't been there. Daddy wasn't quite himself, she could remember thinking. So maybe the woman had said something, upset him, knocked him off course, off the boat, off his life...

She forced herself to carry on, because there was something else she had to see. There was a rented inflatable dinghy at first, grey and splashy, but ah, here was *La Mari*. She made the photo fill the screen, trying to peer into the cabin... She realised she was holding her breath, her stomach hollow and aching. Maybe she needed to stop. And oh God, then there was a photo of her and Daddy grinning on the deck in matching caps – right next to where he would shortly leave this world.

She flicked on by mistake to a full screen of Daddy's face, smiling, tanned, gold hair tousled with salt and wind. She smiled back, touched the screen where that hideous bump would come. Then, as the picture turned to a watery blur, for a moment she thought she saw him wink.

Enough. She closed the file, took out the memory stick. It complained that she hadn't ejected it properly – as if she hadn't said goodbye properly – so she put it in, pressed the little arrow, and took it out again, put it in its little blue box and back into the drawer. But she couldn't seem to eject the image from her head.

Come out and see me.

'Don't be daft,' she said out loud. 'You're not even there; you're a pile of ashes in Eastbourne cemetery. I did try to persuade Mum that you'd want to be left in the Mediterranean, but...'

Don't worry, I'm still here. Come out and see me.

Okay, enough.

She stood up, pushed the drawer closed with her foot and went down to the kitchen – today enveloped in the sickly-sweet odour of un-washed-up Chinese takeaway. *Exploded* Chinese; it seemed to be over every surface.

Alyssa walked in, looking around in horror. 'Absolutely *disgusting*,' she said, putting a hand through her tumbles of auburn hair. 'We need to talk to Abbie about this; I'm sick of clearing up after her. Sure you are too. We need to replace her with another Marina in the flat!'

Hopefully there'd soon be one *less* Marina in the flat. And she wasn't falling for the friendliness; Abbie and Alyssa only ever became chummy with her when they'd temporarily fallen out.

'It's not great, is it,' Marina said, getting on with making herself a cheese and tomato toastie.

'Actually, I wanted to ask you something,' Alyssa started, sitting down at the table.

Oh no, surely they weren't going to start sharing notes about Will? Such as his tedious habit of recounting his dark and nonsensical dreams every morning, or his obsession with nipples – mainly his own. 'What's that then?'

'Well… Will's got to move out of his flat, after an awful row with the dope-head flatmate – but he can't move into his new place until the end of August. I was wondering, would you mind if he moved in with me until then?'

So far, Alyssa and Will had been spending their time at Will's place, but now they would be having sex the other side of her wall. Having sex while they 'saw' each other, as apparently they weren't actually in a relationship as such, even after two months. Or even after *more* than two months, because some logistics had come to light that suggested they may have started trying each other out while she and Will *were* in a relationship and meeting each other's parents.

'So… are you saying I can mind about this and stop it happening, or are you just giving me advance warning?' Marina asked.

'Marina! I really don't want to upset you. But on the other hand, he's literally got nowhere to go.'

'Nowhere at all. I see. Even though his parents live half an hour away in Esher.'

When Alyssa started going on about tube lines for Will's theatre job, Marina got up and took her toastie off to her room, leaving Alyssa calling out after her.

She slammed the door and flumped down on her bed. Took an unwilling bite. Then she saw a missed call from Polly, quickly swallowed and rang her. 'Hello. Car playing up again?'

'No, no. The online one-to-one yoga student cancelled, so I could come now?'

'Yes! Sorry, I was downstairs in a Chinese-takeaway-splattered kitchen – with the She-Devil telling me she's moving Faithless Number Four into the bedroom next door

34

for a month,' Marina said. In Spanish, because Alyssa had come upstairs and was lurking around on the landing.

'*Madre mía!*' Polly replied, then went into a string of Spanish expletives. 'I think that's probably the decider.'

'What? Ah.' She'd already told Polly about Mum and Guido's extraordinary offer, and Polly had struggled to understand why Marina wasn't instantly jumping on a plane.

'I've looked at my diary and I could move things and join you for two weeks, if we could leave it until next Monday.'

She'd have Polly's calming and fun support... but the pictures in the drawer flashed back into her head. 'Oh, Pols, that's great, but... I think I'd really rather leave it until Mum can deal with Daddy's stuff herself.'

'Oh... okay. But shall we go to Shoreham instead of Kew Gardens today? Drive around looking at the location of flats for rent or for sale, then *desplomarnos* on the beach!'

'That sounds like "flop down"? What a great new Spanish word.'

'Yes, we will *flop down* on the beach and dream!'

'Although about *renting*, for now. I'll bring the leftover cake.'

'*Perfecto!* I'll bring tea. I'll call you when I'm outside your House of Hell.'

'It's a bit squished, but here we go,' Marina said, as she opened the tin and put two big slices of Finding Nemo cake on a paper plate on the shingle between their towels.

'*Dios*, the sizes of these! My bikini will snap!' Polly said, patting her tummy and then tying her thick dark curls into a bouncy ponytail.

'Well, if you must wear a... *string!*' Polly was forever trying to lose weight but was so well toned and curved that Marina envied the way she looked fantastic in everything – even a semi-thong bikini.

'Marina, we don't all want to wear a high-waist Speedo sports bikini on the beach!' Polly poured out tea from the flask. 'Anyway, cheers! Happy birthday! Oh, and happy Shoreham life!' she said, as they clicked plastic mugs.

Marina grinned. 'I mean, what's not to like? This gorgeous beach and those river Adur walks...'

'How near Brighton is, perfect for my yoga classes, and your mum and Guido.'

'And still only forty minutes to Gatwick, for you to fly to Madrid to see your family.'

'We can still get up to London in just over an hour when we want to – or find something interesting at the Rop... Oh, I can't say it...'

'Ropetackle Arts Centre. And best of all – apart from being able to afford the rent – there's a...'

'Karaoke place!' they said together, and laughed.

They groaned with delight at the super-sweet cake, washing it down with tea.

'And if you had to choose one of those flats that we drove past?' Polly asked.

'Oh... I think the one with the balcony overlooking where the river goes into the sea.'

Polly looked concerned. 'Wouldn't it bother you, seeing all those boats going past?'

Marina thought a moment. 'Perhaps sometimes, at first. But as long as I don't have to go in one, I'm fine.' She finished her cake and lay back on the towel. 'This is heaven.'

Polly did the same. 'I'm going to look for a place to rent here as soon as I can organise some work.'

'Me too, but tomorrow!'

'God, I'm getting hot again – and I have cake icing down my chest.'

'Same! Let's go in.'

They scrunched down to the sandy edge. The only other people in this square of beach between the two groynes were an elderly couple hunched under an umbrella and a man with three children playing in the sand; the sea was all theirs. They forced themselves into the cold water with squeals of complaint until it started to feel all right and they could enjoy the gentle rise and fall of the waves.

'Oh, you forgot your little square *flotador* for under your arm!' Polly pointed out.

'I know. What an idiot. I'm just being careful not to move it about too much.'

Marina looked out towards the rolling deeper water and reminded herself she was fine, as long as she had her feet firmly on the ground. As usual, she wondered how she could so love the sea and at the same time be so fearful of it. It was beautiful – but not for too long; they soon went back to their little camp.

'I think you have to be English to cope with this!' Polly said, shivering and wrapping a towel round herself.

Marina sat down and poured her some more tea. 'Here you go, you poor thing!' she said.

'What's the beach like below the house in Spain?'

'Oh... super soft with shallow water, and it's called Cala Turquesa, so... turquoise water. From what I remember, anyway.'

'*Twenty years*. I can understand *your* feelings, but why hasn't the rest of the family ever visited the house between renters?'

'Mum and Guido always go to Tuscany – to see his relatives and enjoy all the art. Or they like city breaks in places like Prague or Venice. Ted doesn't really do hot weather; I'm surprised Hannah got him out to Greece.'

'And why is the house "almost unrentable" now?'

'I don't know. Only thing Mum mentioned was the lack of hot water.'

'Well, that wouldn't be a big problem in the hottest part of Spain in August.'

'Maybe it's awful – infested with snakes or something!'

'Marina! It'll be locked!' Polly laughed. 'Anyway, your mum said she'd pay for a hotel.'

'I know. And you and I could have a great free holiday… if it weren't for me having to spend days going through that cupboard of things that will take me back to the past.'

'But…' Polly put down her tea mug and put a hand on Marina's arm. 'Maybe that's what you *need*. I know you hate it when your mum and I suggest you need counselling, and I respect that. But to go back, have some peace and quiet there… I always think you never had chance to grieve enough for your *papá* – it's like you're still a little in the angry stage. This could be exactly what you need.'

Marina looked at her friend and wondered about this. She started to imagine the healing warmth of the *good* memories of Cala Turquesa. Would they help her rub out the trauma of that last day? And… maybe there would be something in the cupboard that would help her remember who that woman was... She refilled their mugs, as if inviting Polly to carry on.

'And if it *isn't* what you need,' Polly said, 'I'd be there to collect the pieces.'

Marina smiled. 'You mean, *pick up* the pieces.'

'Collect, pick up and put together again – all of it, I can do!'

'It's true. And... maybe the sisters *bilingües* need a little *aventura*...'

'So we're going?'

'We're going!' Marina replied, leaning over and giving Polly a hug.

4

Almería, Spain

'Ha! This must have given the luggage men a surprise!' Polly said, lifting Marina's enormous but very light case off the conveyor belt.

'Yes! I put all my stuff in here,' Marina said, wobbling her trolley bag. 'That's for things to take back. Although Mum says it'll mostly be rubbish.'

'In which case, we'll just use it for a bit of cheap summer clothes shopping!'

'*Exactamente!*'

They went through and out into the oven-like heat already waiting for them at a mere ten o'clock in the morning. Marina breathed in that old smell of scorched earth and rosemary. Across the little road with its waiting red-striped taxis, there was the cactus-planted car park.

'*Dios mío*, it's more like arriving at a station – or a garden centre,' Polly said.

'Ah, this must be our car lady.'

A woman with an Indalo Parking T-shirt, clipboard and bag of keys seemed to have guessed who they were and was waving at them like they were old friends. They went over to her and were soon exclaiming with delight at their gorgeously blue Polo.

It had been decided that Polly would drive to the house, because Marina would be too distracted by recognising things and pointing out changes. 'Oh, I don't remember a dual carriageway here!' she was soon saying. 'But let's ignore the satnav and take the old coastal road.'

'*Claro!*' Polly said. Of course.

The glistening dark blue Mediterranean was soon gently lapping at the rocks at the side of the road. 'Oh wow,' Marina said, although not happy about how quickly it became deep here.

'Can't wait to get into it!' Polly exclaimed.

After a while, they were taken inland, and drove through rounded orange-earthed hills fuzzy with baby palms and grasses.

'Aw, it's coming back to me,' Marina said. 'Stark, but I love it. I grew up thinking this was how Spain was supposed to be, not lines of palms and forests of pines.'

'It really has got its own beauty,' Polly agreed. 'And… oh!'

The road had come round another hill, and suddenly they could see San José laid out beneath them, the white houses creeping halfway up the mountains surrounding it, the golden curve of the village's sandy beach. The little port was over to the left, Marina knew, but it wasn't quite visible from here, thank heavens; she wasn't ready for that yet.

'It's grown!' Marina exclaimed, glancing up at the smart villas on the slopes as they slowly drove down the main street. 'Ah, but perhaps not such a bad thing, because so has the supermarket we'll be using.'

'Mm, and looks like there are some good restaurants and shops... Looks very Spanish, though. Can't see any fair heads or sunburnt British backs.'

'Thank heavens for that. All the Brits must still be whizzing up that dual carriageway to Mojácar, which was always their hangout.'

Polly pointed at an estate agency. 'Do we have to pick up keys?'

'No. I've got some. And we did say we were going to have a couple of days relaxing first, having a little tidy-up or whatever, but mostly *desplomándonos* on the beach.'

'Sounds good to me.'

Marina turned off the satnav and looked at the map on her phone. 'Okay, take a left here.' They followed a road out of the village, but when it took a sharp turn, Marina told Polly to go straight on.

'What? Down this... *track?*'

'Yup. Looks better than it used to, believe me.'

They bumped and swayed down the track following the contours of the mountains, a stony dry valley beneath them.

'What happened to the sea?' Polly asked.

'If I remember rightly, you see it again when there's a car park for the lookout place – ah, here it is.'

There were now tantalising glimpses of turquoise sea, but just past the car park, there was a wooden barrier halfway across the road with a sign that had fallen off.

Marina leant forward. 'What?'

Polly stopped the car and Marina got out to pick up the sign and look at it. She got back in. 'Road closed. But it doesn't look very official – and we just saw that car go on ahead. Maybe it's open again now.'

They edged past the barrier and drove on. After a few minutes they saw a car coming towards them, but they weren't sure if it was the same one they'd seen go on ahead. Then they went round the next curve of a mountain and Polly braked hard.

They gasped. No need for a barrier now; the road was completely obliterated by massive fallen rocks, orange earth and a large fallen tree. There would be no getting round it, even on foot.

'Oh bloody hell!' Marina exclaimed, her brain whirring; should they wait a few days until the road was cleared, or...

'Well, that would certainly make the house "almost unrentable",' Polly said.

'But when did this happen? Surely they can't just leave it like this; there are at least four houses in that cove that have been cut off.'

'By road, yes. But you said it was most often visited by...'

'By *boat*, yes.' Marina switched the air con up to maximum, breathed out heavily. 'How long will they take to clear this? How do we find out?' She groaned. 'We don't have any choice really, do we.'

Polly put a hand on her arm. 'You're tired after the early start; you don't have to face that today. We can book in at a—'

'Leaving it will just give me more time to feel sick about it. It's just *a* boat, not *the* boat, and I won't be expected to drive it! Come on, let's get to Cala Turquesa; that water is calling.'

'Well okay, if you're sure.' Polly turned the car round and they bumped along back to the village, chatting about the volcanic mountains so as not to dwell too much on the impending sea trip.

They found a space in the free car park near the port, got the bags out and started walking towards it. Ten-year-old Marina would have been singing and jumping along, holding Daddy's hand, but she now approached with leaden legs. They went past a big blue crane and some wooden supports for boats hitched up out of the water for mending, past small boats bobbing around in the water, then small RIBs like the one Daddy had had at first… Polly spoke to a port staff member and was directed over to a man standing by one of the larger RIBs.

Sitting inside the boat were a middle-aged heavily tanned couple – presumably day trippers. The boat man gave Polly and Marina a smile, asked for twenty-four euros, gave them a flier with his number and asked what time they wanted to be picked up. The girls looked at each other, not having thought about that. Then the man pointed to their bags and said something very gruff and Andalusian consonant-free.

'Yes, we're planning to stay the night,' Polly said, taking the leaflet. 'Can we let you know?'

He chuckled – for some reason Marina would have liked to ask about – then helped them aboard, sat them down, watched Polly link arms with Marina and set off quickly, as if they might change their minds.

Once out between the chubby red and green lighthouses either side of the entrance to the port, he picked up speed and was soon banging over the waves, Marina hanging on tight to the central metal bar. The vibration of the engine, the mounds of scarily dark blue sea… She was soon feeling dizzily sick, fixing her gaze on the rocky coast with its mysterious caves, wishing it to be over. Then they finally rounded the point… to enter Cala Turquesa.

Polly gasped at the sight of the turquoise shallow waters, perfectly rounded little bay backed by pale sand and clumps of rock, and surprisingly dense and green vegetation going up the little valley between the mountains. So dense, nowadays, Marina realised, that you could barely see the four little houses. The nausea subsided, her heart fluttering at the thought that they'd soon be standing on that once familiar flour-soft sand, soon be going into the once adored Casa Palmito.

There had always been beach fans visiting the cove by boat from San José, but there were more people there than Marina remembered – and several little boats hauled up on the sand suggested some had made their own way. As they got nearer, other details came into view: three makeshift shacks – one selling drinks, a small one apparently selling jewellery, and a third one with drapey cloths and clothes. Then they noticed most of the people on the beach were nude.

'Ah. I'm starting to feel a little overdressed,' Polly said, then talked to the boatman and turned back to Marina. 'Apparently there's a hippy colony living here – and because they're nude, it's become a "clothing optional" beach.'

'Hippies *living* here? Where?'

'In shelters they've made, ruins, caves… He says there's natural spring water, they've got solar power, and they live in harmony with nature and sell things they make.'

José mumbled something to Polly.

'Oh, and they don't call themselves "hippies", they're *"turquitos"*. After Cala Turquesa, I suppose. Anyway, they don't sound like people to worry about – but maybe renters don't like this. Didn't the agency email your mum *any* news of the house or the cove?'

'No. Well, they might have; she probably couldn't be bothered to try translating the Spanish. God, I hope they're not squatting in the house!'

'I'd keep your voice low,' Polly said quietly. 'I think our fellow travellers might be… part of this.'

The middle-aged couple were staring at them, so Marina gave them a big smile and said something about how lovely the water was, getting a smile and a nod in return. All she'd noticed before was that they were mahogany-tanned, but she now realised they were in threadbare shorts and tops.

The boat pulled up near to the beach and, following the surprisingly nimble older couple, they jumped out into the warm, shallow water, drawing looks from everyone as the boatman handed them their cabin bags and the weirdly large suitcase.

Polly patted her back. 'You did it.'

'I did.' A dazed Marina scanned the back of the beach for paths. 'Now I just need to…'

'Which way?' Polly asked.

'Um…' There was a wooden board on which the *turquitos* were asking visitors to take their rubbish home with them, and not to use their boats as chairs or places to hang wet clothes. It also had arrows showing the paths to the toilets and massage.

'Let's try this one,' Marina said, picking an unsigned path.

Fortunately, they'd already changed into shorts and T-shirts, stuffing their English clothes into the big suitcase, but they were now dealing with midday heat and wishing they'd stopped at the bar shack for a cold drink before climbing the path.

They reached a clearing, the path splitting between a well-worn one to a hammock and a shack-like dwelling above them, where Spanish *reggaeton* music was being played, and a path that was more overgrown.

'I can see it!' Marina said, looking over to where the white walls of Casa Palmito could just be seen under a monstrous crimson bougainvillea and a large fan palm.

'*Olé!* And the path is flatter now, thank God!' Polly said, and they both started trotting towards the house.

Then they both stopped dead and looked at each other. It was suddenly clear that the music wasn't coming from the shack, but from Casa Palmito.

'Oh no! What are we going to do? Squatting *turquitos!*' Marina said, her heart tapping. 'Can't exactly get the police out here in a hurry, can we?'

'Well, the boatman said they're peaceful, so... maybe they'll just leave peacefully. We'll try being peaceful first.'

'And if necessary, call the boatman, go back to San José and...' Through the branches of the tree, Marina spotted a black-haired round-faced young man in a pair of boxers, unclipping a red-and-white striped football T-shirt from the line. 'Er... d'you think *turquitos* follow football?'

'Hm. An Atletico Madrid top. And I doubt he'd get a smart haircut like that around here.'

A man's voice could be heard inside, calling to his friend – and then he came out too, also in boxers. Taller, more tanned – maybe half African.

'Sound like Madrid accents,' Polly whispered. 'They're *renters*, Marina. *Uf*, didn't your mum check with the agency?'

'I thought so, but it seems not. Uh, why can't she get her bloody head out of a paint pot sometimes?' Marina put a hand to her throbbing temple. 'Can't think straight, let's see... I've got the agency's number, but we may as well speak to these guys first. Although... do we tackle these men in their boxers?'

'That might be more than they'll be wearing later, so... yes,' Polly said, with a smirk.

Marina watched the men joking, the tall one laughing and patting the other on the back. At least they looked good-natured.

The girls came out of the trees on to the open path and approached the house. The music had grown louder – maybe a door had blown open inside – and the men started grooving around to it before groaning and clutching their heads in pain and laughing.

'These *boys*, I should say,' Marina said, because they were reminding of her of the hungover idiots who emerged from the bedrooms of her younger flatmates. 'God, I've had enough of this type at the House of Hell. Let's just hope they're leaving soon.'

The boys heard and looked over – puzzled looks on their faces when they spotted the suitcases.

'Well *hello*, ladies!' beamed the tall half-African-looking one, in Spanish. 'I think you might have made a mistake.'

He looked from one girl's face to the other. 'But come here and cool down, you poor things. We'll get you a drink.'

The girls looked at each other.

'*Ya*-si-el! Maybe if we put on some shorts?' said the round-faced black-haired chap, with clearer and quieter Spanish.

Yasiel looked down himself, gasped, and then looked back at the girls. 'I'm *so* sorry. Come and take a seat while we sort ourselves out.' He pointed to an ancient table and chairs on the L-shaped terrace round the little house, and then they both disappeared.

The girls sat down. Marina stared in amazement at the overgrown bougainvillea, the peeling whitewash of the house, and the terrace with weeds coming up through the tiles. Somewhere nearby, a bird was singing with a sighing whistle – as if he was too hot, too tired or too sad. Her parents had always loved looking after the place, every year painting, mending or improving something, but it now looked like it had been a while since Mum had allowed the agent to organise for any maintenance to be carried out. How could Mum just let the house… *die* like this? Marina fought off a sting of impending tears.

The boys were back, in shorts and singlets. They'd turned the reggaeton down a notch and were carrying Cokes.

Marina and Polly thanked them, snapping the cans open and drinking them down gratefully.

'So… have you got the wrong week?' the quieter one asked.

'My family owns this house,' Marina started, in Spanish, 'and the agency told my mum it would be free for the next three weeks. In fact, that it wasn't being rented at all these days.'

'Which agency was *this*?' Yasiel asked with a laugh.

'Um… I can't remember the name, but the woman is called Francisca… León.'

'There's no way she'd say that!' Yasiel said, laughing again.

The other chap gave him a look and then addressed the girls. 'Somebody in your family has not understood,' he said calmly. 'Every year, we book this house for the first couple of weeks in August.'

So they would be here all but the last few days of her stay after Polly had gone. Marina breathed out heavily with disappointment.

Polly put a hand on her arm. 'We'll have to speak to the agency,' she said to the boys. 'The thing is, the family is going to sell the house, and there are things Marina needs to do.'

It was the boys' turn to look at each other in alarm. 'Really? Oh…' they said in chorus, then looked down at their drinks.

The quieter chap looked up again. 'What things?'

'Well… I'd like to tidy the terrace, and there's a locked cupboard that I need to go through,' Marina said.

'Ah yes, the big cupboard in the double bedroom. I wonder what treasures you may find! I'm Yasiel, by the way,' he said, smiling and shaking each of the girls' hands. The quieter chap introduced himself as Juan José, or 'Juanjo', and there was then confusion over the girls' names, as the boys assumed the English name would be Marina's and the Spanish one would be Polly's.

Marina pulled out her phone. 'I'm going to ring Francisca. I think she manages a couple of the other houses in the valley, and maybe we'll be lucky and—'

Yasiel laughed. 'That would *not* be lucky – the other three are ruins! Two have been taken over by the *turquitos*, and the path to the one at the top of the valley – too far from the beach and the water spring to interest anybody – is so overgrown you can't reach it. Well, other than by coming here and going a long way up the car track.'

'What?' Marina remembered them becoming a bit shabby, but now they were ruins? So that meant clearing the rock fall over the mountain road would have to be undertaken for just Casa Palmito. 'Oh God.'

'They've been like that for ages. How long since you've been here?' Juanjo asked, looking puzzled.

Marina hesitated. 'A very long time,' she said, not wanting to go into this.

'In which case, you'll be wanting to see inside!' he answered.

'I'd love to,' Marina said, excited to see it again.

'We just need to ask Mati.'

'Who's she?' Marina asked. Maybe the other woman at the agency. She couldn't decide what to do first: have a look around inside, or call the agency.

Yasiel was sniggering again. He seemed to find everything they said hilarious, but Juanjo was also chuckling. Seeing the girls' puzzled faces, Juanjo flicked his head over towards the house, as if in explanation.

They didn't have to look that far; the explanation was right there next to Marina. A third lad – but more interested in something cupped between his hands. Long-fingered,

gentle hands, Marina noticed. And when she looked up
from the hands, past a bare, gently muscular chest, she saw
a face frowning with concentration, a profile an odd mix of
sharp cheekbones and boyish curves, topped by an unruly
mop of shiny dark curls.

'You got him?' Yasiel asked. 'The one behind the fridge?'

Mati nodded. 'A female, I think.' He went over to the
rocks and shrubs, crouched down, put his hands down on
the sand before opening them… and out wiggled a lively
pale pink gecko. 'There.' He watched her go, then stood up
and smiled at the girls. But the smile was closed, and the
wide, alert eyes – together with hands on hips as he stood
in front of the door – made him look distinctly territorial.

'Polly and Marina. They thought they'd booked the
house,' Juanjo explained to him. 'Marina's family owns it,
and she needs to empty the cupb—'

'Yes, I heard.' He turned to Marina. 'Of course you
can go through the cupboard in my bedroom,' he said, in
low, resonant Spanish. 'But I don't understand this. The
agency could have arranged to send you the belongings, a
lawyer could have arranged the sale of the house. Why are
you so keen to see the house before selling it? Aren't you
afraid it will persuade you not to?' He wasn't smiling. He
really wanted an answer to this rather personal question –
and the other two boys were also looking over to see her
reaction.

'No, I'm not,' Marina said firmly. 'I'm sorry, I hope you
can find somewhere nice to continue your… annual reunion
next year. How long have you been doing this?'

'Since we were at university together,' Juanjo said. 'We had
a little band together – and still do, when we come out here.'

'Oh, that's lovely,' Marina said.

'It won't be the same, once we have to go somewhere else,' Mati said.

'Shame. But you know, things change,' Polly said, losing a little patience.

'Can I have a look now?' Marina asked.

'Of course,' Mati said, standing aside.

Marina got up. Once walking past him, she realised he was tall for a Spaniard, and she had to ignore both his freshly showered citrus scent and those penetrating dark eyes watching her. Who did he think he was, for heaven's sake? It wasn't *his* house. If they were university educated, surely they had jobs that meant they could afford to rent somewhere lovely in San José?

She stepped inside. The living room was now so cluttered with guitars, a *cajón* drum, heaps of clothes, beach shoes and snorkelling stuff that it was hard to remember… but for a moment she could see Teddy lying on the sofa with his Thomas the Tank Engine books, and then Daddy singing to himself as he mixed a blue birthday cake in the kitchen at the back…

'The locked cupboard is in here,' she heard Mati say behind her, as he opened the door to what used to be her parents' room. He thought she didn't know?

She went in – and gasped at the view of the bay from the doors that led on to the side terrace, almost seeing Daddy standing there looking out, asking *remember this?* The room itself, of course, was not as she remembered it, the bed now angled for the shape of the room, rather than for the view. And of course, *inhabited*. It was somehow inevitable that Mati had taken the double, leaving the other two to sleep in the kids' room. At least he wasn't trashing it – that would have been hard to see, in Daddy's beloved bedroom. There were just a couple of T-shirts on the chair, and a book, phone charger and some papers on the bedside table.

She took the keys from her pocket and put the small one in the door of the built-in wardrobe, half expecting – even half hoping – that it wouldn't work. But it did, the doors squeaking open, and... good God, there wasn't a square inch free of boxes or, on one shelf, items for which there'd either been no box or packing time. She saw a folder of little Teddy's paintings, probably deemed at the time to show too many *boats* to be brought home with them; the bat and ball beach set she and Mum used to love; that boat with a little wind-up engine that you could only use when there was barely a ripple... She took it down and held it for a moment under her arm like she used to on the way to the beach.

'It will take time.'

She jumped. He was still there. They stared at each other a moment, then he dropped his gaze and sauntered off, his low, confident voice soon heard outside – although at least one of the boys – and Polly – were now in the kitchen area, talking about *tortilla*.

She went back to the cupboard, peeked into a few boxes of dinner plates, lamps and sheets. Good; easy, non-emotional stuff for recycling or charity shops – wherever they were. But hauling this lot down the hill and into a boat wasn't going to be fun.

Mati was back – with the closed smile. 'I have spoken to the agency and the others. You and Polly should stay here a few days to go through the cupboard before you move to San José,' he said.

Behind him, Polly was joke-arguing about tortilla technique with Juanjo, like she'd already moved in, and giving Marina a thumbs-up. *What?* They didn't know anything about these boys.

'I will move. You and Polly can be in here, with your own bathroom. The door has a lock,' he added, as if reading her mind.

'That's really kind, thank you... but I need to speak to the agency.'

'Of course. They will give us a good reference, don't worry,' he said with his first real smile, if only a brief one, then disappeared.

She got out her phone and saw a message from Mum asking if they'd arrived all right. She'd deal with her later. She rang Francisca's number and started explaining who she was.

'Marina! I was about to call your mother to get your phone number!' she said in mercifully slowed-down Spanish. 'Why didn't she tell me you were coming? It's a very busy time in the village, but a friend has an apartment hotel and she keeps an apartment free for relatives. I will ask her... Meanwhile, stay there and do what you have to do – maybe until the weekend?'

'But...'

'They are very good people, my nephew and his friends – they will help you and are happy to share the house with you until then.'

'Your *nephew?*'

'Mati. It was his suggestion, even though he is angry you are going to sell the house. I told him your mother was thinking of selling it a few months ago, but he wouldn't believe me. I'm sorry, he can be very stubborn. Come and see me when you are ready, and I will talk to you about the estate agent.'

'But didn't my mother—'

'Meanwhile, do what you have to do, but also have fun with the boys!' Francisca said, and then she was gone.

5

'Well, one useful thing from the cupboard,' Polly said, putting the beach umbrella up, while Marina laid two towels in its shade. They'd found a cosy patch of soft white sand between two rocks near the end of the beach in which to make a camp. 'Once my lunch has gone down a bit, I'll be going in,' she said, laying herself down next to Marina, who'd already splashed around in the shallows.

'God that tortilla was yummy,' Polly said.

'It was funny the way each of you insisted that the tortilla your mother had taught you was the best!'

'Talking of mothers, you haven't told me what your mum said on the phone.'

'Oh, lots of apologies – she'd missed the emails, thinks some of them went to her old email address, thought she'd sent an email to Francisca but hadn't sent it, blah, blah, blah. Hopeless as ever. So really, my fault for not contacting Francisca myself.'

'Was your mum worried about us sharing with three boys for a few days?'

'What? No. You know what she's like – immediately asked if they were all unmarried and did I like any of them!'

'And do you?'

'Do *you?*'

Polly tutted. 'I asked you first, *mujer!* Three good-looking chaps – jeez, something for everyone, isn't there? Sunny sexy Cuban; gentle, black-haired *gitano*; and Mati... surfer boy?'

Marina laughed and shook her head. 'No thanks. I'm not in a hurry for Faithless Number Five. Can't think of anything worse than a distance romance – even one involving fun trips to Madrid. God, I can't even stop guys living a couple of tube stations away from slipping through my fingers.'

Polly sighed. Her own attitude to relationships was a lot more instinctive; she was practically never single, even if some of her liaisons were short-lived. 'Anyway, I can tell you they *are.*'

'They're what?'

'Unmarried. None of them are wearing wedding rings.'

'Oh. Well, even still. And anyway, that doesn't mean they aren't all spoken for... not that I care either way.'

'Didn't you always dream of having a Spanish husband?'

'Didn't you always dream of having an English one?'

'I asked you first.'

'No, I didn't!'

Polly got herself up on her elbows and raised an eyebrow. 'Okay, maybe, but—'

'Oh, I just realised, you weren't in the room when Yasiel was saying what they all did in Madrid. He's an accountant, and—'

'He's never! Seems much too laid-back for that!'

'Juanjo's a psychologist. He used to be in education, but now works as a *terapeuta*. Such a sweetie; definitely your best choice.'

'He is. I mean, he *would* be. Hm, but therapist: oh God no. Imagine being counselled all the time.'

Polly shrugged, probably thinking that would be ideal for Marina.

'And Mati? What does he do?' Marina asked.

Polly lay back down with a grin. 'Guess.'

'Er... something businessy. Got his own business.'

'No. Well, in a way.'

'What makes someone so full of himself? Oh, I know: doctor.'

'No. Well, in a sense.'

'What? Oh – I give up. Professional annoying alpha male, all we need to know.'

'He's a vet, but does research at Complutense university and some lectures.'

'A vet who doesn't cure animals? Why would he want to be that?'

'From the way Juanjo said it, it sounded like Mati might sometimes ask himself that very question.'

Marina remembered Mati's gentleness with the pale pink gecko. An image that for some reason kept returning to her.

'What research does he do? I hope we're not sharing a house with somebody who's got a room full of caged kitties trying out drugs.'

'Well, possibly. Yasiel mentioned those wormy parasites cats get.'

'Ew, ew, ew!' Marina said, pulling a face and laughing. 'Imagine being his girlfriend, chatting with him over breakfast about cat faeces!'

'Maybe this two weeks' escape every year is the only

thing that keeps him sane,' Polly said. 'He's certainly upset about the house going for sale.'

''Coz he thinks it's *his*. Let's hope Juanjo counsels him out of it, because it's going to get really annoying.' Marina sat up, brushed sand off herself and the towel, and looked over at a gracefully nude German couple sitting on a large cotton sheet of gorgeous colours. 'I want one of those things to lie on. Bet they sell them in that stall; everyone's got one. You coming?'

'Yes, let's go and see what he's got.' She looks over the beach, past the nude *turquitos*, Germans and other day trippers, towards the shop. 'Perhaps I should rephrase that.'

Marina chuckled.

They stood up – Polly in her purple semi thong, Marina in the skirted navy sports bikini she used for aqua aerobics – and started walking along the beach. They went past the elegant Germans, the two brown girls with nothing on but matching hair braid bobbles, an elderly couple and their playful dog, and – Marina noticed with relief – a young Spanish couple in modest swimwear. A group of people were waiting for the boat back to San José. When the boatman drew near, he recognised them and asked if they wanted a lift back. He smirked when Polly said they were staying.

They reached the stall and enjoyed looking at the thin cotton cover-ups and shawls before Marina started trying to choose which sunbathing cloth to buy.

'Let me guess, the blue one,' Polly said.

'Nope – not this time. It's going to be the green one with elephants, loads of room for two of us.'

'Big enough for four – or even *five* of us, maybe!' Polly said.

Marina looked at Polly and raised her eyes to the heavens.

'That's *not* going to happen. Sounds like their enjoyment of the sea is of the very active boaty, paddleboardy, snorkelling kind.'

'Good choose!' the man behind the counter said in English, taking the cloth down and folding it. He was tanned and slow-moving enough to be one of the *turquitos*, but had put on some old shorts, presumably so he didn't put off any shy potential customers.

'Do you live here?' Marina asked him in Spanish. 'It's such a beautiful place.'

He replied in rather blurred Andalusian. With translation help from Polly, Marina discovered that he did, but in the winter worked part-time doing mending in a dry cleaner's shop in a town further along the coast. She also learnt that there were twelve in their colony who lived there all year round, and a few more who joined them in the summer. By some miracle, they all got on okay.

'Oh, that sounds wonderful,' Marina said.

Meanwhile, Polly had been looking at some shaggy striped rugs called *jarapas* and selected one in her favourite purple-pink colour. 'Perfect for my yoga.'

'Ah – yoga. I've sold them for that before,' he said.

'Really? Maybe I'll set up a class on the beach,' Polly said, laughing.

The man looked at her seriously. 'You're a yoga *teacher*? Really? Fantastic! I'm serious, there are residents here who would love that. Oh, and when the visitors see you giving a class, they will want to join in and pay – and maybe buy a mat to do it on!'

'Ha! Okay. How about tomorrow morning at ten, before it gets too hot?' Polly suggested.

'Make it half past ten – just after the first boats arrive,' he said. 'I will tell everyone. We can have it just here, where there's space by the shop.'

'But I won't charge – I'm on holiday.'

'You're crazy – but I think you will find you are given drinks and tips. This is great! See you tomorrow.'

As the girls were walking back to their little camp with their purchases, the man could already be heard sharing the news with a woman coming out of the sea with two tiny girls.

Their elephant sheet took up nearly the entire area between the rocks.

'*Perfecto*,' Polly said, pulling the last bit straight, 'but now let's go in. Race you!' She dashed towards the gentle waves, and would have won, had she not collided with a tall, slender young man loping along the edge of the sea. '*Ay, perdón!*' she said, apologising, but then looked up at his face and put a hand on her heart.

'*De nada*,' the chap said, with a gentle smile.

But it clearly wasn't nothing to Polly, Marina saw, and it was easy to see why: the hard 'd' suggested an English accent, and this dorkily handsome chap with sun-bleached fair hair in a ponytail walking nude down a Spanish beach was absolutely Polly's dream type.

Polly joined Marina in the sea, looking happily shaken. 'Well!' she said, looking back and watching the guy slowly continuing on his way.

Marina laughed. 'Hm. Brings a whole new meaning to the expression "what you see is what you get"!'

'Marina!' Polly said, for once coy, and gave her a splashing. 'D'you mind? I've just fallen in love.'

'Oh no, that's it: you're going to join the hippies!'

'No, I'll see if I can take him home and let him wander around Shoreham beach instead.'

Polly did an excited fast crawl up to the buoys and back again, while Marina twirled in the water, admiring the little fish around her.

'I can't believe you forgot your *flotador* for your bad shoulder, *again*,' Polly said.

'Nor can I.'

'Maybe you'll find one in the cupboard.'

'Uh... the cupboard. The thought of having to root around in there under the dodgy ceiling fan while I could be floating around in here! Or having a siesta, as I think that's what I'll feel like once we're back at the house. Oh... but we said we'd go to the supermarket at five with the boys in their boat.'

'No need for you to come; get on with what you have to do in a nice quiet empty house.' She looked over at a small RIB coming into the buoy-marked boating lane further along the beach. 'Here they are now.'

Mati was at the helm of the RIB, coming in showily fast and then cutting the engine to put the brakes on. Typical, Marina thought – but then remembered how Daddy used to do the same and have her laughing with delight.

By the time the boys came up to the house – perhaps having stopped for a beer at the bar shack – the girls were showered, bikinis on the line, Polly making a list on the terrace and Marina in the bedroom putting framed pictures into 'no' and 'maybe' piles for taking home.

Polly came back into the room, shut the door, and shook her head. 'I can't watch.' She lowered her voice. 'Why can't they leave the wet towels outside? Use the hose on their sandy feet before coming in? I recommend that you put on shoes to... *crunch* your way over the living room.'

'My mum would have gone mental,' Marina said.

'And now they're arguing about who is going to be first in the shower.'

'Well tough; they're not sanding up ours.'

'*Claro que no!*' Polly said with a laugh, then looked down. 'Looks like you're doing well. Are these pictures for Shoreham?'

'Possibly.'

'Oh, but *this* one's *gorgeous*,' Polly said, picking out a watercolour not in either pile, 'and that's your mum's signature, isn't it?'

Marina looked over, even though she already knew which one she must have spotted: Mum's painting of *La Mari*. Soon after they bought her, bright blue stripe, cheeky curved nose, shiny white body. Dad had loved the picture – but had also died in the boat after meeting another woman.

Polly was still holding it. 'Can I suggest you wrap it and keep it at the back of a cupboard at home? Maybe one day you'll—'

'No.'

'Or give it to me and I'll put it in my cupboard for you.'

Marina pondered this a moment with a trace of irritation; it was hard enough sorting this, especially with the eczema on her hands getting steadily worse as she did it. If Polly was going to be debating and reprieving things all the time, it was going to take twice as long and be twice as painful. 'Okay, yes. Just don't let me see it unless I ask.'

Polly smiled and put the painting in her drawer. 'Sorry, you carry on.' She came back with an ice-cold can of lemon tea for Marina.

'Ooh, that looks nice, thanks,' Marina said with a grateful smile.

Polly went through to the living room, and Mati could soon be heard telling her friend that tonight he and the boys would be off in the boat to check out a place in San José where they were going to play. *Good,* thought Marina. After their very long day, she and Polly would be able to have a quiet evening in the house.

An hour later, having finished the pictures and sorted through a box of phone chargers, Game Boys and leaking batteries, Marina watched Polly go off down to the boat with the boys. It was the first day, so Marina had tried to do the easier stuff, but the cupboard was both a drag and a minefield of unexpected hurt. A box of Teddy's six-year-old clothing turned out to have an old pale blue shirt of Daddy's that she remembered leaning against while putting a little finger in the hole in the seam. She put it to her nose as if, by some miracle, it might still smell of him… and then looked at the still almost full cupboard, and the piles around her, and felt totally overwhelmed with the task she'd been set. Mum should be doing this, not her. Especially now she had these erupting scaly red hands.

She got to her feet and had another look in her washbag for the Betnovate cream; no, it definitely wasn't there. Yet another thing forgotten; good God, she was turning into her mother. She'd have to get to a chemist tomorrow. For now, all she could do was cool them down under the tap – except water in the cold tap here wasn't anywhere near cold.

Back on the floor with the boxes and piles, she sat there feeling tired and hopeless, pressing each side of her sore hands against the cool can of drink.

'Marina.'

'Oh!' She jumped, spilling the can over her hands and Daddy's T-shirt – which meant she would now have the both painful and pointless job of washing it. 'Bloody hell.'

Mati was giving her his closed smile.

'Did you have to just... *appear* like that?' she asked in Spanish. 'Look what you've made me do.' She stood up and went to the bathroom again to wash her hands, then came back with some tissues to wipe the floor – because he was just standing there doing nothing, one hand on hip, saying something about having to do a bit of work.

She threw the tissues in the bin and came back to the T-shirt, sitting down next to it, folding it up. Maybe if she washed it in mild shampoo, it wouldn't irritate her hands too much.

'Show me your hands,' he said.

'It's *eczema* – I don't know the word for that,' she replied. Still in Spanish, because even though he would surely need English for some of his research work, he hadn't yet offered any.

'Show me.' He stood in front of her now, her head embarrassingly near the level of his denim shorts crotch. Worse, however, were his hands, palms upwards, expecting her to put her hideous pustuled ones in them. The hands shook with impatience, so she went along with it. He then examined them, turning them over and back again. Maybe cats got eczema and he thought he was an expert. He was the kind of guy who probably thought he was an expert in everything.

'You need steroid cream.'

'I know that, but I left it at home.'

'Ah. Then we will have to use nature's cure. Come and sit in here and I'll get some aloe vera.'

Even while they had been talking, the burning on her hands had increased in intensity. 'Okay.'

She padded through to the sofa – the floor as wet and gritty as Polly had warned her. Instead of going off to the other bathroom for some tube of stuff with aloe vera in it, Mati went outside. What? Surely not…

He came back and sat down next to her with a prickly spike of aloe, a knife and a saucer, and proceeded to cut it like a cucumber then peel it to reveal the inner, clear gel-like substance. A bitter, earthy smell filled the room, and made her wonder if this was a good idea. Wasn't it usually just a small, token ingredient in shampoos and creams? Before she could ask if it was going to sting, he quickly took one of her hands and spread the gel on… creating an instant cooling effect that made her sigh.

'Relief, isn't it? Anti-inflammatory and anti-bacterial, vitamins, a magical gift of nature. Cleopatra used it every day, and so should you, while you are here.'

'Thank you, it's really helping.'

'Because your eczema will be worse, with the stress of preparing to sell the house.'

'Oh, don't start that again, *please*.' Why couldn't he just be sweet and kind, forgetting his own agenda, for more than ten minutes?

'I sense you're not thinking carefully about what you're doing.'

'I sense you're thinking carefully about what you don't want me to do – and that you're going to be a pain in the arse about it until you get your own way.'

Judging by his affronted expression, she'd remembered the correct word for arse. 'Marina, that's not fair.'

'Yeah, well *life*'s not fair,' she muttered in English, standing up and going towards the bedroom. Then she turned and was rather pleased to see him still looking a little perturbed. 'But thanks for treating my hands – amazing,' she added, still in English, twirling them in the air in case he couldn't understand. She took hold of the door. 'I'll close this, so I don't put you off while I thump about in here.' And so you can't suddenly be standing in the doorway, like some Ghost of Summer Past, she thought.

Marina and Polly were fast asleep when the boys tumbled noisily back into the house after their trip to the music venue.

Polly groaned and looked at her phone on the bedside table.

'Bloody hell, how do they manage to sound like ten people rather than three?' Marina asked, sick with tiredness. 'And you'd think, in the middle of the night, they could be a bit—'

'It's actually only half eleven.'

'What? Feels like three in the morning.' They could hear the fridge door whumping, cans clonking onto the table...

and then a strum and tuning of a guitar, the low twang of a bass guitar, the fluttering of fingers on the *cajón*. 'Oh Jesus, surely they're not going to—'

After some clapping along with the drums, the three had broken out into some kind of chugging flamenco-rap number.

'Sounds like *Me Maten*, meaning, they kill me?' Marina whispered. 'They're certainly doing that. Although…'

The song had reached the chorus, which had gone into faultless harmonies.

The girls turned to each other.

'They're good,' Marina said.

'They're *really* good.'

'Which two are singing, d'you think?' Marina said.

'We could get up and have a look,' said Polly, sitting up.

'We may as well. It's not like we're going to sleep through this.'

They put back on the sleeveless nighties they'd thrown off in the heat, and crept into the living room, taking a seat on one of the sofas. Juanjo on the *cajón* and main vocals gave them a big grin, as did Yasiel. Mati glanced over but was focused on his guitar and the harmony lines – until Polly and Marina started joining in with the 'Me Maten' bits of chorus, and he half-smiled and nodded.

After the final chord, they all applauded each other.

'More!' Marina said, suddenly no longer tired.

'Yes, what else have you got? Any other recent hits?' Polly asked. The girls, in their true bicultural style, followed both English and Spanish charts. '*Rebelde?*'

'Oh *yes!*' Marina said, because there were three different voices in it, including a Cuban rap for Yasiel.

'Of course,' Mati said, 'although Juanjo and I argue about who has to sing Beatriz Luengo's part.'

'Polly will sing it for you!' Marina said.

'Really?' Yasiel asked. 'That would be great!'

'*Olé*, Polly!' Juanjo said.

With little hesitation, Polly stood up and joined in when they played it, Marina making them all laugh as she attempted the over-the-top flamenco hand movements in the video.

'Let's see, what else shall we play the girls… considering one is English?' Yasiel said with a wink at Mati.

'Yes, what have you got in English? The Eurovision winner?' Marina asked with a laugh, knowing that the quirky electronic Icelandic '*10 Years*' song was a ridiculous contrast to their flamenco fusion songs.

All three boys stared at her wide-eyed, then nodded and laughed – apparently unable to believe she'd guessed.

'Oh my God, that we *have* to hear!' Marina said in English. 'But hang on a minute…' With a laugh and a pat on the back from Polly, she dashed to the bedroom and came back with the daft two-octave mini keyboard she never travelled without. She tried a few keys to check the battery.

The boys cheered, then started their guitar version of the song, Mati struggling with the English but capturing the happy spirit, Marina managing the brash keyboard solo amongst cheers of encouragement.

'Okay, one more, then these girls might need some sleep,' Juanjo said in Spanish, seeing Polly yawning even while she was laughing. 'Something soothing perhaps. You like Bruno Mars?'

'We adore him! Perfect,' Marina said.

The boys started the intro of 'Leave the Door Open', the girls waiting for Juanjo's sweet voice to sing Bruno's part, with the other two doing the answering backing vocals. But it was Mati doing the soulful main vocal over the warm chords, singing – albeit in hard-to-understand English – about sharing a house, kissing and cuddling... What tricks music could play with her, Marina thought, as just for a moment Mati didn't seem quite so annoying.

6

'What are we doing awake at half seven?' Polly asked. 'Don't know, but I'm going to creep into the kitchen and get us some breakfast.'

She opened the door quietly and stepped into the room. Juanjo was asleep on the sofa, face angelic with long dark eyelashes and a lock of shiny black hair over his forehead.

The kitchen area was less angelic. The boys had clearly stayed up for some while after their playing; the recycling bin wouldn't close on the cans, the sink was full of plates and bowls, and there was a line of ants motoring towards a beery meeting point on the worktop. She wiped up the mess, filled two bowls with Spanish muesli, once again admired the Sleeping Beauty, and went back to the bedroom.

Polly had opened the bedroom doors onto the side terrace and its views over the *palmito* bushes to the bay. '*Qué maravilla*,' she said with a sigh.

'I know. Can't wait to get in that sea again.'

'Juanjo asleep in there? I'm guessing it's him who got the sofa bed.'

Marina nodded. 'Sleeping like an angel. Tea a bit later; I didn't want to wake him with that noisy kettle.'

'He *is* an angel,' Polly said, and looked at Marina.

Marina raised her eyes to the heavens. 'I know, but don't start that again.'

'I think he likes you.'

'He likes you too. He probably likes most people in the entire world,' she said.

Polly tutted in that way the Spanish do.

Marina finished her cereal and looked inside at the cupboard. 'God, only a few days to sort this out? Although Yasiel says Spanish people often leave lots of stuff in the house for the next owner, so that could save me time.'

'And *I* told you that, back in England!'

'So you did. Unfortunately, I've still got to go through it all to decide *what* to leave. Maybe I could offer some things to the *turquitos*.'

'I was going to suggest that.'

'I probably need to interest the estate agency with photos, or they might not be in a rush to get on a boat and come and have a look. So I'll have to tidy and get stuff out of each room to snap it. But I'd really like to paint the outside and tidy up the terrace, so I can get some fabulous shots of the house in its location.'

'Without the boys' heaps of clothes, towels and beer cans.'

'Yes. Maybe that *ferretería* I saw in San José has got some white exterior paint. I could ask the boatman to take me back with him after dropping off the day trippers.'

'We could go after my yoga class.'

'Oh no, I don't want you rushing straight off after that – Mr Dork might be loping around!'

'True... but only if you don't mind the boat on your own.'

Marina had already decided that, having done it once, it

was probably best to get on the boat again soon before she lost her nerve. 'I think it's okay, really – especially as the sea looks nice and calm.'

She stopped gazing at the bay and looked behind her at the house. The bougainvillea half-covered the bedroom window and totally obscured the shower room one. Also, the weeds coming up through the tiles were tickling her legs. 'Before it turns into an oven out here, I might make a start on this,' she said.

'What, before tea?'

'Good heavens, no!'

'I'll go and make some, and then give you a hand.'

'Great! I'll have a look in that cupboard outside and see if there are any secateurs.'

'And gloves – these bougainvilleas might look adorable, but they have evil *espinas*,' Polly said.

'Thorns? Oh no, okay.'

An hour or so later it was too hot to continue, but between the two of them they had made a huge difference; even more light streamed into the bedroom and bathroom, and the terrace outside their window – after weeding and filling gaps with sand – looked even more inviting.

'We just need to continue round to the front – which is considerably worse,' Marina said.

'We'll do it!'

They sat down with iced teas.

'I'll come down and give you support for the class,' Marina said. 'Just ignore me when I don't use my dodgy arm.'

'No, no. You know what yoga does to your shoulder. You stay here and get in that cupboard.'

Polly showered, put her hair into a ponytail, and put on her purple yoga tankini and shorts. Armed with water, rug, phone, the music speaker borrowed from Yasiel and a quick hug from Marina, she went off down the hill.

Marina opened the cupboard and positioned the big cardboard boxes the others had brought back from the supermarket. She opened a bag of chews and popped one in her mouth, then had a word with herself about being as industrious as she'd been outside. Ah, but outside... Daddy's T-shirt was still hanging on the line.

She went out of the bedroom doors, along the terrace, round the corner to the line, and unpegged the T-shirt. Then she noticed movement in the corner of her eye... and saw a long dark snake zigzagging along the path.

She stood still, heart patting away. Watched it disappear under a *palmito* bush. *Jesus*. They needed to keep the bedroom doors closed! And wonderful as the view was here, the idea of relocating to a village apartment suddenly seemed a lot more appealing.

Mati walked past her and peered into the bush.

'What are you *doing?*' Marina hissed in English.

'Admiring him.' He turned and chuckled. 'Don't worry, he won' hurt you,' he said in English.

'We need to keep the doors closed.'

'No, they have their home in the *palmitos.*'

'Yes, and *our* home is *surrounded* by *palmitos,*' Marina said, looking around anxiously.

'Exactly, *así*, no problem!' Mati said.

'You've gone into English.' Which, for some reason, now felt annoying.

'Because you had a shock, but now you're okay,' he said,

back in Spanish. He looked at the T-shirt she was clutching to herself. 'I thought that was Juanjo's.'

'It's mine. Well, my father's – who... won't need it.' She held it up and looked at Mati, who was in blue swim shorts, bare-chested as usual. He had her father's broad shoulders and slim, wiry build. It would fit him. 'Would you like it?' she found herself asking.

His serious brown eyes looked at her carefully a moment, then he gently took it from her and put it on. He looked like he was waiting to see what she would say, but she couldn't say anything. 'Thank you.'

'It has a hole in the seam.'

'Good. So already it is old friend,' he said. In English again.

'Right. Okay, I need to get on,' she said, turning and going down the side of the house and in through the open doors to the bedroom. Completely forgetting to look for snakes.

She sat down on the floor next to the cupboard. Tried to concentrate. Crockery. Sheets. A silver Moroccan teapot, tray and little glasses that she wrapped up to take home to Mum and Guido. A box of her mum's hair and make-up stuff, long past their use-by date, that she tipped into the rubbish bag. It was hard to imagine why Mum had bothered, in this heat. Another box, with Mum's clothes – many of which also seemed way over the top for Cala Turquesa. When they'd left, did she really think she was going to come back, as a widow, to wear all these things? She put most of them in the non-*turquito* charity box.

She could hear Mati and Juanjo greeting Polly on the terrace, and Yasiel, whose turn it was to make brunch, say hello to her in the kitchen. Polly came in with a big grin and flopped back on the bed.

'Well?' Marina asked. 'Come on, how did it go?'

'Fantastic. Six of the *turquitos* came, and about the same number of day trippers, who gave me all this,' she pointed to a cloth bag of Coke cans and packets of apricots and almonds. 'But best of all… guess who joined in?'

'Mr Dork?'

'Yes! He's called *Ewan*. Such a natural beginner. Then he took me for a smoothie at the bar, although we couldn't be long because he'd promised he'd take over from the jewellery woman.'

'Wow! And did he explain how he came here?'

'Yes. Last year he had a bit of a breakdown after redundancy from a London newspaper and a marriage breakup. He'd come here the year before with his wife and another couple, and decided to come back and see if he could escape and heal here, if they'd accept a foreigner. They did, and he's thrived: he's done some articles for an online expat newspaper, but the best thing, he said, is that he's learnt how to design and make jewellery! Such a lovely guy.'

'Oh! Did he say anything about meeting up again? None of these *turquitos* wear watches or look like they're aware of anything other than the approximate angle of the sun, so I suppose you'll just have to—'

'We're doing exactly the same tomorrow!'

'Brilliant!'

'How's the cupboard going?'

'Good! I'm putting all the stuff that the *turquitos* might

like in this big box. We could have a sort of *terrace* sale – although without any money of course. Maybe Friday.'

'Great, I could let them know.'

Marina's phone pealed a WhatsApp. She looked at it and said, 'Francisca'. Polly's face fell; obviously she wasn't now so keen on the idea of leaving Cala Turquesa.

'Hello, Marina, how is it going there?' Francisca said in her low Spanish voice, careful not to go too fast for Marina.

'Very good! Oh, except I still have at least… three more days of work to do,' Marina answered in Spanish.

Polly put thumbs up and smiled.

'And you're getting on well with the boys?' Francisca asked.

'Yes. We mostly do our own thing, but it's good. Last night we were making music together, it was such fun.'

'This is what they are telling me,' Francisca replied, then cleared her throat. 'The thing is, I'm finding it impossible to find you anywhere to stay that is pleasant but not extremely expensive.'

'Oh,' Marina said. It was going to be bad enough dragging Polly away from Ewan, and her from her father's view of the cove; she couldn't face moving to some dumpy place.

'So I've come up with an idea. How would you feel about… staying there, but for the days you're sharing with the boys from now on, we will only charge them half the rent? I'm sure they'll take you in the boat to San José whenever you need something, and tidy up if you need to show somebody round, and…'

'Oh! Let me just ask Polly.' She relayed the idea to her friend, who was of course delighted.

'We're okay with it! Have you mentioned it to the boys?'

'Not yet! I'll call Mati now and ask him to discuss it with the others.'

'Okay. We'll try and keep out of the way, so they can talk about it.'

'Good idea! We'll speak soon.'

Polly closed the bedroom door and shared a silent hooray and a laugh with Marina.

'They haven't said yes yet,' Marina said. She heard what had to be Mati's phone ringing in the other bedroom. They looked at each other and both crossed their fingers. Yasiel must have been having a cigarette outside, as Mati could be heard telling him to hurry up because they had to talk about something.

'He sounds a bit serious,' Polly said.

'Oh, he always sounds like that,' Marina said.

'No he doesn't! He's fine with me, and he and Yasiel are always teasing and laughing at each other.'

'Maybe he's just serious about anything to do with the *house*.'

They could hear the boys talking quietly in the bedroom. '*Madre mía*, how long can it take to decide?' asked Polly, pacing the room. 'Maybe one of them isn't—'

'Girls! Girls?' they heard from the boys, now in the living room.

'Where are you hiding?' Yasiel said, with a laugh.

The girls looked at each other and opened the door.

'So…' Juanjo started.

'Well…' said Yasiel.

The boys looked serious and seemed to be waiting for Mati to speak.

Mati turned to Marina. 'We hear you might want to stay

in the house with us. Are you *sure* about this?' he said, with a trace of amusement.

'Well… yes!' she said, Polly joining in.

There was then an enthusiastic kiss on each cheek for her and Polly from Yasiel, followed by Juanjo. Mati then kissed Polly, and Marina – more awkwardly, with one of the kisses somehow landing in her hair. Yasiel said something Marina didn't catch and laughed.

'Shall we celebrate with a swim together?' Mati asked, for once the jolly chap Polly had described, and they all cheered.

Once down at the beach, Mati and Yasiel raced into the sea, diving in like dolphins as soon as the water was deep enough. Polly was not far behind. Juanjo had brought a paddleboard and was soon up on it, the other two boys threatening to wobble him off. Then the boys took turns on it, followed by Polly, looking remarkably graceful for a beginner.

Marina watched from the safety of the water still in her depth.

'D'you want to try?' Juanjo asked, bringing the board towards her.

'No. No thanks.' The paddle would set off the inflammation in her stupid shoulder. She'd had twenty years of trying to avoid talking about her arm while she declined ball games, skiing and yoga – or looked daft doing one-armed swimming or dancing.

Polly swam over to her. 'Let me take you for a ride on it. In your depth. You can just sit on there like a *sirena* – come on.'

Like a mermaid. Like her father's Aqua Marina. But Polly didn't know about that. 'Er… okay.'

She hauled herself up on to the board and sat on it with her legs crossed, while Polly and Juanjo pushed her out to the other two. Marina looked anxiously at the water, but slightly shorter Polly was still in her depth, so it was okay. Then Mati handed the paddle to Marina and shoved her out to sea, shouting 'Off to Africa!' The boys laughed.

Africa. Like she and her father used to joke about. Looking ahead, it was just her, the sea and the horizon. Like on that awful day. Her heart patted away, leaving her breathless.

She turned round to the laughing boys. Not their fault – they didn't know. Polly was facing the shore, waving at someone. Ewan, probably. She waited for her to turn round.

'Get her back. She doesn't like to be out of her depth,' Polly shouted to the boys.

Damn, she was hoping they wouldn't find that out.

Mati swooped upon her so fast that she nearly fell off. 'You can't *swim?*' he asked, incredulously. He started pulling her back to shore.

'Well of *course* I can. I'm just not good with deep water.'

Marina was back on the floor of the bedroom in front of The Cupboard Minefield, but in no mood for it at all. Also, she seemed to be going backwards; Mati had taken off her father's pale blue T-shirt she'd got rid of by giving it to him, and after her shower she'd picked it up from the living room and laid it over her shoulders. Which was a mistake, because the soft warmth of it made it difficult not to cry.

After the swim and paddleboarding, they'd all had a drink at the bar shack, and Polly had turned the conversation round to how Marina needed brushes and white exterior paint to do the front of the house. The boys had happily offered to whizz her off in the boat, to be in San José for when the *ferretería* shop opened at five o'clock, but, despite her boat resolution, she'd gone into some kind of stupor and been unable to answer. Polly had come to her rescue by making up some story about how she wanted to go there for some things herself, so would go with them to get the paint instead, leaving Marina to get on with the cupboard.

'Why am I such a wimp? A phobia-riddled, one-armed killjoy?' Marina asked out loud.

What? Nothing we liked better than hurtling out towards Africa at full speed!

She turned her head to the T-shirt on her shoulder. 'That was *before*,' she said.

We'll go as far as the lighthouse! You can sit on the nose, with your legs dangling over the front.

La Mari cutting into the deep dark blue sea with a hiss, the wind throwing a cooling spray over her. Heaven, *estupendo*... 'That was *then*.'

Are you all right, Marina-Fish? Marinita?

'I'm fine.' She took the T-shirt from her shoulders and threw it onto the bed, where, weirdly, it landed flat – as if someone was wearing it, leaning against the side of the bed.

She opened a box that seemed to be more of Teddy's old books – but underneath, it was her and Teddy's DVDs. Did she really need to go through these? All in English, so probably no good for anyone here. She should take them back for Teddy's offspring – although by the time they were old enough, you'd probably just have to *think* of a film to make it spring up on your telly, DVD players long gone.

She'd just take the better ones back, as she would with his little books. She flicked through and picked out the cute musical dinosaur adventure *The Land Before Time*. Then the Sixties hero puppets in *Stingray, The Complete Collection*. 'I think that one was more for you than us,' she found herself saying to the T-shirt.

No, you loved it too. You loved an adventure. You were never a wimp. She could then hear the thumping drums of the title theme, and the dreamy 'Aqua Marina', as clearly as if someone was playing them in the next room.

'Oh my God, that song!' she said, smiling to herself.

She picked up the cartoon *Tarzan* film. All four of them had liked that. There'd been a song in it... She picked up her phone and went into Spotify. What was she doing? This was such a waste of time. There it was. She pressed it to start. Sort of jungly in rhythm but then... Oh dear. About not crying, being strong...

'You'll Be in My Heart'.

She looked over at the bed. Maybe a little siesta would be good. No more Spotify; she could hear the song in her head, anyway. She went over to the bed, picked up the T-shirt and laid her head on it, remembering for a moment that rise and fall of Daddy's chest, like the swell of the sea.

7

Marina left Polly to her family Zoom call in the bedroom and decided to make a start on the bougainvillea at the front before the sun got too hot. Although she would have to try and press on even when it did, because she wanted to finish it so she could get the painting done and have photos to take in to the estate agent before the weekend.

She soon had a big pile of crimson and green she would have to put somewhere, but two more windows and a doorway to clear. After a while she could hear male voices; the boys were getting up earlier today, even after their night fishing in San José.

There was a smell of warm bread, and then Yasiel and Juanjo came out with coffee and *tostados* – Yasiel with what looked like the classic ham-and-tomato version, Juanjo with a jam one.

'Good morning, Marina! Can we get you anything?' Yasiel said with a grin. 'Or have you had your pony food this morning?'

'I have! Mm, but that does smell good.'

'I've got too much here,' Juanjo said. 'Want some?'

She nodded, and he broke off a bit of toasted baguette and peach *mermelada* and held it out to her.

She came down the ladder, took off her gloves and groaned as the fresh sweetness filled her mouth. 'Oh my God...' she said in English.

'What are you doing up that ladder anyway?' Yasiel said with a laugh, standing for a moment, all over six foot of him, and reaching up to the bougainvillea above the door. 'I'll do those higher bits after my breakfast.'

'Oh! Would you? That would be brilliant – it's taking me an age.' It was also making her shoulder ache.

'I'd rather *paint* – I'll do some for you later,' Juanjo said.

'Great! Yes please!' She sat down with them at the table with her toast. 'This is amazing; I might start having Spanish breakfast from now on.'

They smiled at her. They were both wearing singlets and swim trunks, rather than just their boxers like that first morning. She wondered if they might start having breakfasts as a group – but where was Mati?

'How did the night fishing go?' Marina asked.

'Good,' Yasiel said, and went on to list some Spanish fish names she didn't recognise. 'Mati's uncle Diego and his friend were very patient teaching us.'

'Mati wasn't keen though,' Juanjo said. 'He kept wanting to let everything go – even if it was going to be our dinner.'

'Oh dear! And he's still asleep?'

Yasiel shook his head. 'He got up early, determined to get this bit of work he has to do out of the way before he goes to see his friends at ERTM.'

'Sorry, *where*?' Marina asked, thinking she hadn't understood the Spanish.

'*Equipo Rescate de Tortugas Marinas*,' Juanjo explained. 'It's a voluntary group that rescues turtles found on the beaches. People ring 112 when they find one, and they come to collect the creature and nurse it back to health, if they can.'

'Oh, that sounds good. And also gets him out of the way while we're doing the house up – something I doubt he'll want much to do with, the way he is about me selling it.'

The boys looked at each other, and she wondered if she should have said that.

Juanjo scratched his head. 'Well, *I* think it's nice to help repair it a bit, like a way of saying thank you to the good old house for all the wonderful times we've had here.'

'Yes, me too,' Yasiel said.

Juanjo leant forward and lowered his voice. 'But for Mati, this place is his sanctuary. The place where he... remembers who he is, draws energy. There's so much stress in his work at the university. I wish he'd quit.'

'But it's the family thing... his father is a renowned professor there, and Mati's done very well,' Yasiel said. 'So that's not going to happen.'

Juanjo sighed. 'Anyway, as I've said to him, it's quite likely that the next owner will also make the house available to renters, so we may find we can still come – even if we have to change our month.'

'True!' Marina said.

Juanjo stood up and took their plates. 'Right, I'm off to get ready for Polly's yoga. I've not tried it before, so I hope she'll be gentle with me.'

'Great!' Marina said. 'She will be, don't worry.'

Yasiel watched his friend go in and then turned to Marina. 'He's rather impressed with Polly. Er... *very* impressed, in fact.' He looked at her, waiting for a response.

'She's impressed with *him*. But he should know that although she's *from* Madrid, and still has parents there, she's totally committed to living in England. *Passionate* about it. Also – I hope she doesn't mind me saying, but it'll soon be obvious – she's very impressed with an English *turquito* here. Er... who is in the yoga group.' She gave a gritted-teeth smile.

'Oh. Right.' He put a hand to his head. 'You know, it's the same every year: there's always just one of us in a relationship, the other two single. This time, *I'm* the lucky one. Even though it's very early days. Isa's a beginner at the salsa club I help out at. Not a good dancer, but a lovely person, a teacher – and very musical. She's just taken up piano. Isn't it adults that you teach, mostly?'

'Yes! Good for her. And perfect for you to have a musical girlfriend.'

Polly and Juanjo came out, Juanjo carrying her mat.

'How are you doing with it, Marina?' Polly looked at the bougainvillea. 'Hm, not bad – I'll give you a hand when I get back.'

'No need – we will have finished it by then!' Yasiel said, patting Marina on the back. 'Have fun – or peace, or calm, or whatever one should wish yoga people!'

After they'd gone, Yasiel went off to the shed and came back with some shears.

'What? How did you find those?' Marina said with a laugh.

'You forget I've been coming here for nine years! A couple of times, we couldn't close a window or door, and had to do something. Right, let's get this monster sorted.'

Marina watched as he energetically and skilfully shaped

the rampant shrub. 'Good God, it's Yasiel Scissorhands! You know, like in the Johnny Depp film?'

'I know *Edward Scissorhands*; love it. But don't just stand there!' he said, teasing. 'Get the wheelbarrow, load up the stuff and I'll show you a place off the path where the *turquitos* put their garden rubbish.'

'Okay!'

Just as they were about to unload the first wheelbarrow, Marina heard her phone peal a WhatsApp.

'Probably my mum – or maybe Polly forgot something...' She went in and picked her phone up.

It was her housemate Alyssa, asking if she still had Will's old electric toothbrush, because his new one had broken. Jesus, did that deserve an answer? *No, and nothing else of his either,* she WhatsApped back. There was also an email from one of the Shoreham estate agents, with links to three little flats for rent.

Marina went back out to Yasiel. 'Wow! You've finished! Show me where to dump the leaves and then we could go and have a swim. Maybe Mati will have time to join us before he goes.'

'He's already gone.'

Marina looked down the path, expecting to see Máti's back.

'While you were on the phone.'

'Oh.' As if he'd crept out without having to say anything to her. 'Maybe when the others get back then.'

'You have my services until then!' he said. 'Come on, let me show you the gardening dump.' He grabbed the wheelbarrow and she followed him along a fork in the path towards a large but neat pile of dead plants and bushes in a gulley between rocks. 'You'd think they'd put anything anywhere, but they're very caring of their valley.'

'How long have they been here?'

'Let's see, er... this must be the fifth summer we've come and they've been here. We've never had any trouble with them – but then, we're good customers, and give them our fridge stuff when we go!'

From here, she could see two of the other three houses in the valley, now with makeshift wooden awnings attached to them, tatty bits of furniture on their terraces. 'I can remember those houses being rented out to families – different people each year. Why would people abandon them? Long before the road got blocked.'

'It's a beautiful climate here, but one that is very harsh on buildings, if they are not looked after. People get too old to visit, the younger generation can't agree on repairs, and this happens. But good news for the *turquito* families who have taken them on.'

'I suppose so.' But she didn't want this to happen to *their* house – and that's what could happen, if Mum kept neglecting it. No, it needed to be sold; there had to be someone who would want to take it on.

They had just done the last wheelbarrow load to the dump when Polly and Juanjo came back – with the tall, and thankfully shorts-wearing figure of Ewan coming along behind them.

Polly, looking radiant, introduced him to her and Yasiel.

'Hello, Marina,' Ewan said, with a slight bow. Close to, he had eyes wrinkled from the need to protect them from the sun; a freckled, tanned face; sun-streaked fair hair – and a Bowie-esque other-worldliness about him that would absolutely work for Polly.

'Hi! How are you enjoying the class? I'm told you're a promising beginner!' Marina said, then immediately regretted it when she saw the face of Polly's other beginner smiling resignedly.

'It's been a wonderful discovery. I don't know how I've survived without it,' Ewan said.

Marina turned to Juanjo. 'And how did *you* get on?' she asked him in Spanish.

While Juanjo smiled and mumbled something, Polly patted his back and said he was another natural. Yasiel then urged him to go paddleboarding with him.

'Marina, Ewan thinks inviting all the *turquitos* to come and have a look at the things you want to give away might be a bit chaotic – they have no sense of time or urgency, apparently, and we'd have them drifting in and out of the house for days!' Polly said.

'Oh no!' Marina said, gritting her teeth.

'I know the sort of thing each of them would like,' Ewan said. 'I don't mind having a look through and taking it to them.'

'That sounds a good plan. Just make sure you have first dibs, for your trouble.'

They went through to the bedroom and showed Ewan the *Turquito* box she'd started.

'Whatever you want – and there'll be more. Right, I'm going out to rub down the front of the house in preparation to start painting.'

'Oh...' Polly looked torn between helping her or staying with Ewan.

'Juanjo is going to help later – you two just chill… really.'

She left the two of them sitting very close to each other next to the box, grabbed some Coke cans and went outside with her phone and the speaker. They seemed like they might need some privacy, so she would only do the front terrace, and chip away at the loose paint to her reggae playlist at max volume.

After she'd done one section, she couldn't resist making a start on the painting. On went the glistening white, stunning against the now partially tamed crimson bougainvillea – as Steel Pulse sang 'Shining', about sunshine and flowers and what life is all about. A song more fit for the possible lovebirds inside, rather than a solo Marina selling a pretty little home she used to adore, but somehow seeing it like this made her smile. As Juanjo said, doing it up was like saying a fond goodbye.

The sun was low in the sky when Marina, Yasiel, Juanjo, Polly and Ewan finally sat down at the terrace table with a drink and laughed and cheered as they admired the finished house, complete with its blue window frames that Marina and Juanjo had fought over painting.

'Thank you *so* much, everybody! I insist on taking you all out to dinner in San José!' Marina said, and got an enthusiastic response.

Then, as if perfectly timed, Mati came up the path – wearing her father's soft pale blue T-shirt, but the mop of soft hair tossed into madness by the breeze on the boat, eyebrows pinched with concern above his sunglasses. 'But not me, I haven't done anything.'

'No, but you were off saving...' Marina couldn't remember the word for sea turtles in Spanish, so did flappy motions with her hands, which may have come across a bit dismissive.

'No, I don't save any,' he said.

'Well... you were supporting those who do – that's still a good reason not to be doing this,' she said, pointing to the house.

Mati looked at the house for a few moments. 'My God. Seeing it like this makes it all the more horribly sad.' Yasiel and Juanjo started saying something to him, but Mati walked into the house and, minutes later, a breathlessly plaintive Estrella Morente flamenco song was coming from the speaker in the living room.

Heart racing with anger, Marina charged in, and found him looking at his phone, probably lining up the next song of misery.

'Okay, I've had enough of this. And turn that *off*,' she said in English, pointing to the speaker.

He looked up, surprised. 'Estrella? You just don' know this,' he replied, surprisingly also in English.

'I *do* know it. "Find me in Your Dreams". Not exactly celebratory. What I don't know is why you're continuing to be such a *culo* about this,' she continued in English, but making sure he understood the important word.

He was looking at her, wide-eyed and apparently listening; that was something.

'You think I don't have any feelings about the house?' Marina said. 'All my best childhood memories are here.' *But also, all my worst ones.*

'I only—'

'Why spoil your last time here – the last time for all of us? I don't want to hear one more miserable comment. That's *it*.' In danger of tears, she turned and went back outside, smiling weakly and putting up a hand to assure the others that all was well. She went to sit on a wobbly bench on the path to the garden dump.

She heard footsteps behind her. 'This is good question,' Mati said in English, sitting down next to her. 'Why spoil this time? I'm sorry, Marina.'

Marina stared at the sand beneath her feet. Using a bit of dried grass, she rolled a black beetle back onto its feet. 'Okay.'

The bird with the sighing whistle started up again, soon joined by a second one.

'What *is* that bird that sounds so sad?' She had vague memories of that sound accompanying the mornings and evenings here at the house when she was a child. She'd gone back into Spanish, as if to show she was now back on civil terms with him.

'*Estornino negro*,' he said, then got out his phone and tapped at it, his features a picture of concentration, before breaking into a smile. 'Ha! A... spot-less star-ling,' he read out, and showed her the image – a sort of arrogant Brylcreemed blackbird.

'Oh.'

'He's *not* sad; he's a clever, successful bird,' he said, back in Spanish. 'And very creative with building nests. Fresh leaves, yellow flowers, feathers... Maybe he's commenting on how beautiful you have made the house.'

She looked over at him to check he wasn't going to start up again.

He put his hands up as if protesting innocence, a cheeky smile on his face. 'I won't be saying anything more! Other than I'll take us all in the boat to your dinner at San José so you can thank everyone but me for helping.'

Marina looked over the side of the RIB at the inky dark water. It was still calm. She should be grateful for that – although it made the monstrous number of metres of water below them easier to imagine.

Juanjo next to her leant over. 'It's sandy down there, like a desert,' he said in slow Spanish. 'Beautiful. Some time, when you're ready, you must look with goggles.' He mimed them, in case she didn't know the word.

She hesitated, then nodded. 'Maybe.'

'And meanwhile, I promise I won't let you fall in!'

Mati looked over from the helm, smiled and shook his head.

'Well, if I did, I'd hardly notice, bobbing around in this thing!' she said, tapping her bright yellow life jacket.

'Exactly!' Mati said.

He'd put it over her head before they set off, in a way that so reminded her of Daddy that it almost hurt. In fact, looking at him now, standing there managing the RIB as if it was part of him, wearing a short-sleeved white shirt, there was an undeniable similarity between them – despite their photographic-negative opposite colouring.

She smiled back at him and switched her gaze to the fascinating little cave mouths, and then up towards the towering reddish rock above, now thrown into sharp contrasts of light and dark by the low evening sun. Not only do you get to go to places by water, but you see scenery impossible to discover otherwise; she'd forgotten that. Besides, the RIB, with its rubber sides and lack of pitch and roll, didn't feel like a real, hard, accident-prone boat.

They came into the port, past the stubby red and green lighthouses, the splendid green Guardia Civil boat... and now there would be a new memory here: arriving with Polly and three unexpected new friends for dinner in the village.

They walked down the promenade to a slightly tatty wooden restaurant with overgrown plants, but it was buzzing with life and the waiters greeted the boys like they were old mates. Their round table was on the pavement, overlooking the beach and the pinkish glow forming on the horizon.

Juanjo sat down between the two girls, and then there was an awkward moment where Yasiel and Mati seemed to be deciding where to sit – Yasiel probably thinking Mati and Marina were best separated.

'I will be at the side of Marina,' Mati said in English with a grin, 'just to show I can do this without her to call me a *culo* for a hour.'

'I'll try, but no promises,' Marina said with a laugh.

The waiter brought their drinks – and Marina noticed that Mati had chosen a non-alcoholic beer.

'So I don't drive into mountain later,' he said.

After a big plate of salad for them all to fork into, Juanjo and Polly halved a massive seafood pizza, Yasiel had a plate of octopus, and Mati surprised Marina by wanting to share a selection of meat-free *croquetas* – spinach, cheese and pine kernels; salmon and asparagus; and mushrooms with béchamel. All this was accompanied by the boys' jolly reminiscing about past holidays there, and the girls describing how Marina, doing a short Spanish course in Madrid, had tweeted '*Dios mío*, where d'you find paracetamol on a Sunday night in Madrid?!' and been delighted when it turned out that Twitter friend Polly lived just a couple of roads away. They immediately became the Bilingual Sisters, constantly switching languages in their chats on social media and, once Polly came to live in England, in their get-togethers.

'The perfect way to learn a language!' Juanjo said. 'But being in the country is also the thing. Are you two coming back next year, for Marina to practise her Spanish?'

Polly looked at her friend. 'If Marina's up for it!'

Marina nodded and smiled; even though it was too soon to know if she would want to come back here, she liked the idea of seeing the boys again.

They were now on puddings – *flan de casa*, a sort of super intense crème caramel. Just as it occurred to her that nobody had mentioned her selling of the house, Mati took out his phone.

'Look,' he said in English, quietly. She was intrigued; what made him decide to say some things to her in English? 'You can use these, if you like.' He showed her a series of stunningly creative photos of Casa Palmito, some from today, some from previous years.

'Oh... they're beautiful.'

'Yours are not good.'

'What?' she said indignantly, laughing. He hadn't said anything when she showed them to the boys this afternoon.

'I send them you. What is your number?'

She and Mati exchanging phone numbers: who would

have thought? She said the numbers in English, but he got confused and gave her his phone to put them in for him. Out of the corner of her eye, she saw Yasiel and Juanjo exchanging a look, probably relieved to see this clear sign of a truce.

'You do realise I'll be using them to show the estate agent?' Marina asked, 'Is that okay?'

'Uh-oh, potential *culo* moment!' Polly whispered to her, and the other two boys stopped what they were saying.

Mati thought for moment, then broke into a smile, nodded and patted Marina's arm. 'Yes, is okay.'

8

'You look much happier in the boat this time,' the boatman said, as he and Marina bounced over the waves towards San José.

She smiled and nodded in reply, rather pleased to have almost enjoyed it this time.

He helped her onto the dock. 'Five o'clock?' he asked.

'Perfect.'

She strolled along the little road of restaurants full of late breakfasters. Reaching the corner of the pedestrianised promenade, with its pretty corner of palms and *palmitos*, she got a friendly wave from the waiter who was cleaning tables at last night's restaurant.

She admired the little terrace of seafront houses in ice cream colours, and then found herself on the main street outside the rental office. She walked in.

'Marina?' A middle-aged lady with a handsome face, neat ponytail and swirly blue tie-dye dress stood up to kiss cheeks.

'How did you know it was me?' Marina asked.

'Of course it's you! Welcome. I'm Francisca,' she said, in that low voice some Spanish ladies have. 'The straight fair hair of course, but those eyes! The eyes never change.'

'Ah.' But hopefully she'd grown into those googly things now, as Daddy promised.

'Come and sit down and have a drink. Fanta?'

They perched on a small sofa with their cans. 'Tell me how it's going with the five of you,' Francisca asked, with a big smile. The younger woman with a telephone to her ear looked over with interest.

'Well... it's great!'

'Did Mati bring you?'

'No, no, I came with the boatman. But he brought us all here last night when we went to a restaurant.'

'And he's... behaving about the selling of the house? I've had to remind him that it's not *his*. He gets so passionate about things; he can be rude,' Francisca said, all in easy slow Spanish for her.

'Er... yes, I had noticed!' Marina said with a reassuring smile, but Francisca's face fell. She could be his mother rather than his aunt, with the same mass of shiny curls, the dark, sensitive eyes. In her youth, Francisca must have been stunning. 'But I think it's all okay now.'

'Oh good, good.' Francisca nodded and seemed to be waiting to hear more.

'And he cured my eczema with an aloe vera plant,' Marina added.

She patted her arm. 'That's my Mati – always trying to cure everything.'

'You wanted to tell me about the estate agent?'

'Ignacio Méndez. Yes. Now there's a chap who can be rude. No, who is *always* rude! But he does have the local sales market in his control. Also – and this is what I really wanted to tell you, in case you feel like walking straight out of his office as soon as you've gone in – his son already bought the three ruined houses in Cala Turquesa, so might be interested. The young man must have been brought up by his ex-wife, because he's surprisingly well educated and charming.'

'But when was that? He hasn't done anything with them; two are still inhabited by *turquitos!*'

'Obviously considering his options. This is not unusual here – especially in such a remote location.'

'Yes… but ours isn't a ruin. I'm hoping a local family with a boat might love it.'

Francisca shrugged. 'See what Ignacio says. Let me know how it goes. You need to get there now, before he decides to take a potential buyer off to view five different properties and then take an early lunch.'

'Oh, okay.'

'Lovely to see you!'

Marina walked on along the pavement. It occurred to her that Francisca must remember her father's accident. Had she ever told Mati about it? Probably not, or surely he would have been instantly more sympathetic about her wanting to sell the house.

The estate agency had peeling paint and dirty windows full of faded photos; maybe he was doing so well, with the 'local sales market in his control', that he didn't have to try.

The heavy-featured Señor Méndez was sitting by a computer screen and a squeaky desk fan. He looked up as Marina came in and said something like 'tell me.'

'I want to sell a house,' she said.

He indicated the chair in front of the desk and put a form in front of her.

She filled in her details, then hesitated at the address. Did the road even have a name? She wrote *Cala Turquesa* and looked up for his reaction.

His thick eyebrows rose up his forehead. 'That's not going to sell until there's a road.'

'Are they going to clear it soon?'

'Not that I've heard. Why make a road to ruins?'

'My house *isn't* a ruin. Look.' Marina took out her phone, found Mati's stunning photos and pushed it towards him.

He glanced and shook his head. 'Yes. But there's no road.'

'Perhaps a family with a boat would—'

He leant back in his chair and laughed. '*Perhaps a family with a boat!*' he mimicked. 'Or a helicopter!' he said, twirling a thick finger in the air and guffawing with laughter.

'Well, apparently your son bought the other three houses,' Marina reminded him.

He stopped laughing. 'Who told you that?' he asked, lifting his chin and eyeing her carefully.

'Er… I really can't remember,' Marina said, wondering if she'd missed Francisca telling her she wasn't to say anything about it.

'Anyway, that was before the road…' He made a swooping down motion with his hand and a tumbling sound.

Marina stood up. 'Well, I'm glad you find it all so funny. I'll just have to sell it on the internet. Goodbye.'

She swept out and strode along until she came to an inviting little turquoise-painted café that seemed perfect for calming her down. Taking a shaded table outside, she was soon consoling herself with a prettily garnished cheese *empanadilla* and a peach-and-kiwi smoothie.

She got out her phone and went into Idealista, tapped San José in there, and was soon gazing with horror at the stream of flats, houses and new-builds available. None of them were remote. All of them were on a *road*. She could put Casa Palmito on there and see what happened, of course, but selling it herself – hosting people offering the price of a garage or just having a nose around – didn't sound fun. And if the boys weren't there, it didn't sound safe, either. As Ignacio said, she'd have to wait for the road to be cleared – if that ever happened. Her flat in Shoreham clearly wasn't going to happen any time soon, but she could find one to rent; it wasn't the end of the world. Meanwhile, she should enjoy her time here – especially now she was getting along with all three of the boys.

She had nearly four hours to wait for the boatman. Without your own boat, Cala Turquesa was certainly an awkward place to stay. Mati had some kind of special deal on his hired RIB because his uncle worked at the port; most people wouldn't be able to afford to add boat hire to their holiday. No wonder Casa Palmito was almost unrentable as well as unsellable. She breathed out heavily. Poor little house – what was to become of it?

She decided to talk to her mother about this later and meanwhile just try and get on with the day. She could either take the car for a spin, or – if she could hire one of those sunbeds with a bamboo shade over it – flop on the beach. After her late night, it was going to be the beach, possibly with a little kip.

She paid and thanked the two women who ran the café, started to look forward to the afternoon, and turned towards the seafront – only to see Ignacio Méndez locking up his office for the afternoon and coming towards her.

'Señora Meyer. What a shame, you now have four hours to wait for the boat back to your house.' He shook his head, with an amused half-smile.

'I know that. It doesn't matter; I'm off to the beach.'

She carried on along the front, back past the ice-cream-coloured houses, then along the wooden walkway over the sand. She was in luck; six euros gave her a place in the front row for the afternoon.

She angled the sunbed so she could tan her legs a little. She soon got too hot so, tucking her skirt into her knickers, she went for a paddle in the little waves. Coming back and sprawling on the sunbed, one leg on, the other leg off so she could enjoy the feel of the soft warm sand on her foot, she nodded off.

A cloud. She opened her eyes. It wasn't a cloud, it was somebody blocking the sun. Looking down at her. Saying something.

'Sorry, what did you say?' she managed in half-asleep Spanish. She put a hand to her eyes but could still only see a silhouette against the sun.

'I said, I'm sorry to come to you like this, but you didn't answer your telephone and I didn't want to lose you.' English, with only a mild accent. But surely he meant 'miss' rather than 'lose'.

She sat up, and he perched on the sunbed the other side of the pole. She could now see his face, and... it was worth sitting up for.

He held out a hand, English style. 'Agustín Méndez.' She

went to shake it, but then realised he was handing her a card with his name and a hill of white houses against a blue background. 'You talked with my father about your house. By chance I am in San José for a few days.'

'I hear you own the other three houses,' she said. 'In Cala Turquesa.' She still wasn't fully awake. She was distracted by this Angel-Gabriel-Agustín visitation, and indeed the angel's appearance. His mother must be extremely refined, because the liaison with her toad of an ex-husband had produced a creature in whom the father's heavy features had been softened into strong ones, the jowled face sculpted into a wide but classically bone-structured one.

'Yes. I understand you are waiting for the boat at five o'clock. If you like, I could take you in my boat and you could show me the house now. Or if you prefer, I could visit later.'

She hesitated. You shouldn't get into boats – any more than cars – with men you don't know, but Francisca seemed to have a good opinion of him. Also, if he visited now, mid-afternoon, there was a good chance that the boys would be out.

'That would be great, as long as you can ignore the mess. My friend and I are sharing it with three guys at the moment.'

He looked amused. 'Really? Does that go well?'

'Mostly!'

She stood up – and quickly pulled her skirt out of her knickers. 'Sorry, was...' She didn't know the word for paddling.

He smiled. 'Of course. Would you like to go for a drink or an ice cream before we go?'

Probably yes, in usual circumstances, even though they would look an odd pair – her in her crinkled skirt and wind-blown plait, him in his smart chinos, crisp white shirt and sleek dark haircut. But she was here to sell the house, not cloud the issue with half an hour admiring the only possible buyer's physical attributes before starting negotiations with him. She packed away her sun cream and water bottle.

'Marina?'

'Oh… no, no. Unless you…'

He smiled again. 'Then let's go.'

They walked over the sand to the port car park, where Marina's rented blue Polo was gathering orange dust. She tapped it. 'I hired a car, but…! When are they going to clear the road to Cala Turquesa?' she asked, in case he knew more than his father did about it.

He shook his head. 'That doesn't have to be a problem.'

She looked at him.

'I'll explain later.'

They passed the boatman's RIB. 'I better tell him I won't need the boat,' she said, getting out her phone.

'He will go anyway, to collect the people on the beach. But of course, it is polite to say.'

Heavens, you'd think he was English. They waited for her to tap out a message on her phone and then went a few boats further along. He had a similar but newer and more comfortable RIB, with proper seats.

He went aboard and then held out a hand for her to take as she followed him – just as the boatman did, but somehow it was embarrassing.

'The best seat,' he said, pointing to the one beside him at the wheel.

They set off at a genteel pace – and continued that way. The water had more of a swell out here now, but not a drop ever reached her; none of the splashy bumping along of the boatman, or excited speeding up, slowing down and occasional laughing drenchings of Mati's boat.

After what seemed an age – in near silence – the RIB cruised between the buoys to the shore, and he dropped anchor. She went to the edge, swung her legs over, and paddled to the beach, then looked back to see how he was going to cope in his chinos. He swiftly rolled them up and kicked off his sandals, easily morphing from formal businessman to a casual boatman with admirable calf muscles.

Which may have been what the staring people on the beach were thinking – except some of the darkly tanned and nude *turquitos* looked like they were thinking something much more negative, once she was close enough to see the expressions on their faces. One of the older ones even said something to him, but got a gracious smile and a response in return that she didn't catch.

She followed him past the floaty cloth shop and then the busy bar, Agustín seeming to know the way. He also seemed to be accustomed to the hostile muttering from the people in the bar – who included, Marina noticed with a sinking heart, the three boys, looking dismayed.

Agustín put on his sandals and made a gesture inviting Marina to lead the way up the path. They climbed up into the quiet of the valley. When they came out of the bushes to where you could see the house just above them, he stopped. 'Very nice.'

'I've got photos in my phone, if you'd like me to send them.'

He didn't answer, concentrating too hard on looking at the front and, from the side, the view over the whole cove.

'Come in, we've got Coke, lemon tea, beer with and without alcohol...'

'Ah... Lemon tea, please.'

He was careful to follow Marina's example of hosing down her feet before going into the house.

The living room and its pretty Spanish arch didn't seem to interest him, and he wasn't measuring anything or writing anything down.

She handed him the glass. 'It's a bit of a mess, because one of the boys sleeps in here. This is the smaller bedroom,' she said, opening the door to Mati and Yasiel's room, which was a lot tidier than she'd feared, '...with a bathroom next door, and over this side, there's the main bedroom with its en suite.' He followed her over and crossed through the bedroom to open the doors to the terrace. Again, he seemed more interested in the views than the house; it made her wonder why he'd been in such a rush to visit it.

'Shall we sit here and talk?' he asked, pointing to the little table and chairs for two, now in semi-shade.

They sat down with their drinks.

He patted his hands on the table for a moment, then looked up again. 'Marina, I don't know how much my father told you.'

'Nothing, other than that you bought the others before the road...'

'You need to understand: I am not an estate agent but a

developer of property. I'm in the business of creating, not buying and selling.'

'Are you saying you'd tear down the house and build something else?' she asked, desperately trying to control her trembling anger at the thought of that.

He looked mildly insulted for a moment, and then laughed – which made him seem worryingly more like his father after all. He put his hands together as if in prayer. 'It's a question of *vision*, Marina. What would be the best for these homes, the people, this cove?'

'You mean, what would be best for making you the most money?'

He shook his head and laughed again. 'How *escéptica* you are! And... *brutal!*'

'I'm sorry. My mother says the brutal honesty is due to my Dutch half. Do go on.'

'It's not all about money. Although, it is strange, and maybe you don't believe it, but if I do the best for the place and the people, in the end this is always the best for the business too. And if I don't enjoy the creative part of my business, why I get up in the morning and do it? I could work for my stepfather's agricultural business. He would pay me well for much less time and stress.'

Marina bit her lip, wondering if this was genuine or complete *mierda*.

'What I see here is four houses redesigned into a unique, eco-friendly mini resort.'

'*Resort?* What d'you mean, *resort?*'

'People would rent a house for between one to four weeks, for a unique experience.'

'A resort means a pool. Where's *that* going to go? It would ruin the look of the valley.'

'I agree. Each house would have a small plunge pool. The sort of people who would want to come here, want their privacy. Also, we wouldn't be allowed to build where there isn't already—'

'And a *boat?*'

'Boat hire would be offered. But they would also be able to drive. With the development of the houses, the road would be repaired.'

'But people might want to *buy* these houses.'

He shook his head. 'They might. But is that fair? Is that the best for the people and the cove? Using the place just two weeks in August, one week at Semana Santa, and the rest of the year the place lies empty and decaying? Winter days here are sunny and beautiful for walking, observation of birds... If the houses are rented, more people can enjoy them.'

'And the *turquitos?*'

'Obviously those living in the ruins will have to leave. And so these people don't continue to make homes out of ugly pieces of metal and plastic, we would make some wooden structures for them near the beach.' He finished his drink and beamed at her. 'It seems you also don't only think of the money!'

She shrugged.

'You haven't even asked how much I would give you for the house.'

'Okay, how much *would* you give?'

'Enough for you to... buy a small flat in San José.'

Marina's mouth opened. It was a lovely thought, but there was no way Mum would go for that. If she and Guido wanted to buy another second home – not that they'd ever mentioned it – they'd choose Tuscany near his family, or maybe in their beloved arty Venice. Not the humble seaside village where her first husband died.

'If you're interested, I will look for permission,' he continued. 'With the houses already here, that won't be a problem – but these things take a lot of time, of course. Maybe a year or more, by the time the plans have changed a few times.'

'I see. Okay, I'll talk to my mother.'

Voices could be heard on the hill.

'I think your friends are coming. Anyway, I have to go. Thank you for the drink.'

'God, I should have offered you something to eat, I'm sorry.'

'I will survive.'

The boys were singing – something pop flamenco that sounded familiar. Loudly, as if to scare off unwelcome visitors.

'So, they like flamenco?' Agustín asked.

'We all do. And tomorrow the boys are playing in the San José campsite bar.'

'Ah. So you will be in the village tomorrow. Would you like to talk more, over dinner before the boys play?'

'Oh…' It would be good; she'd have spoken to Mum by then. 'That would be lovely, thanks.'

'Let me know which boat you will take and I will collect you from the port, okay?' He stood up and gave her a kiss on each cheek. 'Until tomorrow.'

She watched him walk down the side of the house and down the path, meeting the boys coming up it. He said '*buenas*', but it sounded like only one of the boys answered. *Buenas. Buenas tardes.* Good afternoon, but here they just say 'good' for short. She suspected there wouldn't be anything *buena* coming to her in the next few minutes.

She went back into the bedroom and opened the cupboard, still only half emptied – but it didn't look like there would be an urgency for that now.

'Marina?' Mati called out, sounding concerned as well as cross.

'Yes?' Bracing herself for an irritating tirade from Mati, she went through into the living room. They were coming in, sandy and wet; it looked like they'd just been in the sea.

Mati looked her up and down. 'Are you okay?'

'Well of course I am; he's a property developer, not the son of the devil.'

Mati's eyebrows pinched together. 'I *know* who he is. He's got developments all over the place, and has looked at Cala Turquesa before.'

Yasiel and Juanjo took drinks from the fridge and made a speedy exit onto the terrace.

'Your aunt speaks very well of him,' Marina said. 'He wanted to see the house, since he owns the other three. I'm just considering all the options, that's all.'

Mati nodded and took a swig of beer, but for all his manly bare chest and hand-on-hip stance, he still looked perturbed.

'To be honest, after talking to everyone today, it looks like selling the house is going to take a long time. I'd put money on us all still being able to rent it next August.'

His face broke into a wide smile, and he cheered as his hands went up in celebration. Then he suddenly gave her a damp and salty hug... that unexpectedly left her breathless and tingling all over.

9

Mum had turned down the option of a video call, probably because she'd no doubt be seen surrounded in paints or mouthing 'I'll just be a minute' to a client in the gallery. She didn't seem to be fully concentrating – but then, nor was Marina.

'As I said, the road won't get fixed until there are rentable houses, and the houses won't be rentable until there's a road,' Marina repeated.

'Which is why this Augustine chap sounds like the answer. And it's a pretty good offer, all things considered. I'd accept and get things going, darling.'

'I... just want to ask a bit more about his plans.'

'Over dinner, yes. That sounds wonderful, very kind of him. Is there... a little chemistry between you two then?'

'Oh Mum, *please*.'

Marina could hear Juanjo calling her, Yasiel joining in. 'Ah, I've got to go. Breakfast is ready.'

'You have it all together, the five of you?'

'Yes.'

'Okay, off you go. Enjoy. Look after yourself, darling. Lots of love.' She was gone before Marina could even say goodbye.

She looked outside and… yes, the empty seat at the table was next to Mati – wearing just his red trunks, and water-tamed hair suggesting his lithe body would be scented with citrus shower gel. She'd suddenly lost her appetite. What? Oh good God, *no*. How was this possible? One damp and salty hug with him yesterday, and now here she was, burdened with an unfeasible but totally undeniable attraction to this annoying man. It had been happening for a while of course – the low, melodious voice; those dark, serious eyes; the fluidity of his body anywhere near water; those sensitive, caring hands…

'Ma-ri-na!' Yasiel shouted.

Mati turned round, grinning. 'Yes, what *are* you doing?'

She went out and took her seat – apologising too much when her leg bumped against his.

'Pony food and half a tostada, both. There you go,' Juanjo said, pushing the bowl and plate towards her, 'and Polly made you some English tea.'

'Aw, thank you!' She had no idea how she was going to get them down. *Crunch*. Jam all over her mouth. She reached over Mati for a piece of kitchen roll and said sorry again.

Polly was looking at her quizzically, as she had done last night, when Marina insisted on doing the cupboard rather than sitting in on the rehearsal as the boys had invited them to do.

'I don't get it; are you cross with him, or in love with him?' Polly had whispered to her in the bedroom.

'What?' Marina had replied, and then just laughed.

She shook herself back into the moment. The boys were now discussing the day ahead. They were going to rehearse in the morning, swim, have lunch and maybe siesta before setting off at about eight for San José.

'The six of us, if Ewan wants to come,' Mati said.

'I'll already be in the village,' Marina said, 'I'll see you there.'

Mati turned to her, looking puzzled. 'Oh?'

'I've got to find something for my mum in the shops,' she said, as she and Polly had planned; she didn't want the boys – particularly Mati – jumping to the wrong idea about her dinner with Agustín.

'Are you going to be our rehearsal critic today, or are you going to be back in that damn cupboard?' Yasiel asked.

'Haven't you nearly finished, now?' Juanjo joined in.

'Yes! Well, the household stuff. Ewan, Polly and I are going to give away the last things today. Then it'll just be all the family papers, twenty-year-old bills and things – mostly for barbecuing!'

'It's been *twenty* years since you were here? I didn't realise. Careful – there might be some lovely photos of little Marinita,' Mati said.

Only her father – and maybe Diego at the port – had called her that.

'How old were you?' he asked. 'There were so few people around in those days, maybe we met on the beach!'

'Ten.'

'Ha – we're the same age. But you left a few years before my brother and I started being sent down here to stay with Francisca for a few weeks every summer.'

'Ah.' If Daddy hadn't died, maybe they would have met, talked about boats... but Daddy *did* die, and some now-middle-aged Spanish lady in the village – maybe even

Francisca, for all she knew – was there when the accident happened.

'He's waiting for you.'

She turned to the boatman, confused for a moment.

'Your gentleman.'

They were coming into the port, and yes, there was Agustín, looking elegant as ever, waving. She waved back. He had a slim case under his arm, no doubt with images of the house Casa Palmito was to become – although maybe not until she and Polly had had another holiday in it with the boys.

José the boatman helped her onto the dock. 'Shall I see you tomorrow morning?' he asked.

Good God, he was assuming she was going to stay the night with her gentleman. 'No, no. I'll come back later with the boys. They're playing at the campsite tonight.'

'Ah, very good. Maybe I'll come along to that.'

Agustín came forward and kissed each of her cheeks. 'How are you today? Did you survive the boys' inquisition?'

'Oh…' She smiled with gritted teeth.

He laughed. 'It's okay, I am accustomed!' he said in his near-perfect English. He patted the case under his arm. 'I have the first drafts to show you. I was thinking we could go for a drink at the hotel before we go into the restaurant.'

'Ah, okay.'

'You will love the restaurant – it's my favourite place to eat, and right over the beach.'

'That sounds wonderful.'

They walked along the front, up to the main street and

then up the hill – slowly and keeping in the shade – with occasional glimpses between the houses of sea, golden sand and rock pools. She was pleased to see a few people smiling or exchanging a few words with Agustín; not everyone hated him.

'Miss Meyer?'

She turned to find an Indian-looking lady with a daughter of about ten or eleven who looked familiar…

'Zara!' Marina said, and watched the little girl break out into a big grin.

'I'm Shefali,' the mother said, 'we once met at a parents' evening at Oakfield House.'

'Oh yes. Are you enjoying your holiday?' Marina asked Zara.

Zara bit her lip.

'It's really funny we should bump into you today. We had a few tears this morning about a piano piece she's stuck on.'

'My piano teacher says I have to learn it before next term or I can't do my grade two,' Zara said, sadly.

'Oh dear! But you shouldn't be worrying about that on holiday.'

Shefali turned to Agustín. 'I'm so sorry to interrupt—'

'No, no, don't worry!' Agustín replied.

'Thanks,' Shefali said. 'The thing is, we have a piano in our second home here, because she likes to play a little each morning. But it's now become a daily torment!'

'Goodness, which is the piece that's causing all this misery?'

'"O Waly, Waly" – and that's exactly how we feel about it!' Shefali said. 'Oh, I don't suppose… we could pay you to give her just one lesson so you can explain it?'

'Of course!' Marina said. Zara had been a happy, responsive and quite musical pupil; it was a shame to see her like this.

Zara jumped up and down, and Agustín patted Marina's arm and said, 'Marina to the rescue!'

'I've had an idea,' Shefali said. 'If you could make it next Friday late afternoon, you could come with me to the expat bar afterwards – temporary expats are allowed! They're a small, lovely crowd, with some Spanish friends too – a great way of finding out what's going on in the village!'

'Ooh, that sounds good, but the bar might be a —'

'I'm in San José for a local concert next Friday; I can take you back,' Agustín said.

'Oh, you shouldn't—'

'Well, I can take you home, no problem,' Shefali said.

'Thank you, but… you'd need a boat!' Marina said. 'I'm staying at my mother's old place in Cala Turquesa up the coast, and the road is closed.'

'The place with the hippie colony? How exciting! We've been meaning to get the boat to it. Everyone will want to hear about that at the bar! Look, here's my number,' Shefali said, taking a receipt and a biro out of her bag. 'WhatsApp me.'

'Thanks, I will.'

As they said goodbye, Zara called out 'hasta pronto!' – reminding Marina of her own attempts to speak Spanish at her age.

'Hasta pronto! And meanwhile, I'm going to send you someone singing it as a folk song, with its other title: "The Water is Wide". You'll love it, and then I'll show you how to play it, okay?'

'Okay!'

'Why didn't I know you are piano teacher?' Agustín asked as they carried on up the road. 'It seems that you enjoy it. I don't think the piano teacher I had as a boy enjoyed it; the lessons were all pressure and no fun.'

'What a shame! Half my piano pupils took between thirty and fifty years to have another go at piano after having a nasty teacher like that as a child.'

'I can imagine!' He stopped outside a smart white and dark wood hotel but took her down a side entrance to a quiet terrace overlooking the beach. They sat down at a large wooden table and ordered drinks.

'You don't want wine?' he asked.

'No, I much prefer the *mosto* grape juice; for me, most wines are just grape juice gone horribly wrong!'

He looked shocked. 'But Marina! Wine is one of the most beautiful things on earth! I'm sure I could show you—'

'No. Well maybe...' She was going to say *another time*, but would there be another time? 'So...'

'Are you ready for this?' he asked, pulling a laptop out of the case. 'I think you're expecting the houses to look the same but more white.'

'It's crazy of me to care at all – it'll be nothing to do with me.'

He looked up and stopped tapping on the keyboard. 'You care because you would feel responsible if what I build is horrible. I've been waiting for your house before doing anything. In fact, I was about to contact your family through Francisca – such a coincidence, no?'

'It is, yes.'

'So… come and sit this side of the table with me, so you can see.'

She moved next to him. He was wearing aftershave, something the boys didn't bother about in the house.

An image of four houses dotted up the Cala Turquesa valley filled the screen. They were sleekly modern with wide glassy eyes to them. In fact, more glass than anything else. 'Oh.'

'What d'you think?'

'A bit hot, with all that glass. And people can see you changing your clothes.'

He laughed and started talking about one-way glass, blocking of solar radiation, reducing need for lighting, maximal views. Glass was the 'ultimate green material', apparently. And of course, each house would have its own solar power.

'Yes, that's good. I just think it's a shame there isn't a nod to the former designs – red roof tiles, the odd arch. But hey, what do I know?'

Their drinks arrived.

'Energy-efficiency is priority. Anyway, it's only an early draft.' He flicked through the possible layouts for each house, all now managing to have three bedrooms rather than two in the same plot size.

'Wow.'

'So… did you get my email?'

'Yes.' The email with the offer. As he'd said, it was enough to buy a small flat in the village. It just didn't seem very much, for that heavenly if tatty little house. 'I'm sorry, I should have replied. We… need to think about it.'

He laughed gently. 'Marina! At this point, you're supposed to throw your hands in horror and insist on twenty thousand more!'

'Oh God, so I probably am.'

'I'll take it that you have, and revise my offer to ten thousand more, okay?'

'Okay!' she said with a laugh and patted his arm.

'And how long might it take you and your mother to decide?'

'How about this: I'll let you know before the end of the month.'

'Perfect.' They clinked glasses, and went through to the restaurant, Agustín having reserved a table looking over the bay. There was a crisp white tablecloth and glistening tableware. She felt rather underdressed in her faded old seahorses sundress and boat-friendly Crocs.

Over a shared salad, he asked her if she'd been browsing the internet for little San José places.

'No. My mother's husband is from Tuscany; if they do buy another second home, it would be in Italy. I definitely want to come back here, but I'll be renting.'

He nodded slowly. 'What a shame, you could visit every time the pupils have holiday.'

'It would have been even better than that. I could have had a digital piano here and taught online, as I do at home, and come whenever it wasn't rented! Ha – what am I talking about? It's out of the question.'

'You teach *online?*' He looked surprised.

'Yes. It works well – the pupil and I both have a stand so we can use phones as keyboard cameras,' she explained.

'But if you teach online, and lots of adults... could you take one more? I would love to be able to play, to make my own music, not just go to concerts!'

Agreeing to have Agustín as a piano pupil? Wouldn't that be, well, some kind of conflict of interest? On the other hand, having dinner with your house buyer was probably already that. 'Have you got a piano?'

'No, but I could get one. *Two*: a good one for my home in Almería, and a small electric here.'

'*Here?*'

'I also have a house in San José.'

'Oh, I didn't realise. That's nice.'

Agustín looked down at the table, smiling to himself. 'I have an idea. Sometimes I rent out the little flat below mine – only to people I know, these days.' He looked up at her. 'If you rented that, I could store your electric piano for you – and we could make your San José teaching happen!'

'Oh! That sounds brilliant!'

'It's on the road going up from the corner of the promenade before it turns towards the port. I could show you this evening, if we have time.'

'Okay!'

Their main courses arrived: a vegetarian hamburger for her, tuna steak for him. After a day of Mati-affected appetite, she was starving.

'You should go to this expat group next Friday, with the piano pupil mother. Make some friends, talk to them about living here part-time.' He smiled at her, looking into her eyes. 'This is all coming together, Marina, I can feel it. And it makes me very happy for you. Well, and for me!' He put a hand on hers.

It did feel like that. Although just possibly not completely in the way he saw it. Surely such a handsome, eligible chap couldn't be interested in a Croc-wearing Englishwoman who would seldom be here? Flattering as that would be, it would be very awkward.

She withdrew her hand. 'Certainly lots to think about!'

'Ah, and almost I forgot; next Friday there will be an incredible concert at the *anfiteatro* in San Rafael. A flamenco guitarist and a classical guitarist who play together. It starts late, so you could still go to the expat group first.'

'Great! I'm sure the boys will want to come to that too,' she was glad to add, rather than making it a date.

He nodded. 'But maybe they will have another concert themselves? Anyway, let me get you a ticket, please; you mustn't miss this. I have heard them before and have their CD.'

'Oh... well that would be lovely, thanks!'

They had finished their meal, and Agustín was asking if she wanted a dessert.

'No, I'm fine thank you, but if you—'

'I'd rather have more time to show you the flat.'

'How far is the campsite from there?' she asked, getting her phone out to look at the map.

'Ten minutes? Don't worry, I'll walk with you to there.'

She was going to have to take him up on his offer; there wasn't going to be time to get lost. If the boys saw her with him when she arrived, she'd just have to make out she'd bumped into him by chance.

They walked back down the hill, the glimpses between the houses now showing an impossibly romantic pink-orange glow over the sea. Then it was along the seafront, and into

Agustín's road – a cul-de-sac of attractive gleaming white buildings, each with a gate to a private ground-floor patio, and steps going up to an apartment on the next two floors that had a wide balcony and, by the look of it, a roof terrace. He stopped outside an immaculate one with a leafy green tree coming over the wall.

'Your... *higuera!*' he said, touching its leaves.

'Fig! I love figs.'

He opened the gate. There was a neat patio with a border of succulents, a barbecue and a seating area. Then he showed her round the modern white and terracotta two-bedroom apartment, even pointing out a space by the bookcase where her keyboard could go. All this at a price considerably less than she was paying for her room in the House of Hell back home.

'It's... gorgeous,' she said, overwhelmed.

He beamed, then looked at his watch. 'Okay, let's get you to this concert.'

They went back to the promenade, took the next road, then through the welcome shade of a park of eucalyptus trees. They could hear a band playing... the boys' unmistakable 'Me Maten' song.

'What? They've started early!' Marina said.

'Well, we're here now.'

They went through the gates to the lit-up bar area, where there was a crowd of about fifty or so people behind the lucky ones with tables.

Much as she'd enjoyed his company, it was now time to lose Agustín. Wasn't he just going to walk her here? But he looked like he was intently watching and listening to the band.

'They're very good,' he said during the applause at the end of the song.

Polly grabbed her arm. '*There* you are! I WhatsApped you – they had to go on early because the first band's van broke down.'

'Ah, that explains it,' she said, as Polly and Agustín said hello to each other.

Polly nudged her and tilted her head towards the band. Yasiel was blowing her a kiss, Juanjo was waving, and Mati nodded and smiled.

'I'll leave you to it,' Agustín said to Marina. 'I'll send you message about next week.'

She thanked him for dinner, they did the Spanish double-kiss, and he made his way towards the gate.

'I think we might have some catching up to do?' Polly said.

'Well, yes, but not in the way you're thinking... Where's Ewan?'

'He's not ready to handle a crowd. Says he'll stick with being a practice audience in rehearsals, for now.'

'Bless him, fair enough.'

The band had started a new song – an old flamenco-pop song of Ketama's called 'Agustito'. She couldn't make out the rest of the words, and had no idea what the title meant, but something about the way the boys were singing the chorus while watching Agustín leave made her wonder if they were having a joke about him.

10

Marina and Polly were having breakfast on their terrace, unable to wait for the boys to wake up.

'So, are you going to accept his offer?' Polly asked.

'Well Mum's given the go-ahead. I'm sure I will, I just want to wait a bit longer, in case I think of some other way of doing things. Or maybe until I know more about his plans.'

And Agustín's *other* offers?' Polly asked with a wink. 'Concert, special price flat rental, himself as a pupil, himself as a… handsome eligible suitor?'

'That last one has *not* been offered.'

Polly raised her eyebrows.

'I know how it looks, and maybe there's a little spark there between us, a little romantic schmoozing going on, but nothing more.'

'Such a great-looking guy. I don't know how you can say that with such confidence!'

'Never mind me, how's it going with Ewan?'

'Great. Even if he does have issues. He's talking of coming over to see me in England! Although I've been painting a picture of Shoreham seaside tranquillity, so I need to make that happen as soon as I get back. Oh, and by the way, after yoga we're going for a swim and then to his place, so the bedroom's all yours.'

'Okay. Yoga? It's Saturday. Don't you get weekends off?'

'The *turquitos* don't know one day from the next. They're only aware of the hours of the day by when José turns up in the boat. Anyway, it's good for me, and wonderful for Ewan.'

'I'm going to come down with you, find something for Mum in the floaty cloth shop.'

Polly frowned. 'And pretend you bought it in San José?'

'Oh God. I'm surprised none of them asked how my shopping went! But I *would* like to get her something – especially if I can support the *turquitos* while I'm at it.'

'Ooh, there's José now,' Polly said, looking out at the boat coming into the bay. 'I better wiggle on.'

'No, the expression is *get a wiggle* on!'

'That! Come on.'

'Okay – for once let's just throw our breakfast stuff in the sink with water in, like the boys always do.'

'Yes!'

Down at the beach there were six *turquitos* – the older couple on the boat with them when they arrived; the affectionate two girls, today with matching shorts; Lala, the forty-something woman who had inspired Ewan to design and make jewellery; and Ewan himself. One of the others was welcoming the boat and telling the trippers about the yoga.

Apart from the smile from Ewan, Marina didn't get much response when she said '*buenas*' to the *turquitos*. This sometimes happened, if they were a bit in their own world, but today not one of them even nodded.

Dani in the shop was also unresponsive. She chose a tiny fish bathmat for a no doubt tiny Shoreham shower room, a short tasselled turquoise dress she could use for a beach cover-up, and two colourful headscarves that her mother would love for tying her hair back when painting – but he clacked her change down on the counter and asked, 'Why?'

'My mother will love using them for—'

'Why are you letting a developer build a hotel here?' he asked irritably in consonant-free Spanish.

'A *hotel*? Nobody's going to build a hotel here. I don't know where you've—'

'You will sell it to your handsome developer boyfriend to make a hotel; everybody knows. And then he will drop you.'

'Well, everybody's *wrong*; he's *not* my boyfriend. And I'd never…'

'She loves the cove. She will do everything she can not to spoil it,' Mati's low voice said in Spanish behind her. 'Come on, Marina, don't listen to this; let's go for a swim.' He put his warm hand on her arm a moment, and then they walked down the beach towards where the boys had left their things.

She turned to him. 'Do you actually believe what you just said there?'

'I have to.'

She groaned.

'No, no, of *course* I do. You'll do your best for the cove. Whether you'll do the best for *yourself*, I don't know.'

She stopped. 'Oh no. Please, *please* don't start this up yet again.'

'Then tell me…'

They'd reached the boys' pile of belongings, and Marina put the paper bag the shop had given her into the beach bag. Yasiel and Juanjo were splashing around in the water. She thought she and Mati would sit and chat there, but he couldn't seem to be near water without being on it or in it. She followed him in.

'What kind of development is he proposing?'

'He wants to replace the four houses with modern, one-storey energy-efficient ones, each with a little plunge pool. Lots of glass. Personally, I didn't like the look of them, however eco-friendly they are. They will all be short-term rentable, so lots of people can enjoy them rather than just a family coming for a couple of weeks a year.' There, he had the facts, so maybe he could now shut up about this.

He nodded slowly. 'And he describes this... over *dinner*. Wine. Let me guess, looking over the water. Ha! Or looking into each other's eyes! Well, all fine of course, but not a good way of doing *business*, Marina.'

Madre mía, the guy was reaching a whole new level of patronising arrogance today. 'That's *not* what—'

'And you know I'm right about this, or you wouldn't have made up the lie about the shopping.' A wave broke over them – more on him than her. *Good,* she thought, laughing with delight, but maddeningly he only looked even more gorgeous as he pushed the wet hair out of his eyes, body glistening in the sun, waiting for her response.

'I just didn't want you... and the others... to think I'd made up my mind, or – well, like *everybody*, according to Dani – get the wrong idea.'

Watching another fair-size wave wobbling towards him, he said something like 'we'll see.' Then he snatched Yasiel's surfboard out of his hands, and let the wave carry him back to the beach. Yasiel caught up with him and dunked him, which had Marina laughing again.

'Okay, come on, let's go right to the other end of the bay where there are bigger waves,' Yasiel said.

'Come with us, Marina,' Juanjo said. 'Just bodysurf, or we'll let you have a go on one of these.'

Marina looked over to where the waves were rolling and curling over like adverts for washing machines. It was also a place where the water became deeper more quickly.

'No, I'll leave you to it. I'm going back up. The cupboard's calling.'

'*Now?*' Mati asked. He put a hand to his hear and wrinkled his eyebrows. 'I can't hear him! But okay. See you later.'

Showered and wearing her new little dress over her bikini, Marina had put the wonky sun umbrella up over the bedroom's terrace table and had a box file of papers to go through with her Coke. She was doing well, she thought, as she hurled ancient vacuum cleaner and fridge manuals into the recycling box at her feet. Fridge? How would you replace one now? You'd have to hire a boat so large it would cost ten times the price of the appliance. Perhaps she should tell Yasiel to stop hanging on to the door as he swooped down to pick out a beer.

She flicked on. Long-replaced microwave, vacuum cleaner, and... what? *What?* Only Mum could have thought it was okay to put the *boat* manual in here with these. *La Mari*, in here like a hyacinth macaw with a bunch of sparrows.

She stared at the shiny manual cover showing the 'Grady-White Adventure Walkaround' – *La Mari* – and it took her breath away. Just like the first time she saw her.

'What d'you think?' Daddy had asked her with a big grin on his face, as they stood on the dock.

Marina was six and holding her breath with excitement. *She* – because boats are girls, Daddy had said – was so pretty, with her blue stripe like a special hairband. And you could walk right round her, sit on her nose, go whizzing off over the waves, park her where you want, discover places! 'I love her! Let's go now!'

Marina smiled at the picture... but then she remembered the *last* time she saw her.

'I'm not going!' she shouted to the green Guardia Civil men who had boarded the boat before she reached the harbour. 'I'm staying with Daddy!'

The green men looked at each other. One with no hair and a big face bent down to her and put his hands on her shoulders. 'We take father to help him, okay, María?' he said in throaty English. 'You go in the little green boat; it take you to your mami.'

'Daddy wants me to stay!' she screamed at him.

The little boat was tying up, and it looked like the big-face man was going to lift her into it. She wrenched herself out of his grasp and ran round to *La Mari*'s nose... but the blue and black bits in her eyes were back. She hit the bar too hard and was suddenly somersaulting over it, thinking, in the air, that Daddy would be cross, but also wondering if she'd now hit her head and join him in the hospital. But there was just a slap as she landed on the hard water, and then it was in and in, down and down...

She opened her eyes and – only just remembering not to gasp – wished she hadn't. Because she was on top of a scary mountain of water. A long, long way beneath her, there was sand and swaying grass like another world... A thick arm roughly yanked her up. She wailed in agony as somebody pulled her hurt arm... and then she was in the little boat, hearing 'hospital', and soft words, maybe English. She leant away from them so she could look at *La Mari* and held her breath as she willed the world to turn back so it could be Daddy, not a green man, at the helm.

She went to the bathroom, blew her nose, washed her face in tepid cold water. Quickly, so she might not think any more about it, she wrapped the *La Mari* booklet in the paper bag from the shop and put it in her flight bag. She couldn't keep it, but she couldn't throw it away – like all the memories of those days.

She sat down again, threw out some old household bills, but decided she'd had enough. Besides, she had something much more urgent and pleasant to do. She picked up her phone and tapped 'O Waly, Waly' into Spotify. The Rutter strings version was divine, but little Zara needed to hear the *song* before she could hopefully come to love the dour arrangement in her grade two exam book.

She tapped a vocal version, with its alternative title, 'The Water is Wide'. Hm. At least it wasn't The Water is *Deep*. Ah, Eva Cassidy had an acoustic version. She grabbed the speaker and let it fill the terrace. Such a pure, expressive voice, such beautiful phrasing of the melody... how could Zara and her mum not love it? But oh God, the lyrics – deep love, asking for a boat for two, and it didn't sound like it ended well...

'What's this?' Mati asked.

She jumped. 'Can you stop creeping up behind me?'

'What *is* it? So beautiful.'

'Eva Cassidy. It's a folk song. Scottish, I think.'

'You must send me the link,' he said.

'I will.' She'd be sending her first WhatsApp to him. With a boat and a tearful emoji.

'Marina...' he said, looking at her carefully.

She sniffed. 'I'm not *trying* to make myself miserable, honest!' she said with a watery smile, and explained about Zara's piece and the lesson she was going to give.

She turned off Spotify, which was now going into Eva Cassidy's last song before she died at thirty-three – two years younger than her father had been.

'All about boats – which you're not happy with. You don't seem to be a huge fan of the sea.'

'What? I *love* it.'

'Then why don't you... throw yourself in there?'

Oh, she'd thrown herself in there, all right.

Her shoulder – the easiest explanation. 'I've got a long-term shoulder problem. I forgot to bring my floating square thing I usually put under my arm when I swim, to stop it moving about too much and getting inflamed.'

'Is there nothing anyone can do about that?' he asked.

'They've tried. I damaged it as a child. But I do aqua dance aerobics and swim with three limbs!'

'Then you should get a floating thing from the village.'

'Yes. Don't know why I haven't.'

'And some goggles and a snorkel, so you can see underneath and not be scared.'

She'd seen underneath, all right.

'And boats... are not just transport! They can be such fun. You should try taking the helm.'

Oh, she'd... *Jesus*.

'Listen,' he said, sitting down at the table and finishing her drink. 'Before you decide about the house, you need to discover the sea here. The wonder of this coast. I will show you it – it's my mission.'

Her heart began to pat away, at the thought of the deep water she didn't want to be talked into, but also the thought of time spent in close proximity to this attractive but frequently annoying man. Maybe she'd get to know him better and... *like* him. 'Er...'

'We'll start taking the boat out together, every day we can, until you love her. I'll show you the caves, the volcanic rocks, the secret coves. Let you drive. Have you swim with your floater and meet the fish.'

'Oh...'

'What d'you think?' he asked her, with a big warm smile on his face.

11

'So, what'll be the first lesson in Marina's maritime orientation programme?' Juanjo asked as she and the three boys glided over towards San José on a calm sea.

Yasiel laughed. 'Surely it has to be how to drive the boat?'

'We don't mind going a bit slower while she has a try,' Juanjo said.

'Or maybe it should be the basics first – like, how to skinny-dip in a remote cove!' Yasiel said, giving Mati at the helm a nudge.

Mati laughed a little too loudly for Marina's liking, as if this was the most ludicrous idea imaginable.

Marina put out a disbelieving palm-upwards hand. 'Boys, I am actually *sitting here*, you know.'

'Maybe she should start with a canoe,' Juanjo suggested, then turned to her. 'You could both come with us before going off to do your *lesson*.'

'Hm, not sure,' Marina said, thinking of the thing overturning in deep water, 'but I do feel bad you're missing out on that, Mati. I really don't mind if—'

'No, no, I have plenty of time for that. We'll keep to the plan.'

'Which *is*…?' Yasiel asked.

Mati tapped his nose.

They'd arrived at the port, and a middle-aged man in the dark blue shorts and polo shirt uniform of the port was waving at them enthusiastically.

'That's my Uncle Diego, Marina,' Mati said. 'He's been working here forever. He would have been here when you were a child.'

Diego. Oh God, her father's friend, the smiley port man. They'd sometimes go for a drink at a place next to the port – much to Mum's annoyance. Diego would remember her father's accident – and maybe her name, and that she was on the boat... Luckily, Diego was called away to help with a query at the office before Mati could introduce her.

Yasiel and Juanjo patted her on the back and went off to the beach. Then it was just her and Mati – walking the same route she'd taken with Agustín, but it felt much longer. She was so aware of him, and the care she was taking not to bump into him was as if he were carrying an electrical charge.

He turned to her as they stopped outside a kiosk of beach paraphernalia. 'Here we are, but I thought you might like to go to the Sunday market first? Lots of those colourful drapey things you like, and we can pick up some snacks for our trip.'

'Er... Oh, yes!' They walked on into the *rambla* – a road with high walls that apparently took occasional storm water off to the sea. This was where they'd set up the *mercadillo*, a little market of stalls selling kitchen equipment, cheap colourful summer clothing, fruit and vegetables, and the inevitable trainers and designer boxers that you assumed were off the back of a lorry.

The market people had strung cloth between the stalls to give some shade, but Marina was soon boiling in her shorts and T-shirt and touching some of the soft, thinnest-possible loose dresses.

'Good idea!' Mati said, as the stall woman swooped through the forest of hanging dresses and took down one to put up against Marina. He helped her pick out a purple tie-dye one with an embroidered neck and a turquoise one with palm trees on it.

'Oh, and Polly keeps telling me to get a new bikini,' Marina said, coming to a stall of colourful swimwear.

'Look, a flamenco one!' Mati said, pointing out a blue bikini with white spots from a swimwear stall.

It was a modest design, but not as Fifties-style as her sports one, and it had a pretty frill. 'I might have to have that! Can you wait while I...?'

'Of course! All part of the programme!' he said.

She disappeared into the tent changing room, tried it on over her underwear, and came out grinning as she took it over to the till to buy it.

'*Olé!*' he said, and insisted on buying her a second one in the same design but in crimson. 'In exchange for that T-shirt you gave me – and well, a peace offering!'

She laughed. 'Oh, okay! Thanks.'

Then they went to the food stalls, and in a dense aroma of olives and roasting nuts, bought bags of salty pistachios, still-warm sugar-roasted almonds and some chewy fruit sweets with exotic flavours.

'Mm, delicious,' Mati said, making a start on the almonds as they walked back to the beach kiosk.

'They really are,' Marina said, putting another handful

in her mouth. 'Now, let's have a look... Ah, perfect.' She picked out a little yellow square float.

While Mati went over to examine the snorkelling stuff, Marina found herself looking at boxes containing large rubber rings for bigger kids – or regressing adults.

'This is what you need,' Mati said, coming over to her with a mask snorkel like she'd seen the boys use. 'You can breathe normally in it. It's expensive, but you could leave it with my aunt and uncle, for your next visit here. We'll come back and buy fins if you get keen!' He picked up the box with a large inflatable rubber ring with an orange-segment design that she'd been admiring. 'We need this too. We had one – Juanjo adored it – but it broke.' Without asking, he also took the float from her and got out his wallet at the counter.

'Hey, no! You can't pay for these,' she said, and quickly got out a note and put it on the counter. The shopkeeper looked from one to the other and took a note from both of them and gave Marina the change.

'What?' Marina said, as they came out of the shop with their bags. 'That's not fair. Not when you're already going to be giving your time to helping a floundering human dolphin.'

He looked at her. Maybe she hadn't used the right words.

'But I am *making* you do this – and I *like* to help *varamientos!*' he said in English.

Wasn't that the word they used for animals found hopelessly stranded on the shoreline? That was a bit much. She would have complained, but she was distracted by the tingly imprint left by the pat on her shoulder.

They went back to the boat, now with two bigger ones

close either side of it, and – her heart thudded – the large green Guardia Civil boat, which she'd once thought super-awesome, looking like it was nearly blocking the entrance as it filled up with fuel.

'D'you want to drive?' he asked with a cheeky smile, back in Spanish.

'Er...!'

He laughed. 'Fine, isn't she?' He tilted his head towards the Guardia Civil vessel with its sleek, go-fast shape. It had finished refuelling and started a baritone purring.

They got into Mati's boat and stuffed most of their purchases into the two flat box cupboards. 'Yes. It looks like we might have to wait a bit,' Marina said.

'What? No.' He untied the ropes, started the engine, and effortlessly swung the RIB past the Guardia Civil as well as an incoming fishing boat. Manoeuvring fluently, like the boat was part of him. Like her father used to do.

She was relieved to see they were heading back towards Cala Turquesa; she wasn't yet ready for the other direction. Once they were some distance from the shore, he slowed and put the engine in neutral.

'D'you want to try?' he asked Marina, pointing to the wheel.

'No, no, I'm fine.'

'And you will also be fine driving the boat, with me here next to you.'

'Oh... well... okay.'

They stood up and changed places, but the continuing effort to avoid Mati's force field somehow made Marina clumsily bump into him, and he grabbed her arms. 'But you'll need to keep on board to do it!' he said with a laugh.

Jesus. Once she was straddling the central captain seat – and glad that at the last moment she'd changed into shorts – he showed her how to push the gear into forward and she was off.

'That's it, great!'

She wasn't doing 'great', with her hopeless left and right oversteering, but he was right next to her, helping to settle her nerves, and after another little encouraging pat on the arm she found herself going round in a daft circle, giggling with the fun of it. The water was calm and willing to let her fool around on it. She was back pointing in the direction of Cala Turquesa, but then turned towards Africa so she could push the stick forward and go faster. And faster…

'Marina! Madwoman – I had no idea! Enough!' he called out, laughing.

She slowed the boat and turned it in a gentle circle, grinning unstoppably as the fun of it came back to her. 'I'm not sure I'd be happy trying to moor it though!'

'We can try, I'll show you. There,' he said, pointing straight ahead.

'What, tie up to the mountain?' she said.

'The cave, look.'

As she got a bit nearer, she could see it. Or rather the entrance to it, with its bright turquoise water.

'I don't like caves.'

'Nor do I!' he surprised her by admitting. 'Dark, and how d'you know a stone won't go…' He mimed a rock hitting his head and a silly face going unconscious. 'Yasiel and Juanjo love them – but usually leave me behind, saying I spoil it for them! But this one has an open entrance, sky on top the way I like it. Just go very slowly, I will help.'

He stood next to her, ready to take the stick and the wheel.

They were getting nearer. 'No! I'm going to bump!' she said in English by mistake.

'Is okay, we are in a bump boat!' he replied in English. 'And you won't do that, look.' He showed her when to go into neutral, reverse a little... then he used a hook and pulled them to a little ledge, tied the rope round a stone, and, after reaching down and getting something from the box, encouraged her to join him on the ledge.

They sat on it with their feet in the clear water, the cave mouth and its dark water and rocks to one side of them, while they sat in the shady but open little inlet.

He handed her nuts and sweets, and he'd brought along some lemon teas in a little cool bag.

'Perfect!' she said.

'And it's good, because you shouldn't be in the sun at this time of the day, with your colour,' he said, back in Spanish.

'Even with cream on?'

'Even with cream on. Or one day you could regret it.' He looked at the skin of her chest above her T-shirt, and then her face.

She wondered what he thought of all her freckles, so different to his clear, golden-brown skin. Maybe the Spanish find '*pecas*', as they called freckles, ugly.

'But you never complain about the heat.'

'No. I only ever complain about cold. And I do a *lot* of that,' she said.

'So you are living in the wrong country! Did you ever think of leaving it to live somewhere warmer?'

Marina thought about this a moment. 'Only when I was a child. I used to ask my dad if we could live here.'

'And what did he say?'

'He said... when he and Mum got older. Meaning when they retired, I suppose.'

'But they didn't.'

She may as well say it, without giving details. 'He never retired. He died... some years ago.'

'Oh, what a shame. I'm sorry. Were you close to him?'

'Very,' she said quietly. It was time to get off this subject. 'But I have a wonderful Italian stepfather, and he and my mother are very happy in their art world in Brighton.'

'Ah yes, I have heard about Brighton. But you said you live in London, I think?'

'On the edge, yes. But both Polly and I are planning to move to the seaside when we get back.'

'San José!'

She looked at him and laughed. 'No! *English* seaside. We'll each have our own place, but in the same village.' She needed to get off this subject, in case it occurred to him that money from the house would be going towards a purchase. If she told him about that, they'd soon be talking about the house sale and possibly ruin this lovely moment. A lovely moment that was probably part of his agenda to persuade her not to sell it.

He opened his mouth, as if to say something, but seemed to stop himself. Maybe he too didn't want to spoil things. Silence fell between them, with nothing but the echoey claps of the water inside the cave, the swoosh as they moved their legs in the water. Out of nowhere, she wondered what she would do if he leant over, turned her face towards him with one of those sensitive hands, and kissed her.

'So, how about you, are you happy living in Madrid?' she asked.

He took off his white T-shirt, dropped down into the water up to his shoulders, and turned to look at her with a wry smile. 'I think you've probably already guessed the answer to that question – or my friends have been talking! It's a wonderful city, it's where my work is, I have a lovely flat near the Parque del Oeste, and fabulous music venues, a lake for water sports, *but…*'

'And your parents live there too?' she asked, even though one of the boys had already told her about how Mati's father was a professor at the university.

'Yes. Although I'm not sure living too near parents is a good thing. And as for working with your father at the same university… Sometimes we could do with some distance. And I'm much too far from Francisca and Diego, who are very important to me.'

'And… the sea.'

'Yes, Marina, the sea!' He swept the water with his hand, splashing her and making her laugh. 'Are you coming in?'

'Er…' She looked down into the clear turquoise water. If he was up to his shoulders, she would be up to her nose. And she wasn't sure how she would get out.

'No. Don't,' he said. 'This isn't the time to try deeper water. I've got ideas for that.'

'Oh?'

He grinned, then disappeared like a seal under the water, coming up by the end of the boat, and then, with one movement, hauling himself aboard over the inflated edge of the RIB straight onto a seat.

She laughed. 'That's just showing off – you could have used the step at the back!'

'Come on, let's go back now; we've got those toys to play with!' He came over to her, took the bags and stowed them. After offering a hand to help her, he shrugged and smiled when she managed on her own.

'D'you want to reverse her out?' he asked.

'If you could start the engine.'

'Okay. Sometime we'll have to teach you how to do that using your left arm.'

Marina took them along the coast, past several more caves and a jutting-out piece of rock that looked like a face that she'd never noticed before, and into Cala Turquesa – where José was dropping off the one-o'clock trippers – including Yasiel and Juanjo.

'You better take over – I don't want to ram into José.'

'Really? He probably deserves a little thump for spreading gossip about you.'

Of course – how else would the *turquitos* know about her spending time with Agustín?

'A *big* thump, in fact,' she said. 'But there are some swimmers in the boat lane. Let's swap over.'

Once they'd changed seats, he surprised her by leaning forward and kissing her cheek. 'For José – and several others – who're looking with their mouths open. That'll confuse their theories!'

It was just a kiss on the cheek, like half the usual Spanish two-cheek kiss, for heaven's sake, so why was she blushing and speechless?

'But mainly for being such a brilliant new captain, of course,' he added, and patted her arm.

They got out of the boat, and in a daze she started helping him use the winch to pull it up on the beach – until Yasiel and Juanjo took over.

'How did it go?' they asked.

'She was amazing,' Mati said. 'And now we're just going to take our things to the house and then come back with her snorkel mask!'

Jesus, she might have had enough today, but the other two were talking about joining in.

'I've seen how far you go out – particularly you, Yasiel!' Marina said. 'I'm just going to stay in the shallow water and get the hang of it, today.'

Once back on the beach, Juanjo and Yasiel admired her blue mask but went on ahead towards the rocks.

She got the mask on and waded in until she could get down in the water and try it. She was soon breathing normally and admiring a shoal of little silvery-blue oval fish with black dots on their tails. She came up and gesticulated to Mati in excitement, saw him give a thumbs-up, and went down again. More silvery-blues... and then a slightly larger stripy grey fish. Great, and she'd only been doing this for about ten minutes! But it had only taken ten minutes of swimming like this to set her arm off into lightning flashes of pain. She stood up, not wanting to mention it.

He stood up too. 'Your arm? But the float will make you too high in the water... I know – hold my ankle and I'll pull you along.'

'To where?'

'Not too deep, I promise.'

And so that's what they did: she held his ankle as he swam, but it wasn't easy.

He turned and stood up again. 'No, try the waist of my trunks.'

'What? Supposing they come down?' she said, grateful to the mask for covering her blush.

He laughed, shrugged, pointed to the waistband, and went back under the water. She followed him under and grabbed his waistband, her fingers against his waist... oops, and her forearm briefly making contact with his neat *culo*. Bumping her leg into his, she was about to give up – but then he pointed to a long greeny-blue fish with an orange strip down its side, and she nodded with enthusiasm in reply.

He stood up. 'You see what fun it is?' he asked.

The other two came over, and seemed to be talking about starfish and something else with prickles – did she want to see?

'No, I...' She took the mask off. 'That's enough for me today, but wow!' She turned to Mati. 'Thanks for the tow!'

He grinned. 'Any time.'

Marina flopped onto the bed after her shower and gazed out of the double doors to where the sea was now taking on a pink glow. 'I think I'm sea-spent. Water-wasted. Completely and utterly marinated,' she said to Polly.

Just when Marina had finished snorkelling, Polly and Ewan had floated up on lilos donated to them by an English couple on the last day of their holiday. Polly had told her to nip back to the house and swap her mask for the rubber ring – which she and Ewan had blown up for her with a pump Polly had spotted in the shed. They'd then spent ages floating around the bay, the three of them – and gone back for more, after lunch.

'Or just…' Polly, already collapsed on to her side of the bed after a late afternoon of passion at Ewan's, put her hands behind her head and looked at her friend '…*Matinated.*'

Marina put a finger to her lips and grinned with gritted teeth. The boys could be heard setting up their instruments next door.

'Well?' Polly whispered.

Marina shrugged. 'Unbelievably, he was really nice. Bossy, showing off, but kind and fun to be with. And although we all know there's a Casa Palmito agenda here, he had the grace not to mention it, not even once.'

'That's quite something. Maybe he was distracted by a competing second – or maybe now *primary* – agenda.'

'Oh no. I'm still the woman who wants to sell "his" house of nine summers, make no mistake,' Marina whispered.

The boys had been discussing something, and now all three of them were calling them into the living room.

Both lolling in their underwear, they each put on a dress – Marina insisting Polly was welcome to wear the purple tie-dye one, while she wore the turquoise one with the palm trees.

'Well look at you two!' Juanjo said, sitting on his *cajón* drum and giving a burst of excited rapping of his fingers on it.

They curtsied.

'Perfect for the next campsite gig,' he went on.

'Oh? When's that?' Marina hoped it wasn't going to clash with Friday's classical-flamenco guitar concert.

'Sunday,' Yasiel said. 'But what we mean is… for you to join us, as guest artists!'

'What?' both girls asked, laughing.

Mati beamed at them. 'Just a few numbers. Wouldn't you like to? We've been thinking of how to make it a bit different this time, and…'

'Mati came up with the perfect solution!' Juanjo said.

The girls looked at each other and started asking which songs they had in mind.

'Well obviously Polly's fabulous Beatriz Luengo for "Rebelde",' Juanjo said, smiling at her.

'And we'd do the Icelandic Eurovision "10 Years" this time, if we had Marina's keyboard solo!' Yasiel said.

'They could join in the chorus of "Me Maten"…' Juanjo suggested.

The girls grinned and agreed.

'But also…' Mati started. 'You said you do karaoke? So maybe you have a song you'd like to do, that we could work out? We've got a week to get it right.'

'Oh…' Polly looked at Marina. There was an obvious choice, the duet they'd been obsessed with the last few months – and for which they'd got rapturous applause the one time they'd dared perform it, using slightly less offensive lyrics.

Marina bit her lip, trying to think of an alternative. Apart from anything else, did she really want to sing this to Mati right now, the way she was feeling about him? But… it would be such fun. 'Doja Cat's "Kiss Me More". Could you do that?' she asked the boys. 'The keyboard figure would sound lovely on the guitar.'

The boys looked stunned.

'You know it?' Polly asked.

'Of course!' Yasiel said, looking for it on his phone.

'Come back in about an hour so we can work out the chords, and we'll have it ready for you two divas!' Mati said.

'Okay,' Polly said, 'but it's our turn to make dinner, so you'll have to put up with us in the room.'

Polly looked in the fridge and, finding Yasiel and Juanjo had bought some enormous onions, tomatoes and green peppers from the *mercadillo*, suggested making a soya-based Bolognese sauce. They laid the table, chopped and fried while the boys sorted out the song, and were about to put the spaghetti on when a recognisable 'Kiss Me More' accompaniment started filling the room.

'Okay – let's have a first go,' Polly said.

'Really? Smells so good, I'm starving!' said the ever-hungry Juanjo.

'I can't wait a minute more to hear Polly doing those saucy rapping verses!' Yasiel said, and Juanjo laughed and agreed.

Polly winked at Marina, who tried to keep a straight face. Once the song started, the boys were clearly surprised to hear it was Polly doing the sweet, plaintive verses, harmonised by Marina... and then awed, laughing and cheering when the usually more demure Marina came out with a very sassy bit of rapping, complete with a few of the slinky moves.

At the end, the boys whooped and cheered.

'My God, this needs to be near the end – they're going to

steal the show!' Yasiel said, wiping tears of laughter from his eyes.

'Fantastic… utterly fantastic,' Juanjo said.

Mati blew them each a kiss. 'Beautiful. And my God, Marina, the piano teacher turned rapper!' He shook his head. 'Who would have thought!'

They had a celebratory dinner, talking about booking more gigs there the following year with whatever had inspired them in the Spanish, English or other charts in the meantime.

Afterwards, they settled back down to rehearsing other songs.

Marina's phone buzzed on the table. She picked it up. Mum saying something about how she hoped she wouldn't be too upset. What? She went into the message. *It's just a date, darling. As I say every year, remember Daddy wouldn't want you to be upset.*

The anniversary of her father's death. Of course. Oddly, despite being actually here where it happened, she'd for once lost track of the dates. It was tomorrow. Somewhere in her mind, Daddy seemed to be telling her he wouldn't have minded if she had forgotten; her getting out and happily enjoying the sea, like she'd done today, was much more important to him.

Then Mati said they were going to play them a song they'd left out last time, and the boys started performing 'Mencanta', written by a pop-flamenco artist after his father had died. It was full of the beautiful pain of remembering him, how he couldn't go back to how things were before… The girls were invited to join in, but Marina's throat was so tight she could barely sing. Polly next to her squeezed her arm. Somehow she'd have to go through the anniversary tomorrow, with further sea discovery with Mati, and keep her feelings in check.

12

'You could just tell Mati you don't feel like it today,' Polly said, watching Marina take a photo frame out of her bag and letting her father smile at her from the bedside table.

'The water's still lovely and calm. He wouldn't understand,' Marina said.

'Unless... you told him,' Polly replied, as she had done many times before, on hearing about tactless or perplexed flatmates and boyfriends – but Marina hated telling people about what had happened to her father. And of course, nobody – not even Polly – knew the *full* story. Nobody, other than that woman. Marina often wondered how bad the woman must have felt on hearing that Daddy died after she'd left them. Was the woman thinking about him today? Was she still living here? Who was she? It all happened so quickly, Marina probably wouldn't have recognised her days later, let alone twenty years on; she'd almost certainly never know.

'Marina?' Polly looked concerned.

'I'll be okay later.'

The boys had just gone off to take the boat out for a cave-exploring adventure – which Marina had declined – while Mati had some work he hoped to finish by lunchtime.

Once Polly had left to go and do her yoga down on the beach with Ewan, Marina knocked on the other bedroom's half-open door. 'Would another coffee help?' she asked, in English by mistake.

'Please!' he replied, also in English.

She went off to grapple with the old coffeemaker and to pour the remaining almonds into a little ceramic bowl.

He looked up as she came in and put her offerings on the bedside table. 'Ah *yes*. Thank you.' He was sitting propped up on the bed with the computer on his lap, surrounded by papers.

'Why don't you work in the living room?' she asked, back in Spanish. 'Nobody will be around for hours.'

He looked puzzled. 'Why? Have you decided to go to the caves with the lads, after all?'

'No! I meant nobody apart from me. And I'll be in my cupboard or in my rubber ring on the sea.'

He nodded and smiled. 'Ha, that's the thing with working here. You can always go for a quick swim for a break. Or in the winter, a sunny walk wearing a T-shirt.'

'You come in the winter?'

'Once or twice. Three or four days, staying with my aunt and uncle.'

'How lovely.' Like they used to, at Easter. 'Well, I'll leave you to get on. Looks important,' she said, seeing a veterinary research journal, and a draft of a scientific paper with Matías Ramírez León as the first of about five authors – including a Juan Carlos Ramírez something, who could be his father.

'It is. The disease can pass from cats to humans. Somebody has to work on this. I just sometimes wish it was somebody else.'

'So you could be a vet curing people's adored dogs, horses and rabbits instead?'

He smiled. 'Yes! If I could cope with the fury of my father and colleagues. But maybe I would regret it.'

'It's what my father did,' she said, surprising herself. 'He had a well-paid job at Shell in London – where *both* his parents worked – but gave it up to be a lifeboat...' She tried out the word coxswain, with a Spanish accent.

'A what?'

'Er... captain of a lifeboat.' She started explaining the RNLI to him.

'Oh yes, I've read about this. Most are volunteers, aren't they?'

'Yes, but some are full-time – like the boat drivers.'

'Ah. And was it a good decision?' he asked.

'Definitely. Well, for *him* – and my brother and me, as we saw much more of him. We moved to a little narrow house on the harbour, which I loved. But I don't think his parents and my mother were ever happy about it.' She took some almonds from the bowl he held out. 'So, are you moving?'

'Moving?' His eyebrows went up.

'I mean, to the living room!'

'Oh!' He laughed. 'Yes.'

She helped him set up at a table in the other room, once it had been cleared of sun creams, caps and a couple of vests.

'I want to hear more about your father,' Mati said. 'He sounds like an incredible man.'

'He was... but there's not much more to tell, really,' she said, hoping that would put an end to it. 'Right, I'm off to the cupboard.'

★

'D'you want to start the engine? A bit awkward with a left arm, but I'm sure you can do it,' Mati said.

It was a much smaller engine than the one on *La Mari*, or maybe that was just because she was a lot taller, and not in a breathless panic... She looked around. José was doing the three o'clock drop-off and pick-up but looking over at them and waving. She waved back. 'Perhaps not with an audience, the first time.'

'Yes, true. Ha! Two days in a row, the two of us in the boat – that'll give José something to think about!' he said with a laugh.

'Hm.' And why shouldn't it? It had given *her* something to think about. Was there any more to this than a sea-mad guy helping an apparently timid landlubber get afloat? *Re*-floated, that was; what he didn't know, was that her love of the sea was as strong and as old as his – but had been broken.

'But what will he make of it if he sees you with Agustín again?' Mati continued.

She busied herself storing the drink and pistachios in the little boat box. 'He bought me a ticket for the classical-flamenco guitar concert on Friday,' she decided to say; he'd have to know sooner or later.

'*Why?* We're all going to that – you could come with us.'

'Well, no, I'll get the boat earlier, because I'm giving that little girl a piano lesson. After that I'll go for a quick drink at the expat bar with the child's mother, and then Agustín's going to pick me up from there and drive to San Rafael.'

He looked puzzled, possibly annoyed – and wasn't starting the boat, as if in protest. 'So we'll all be at the concert, but you'll be sitting somewhere else. That's *weird*.'

'No! We can all sit in a line. Well, unless you have a moral objection to being within two metres of a developer.'

He started the engine.

'He's really not a bad person. You might even like him – he loves music.'

'I'm sure. He'll be asking you for piano lessons next.'

'He already has,' she said, without thinking – and immediately regretted it.

'*What?* What the hell's going on here?' he said, eyebrows pinched together in fury. 'You can't possibly discuss business like this. What you're doing, letting your attraction to him influence such an important decision, is very unfair on your family – and others affected by it.'

'Oh, for heaven's sake – back on your agenda again! When will you stop?'

'When will you stop letting him romance you into the sale?'

'He's not romancing me. We're *friends*.'

He tutted and did that Spanish dismissive fling of the hand over the head.

'You seem to think I'm a complete idiot,' she said. 'And anyway, for what it's worth, despite his good looks, I don't have an "attraction to him".'

He glanced at her, and then back at the sea. 'I'm just trying to help.'

'Okay, I'll accept that as the nearest I'll get to an apology.'

He nodded, still looking perturbed.

'So, are you going to let me take over?' she asked. They had already come out of the cove.

'Of course.' He put the boat in neutral, and they switched seats. 'I thought we could go past San José to the series of wild beaches, maybe even as far as the lighthouse. Then stop off and swim at a little beach on the way back.'

Good God; exactly what she and her father had done. Doing this again, today of all days.

'Okay?'

If she didn't do it today, he'd only suggest it another day. Who wouldn't, when they could admire extraordinary volcanic rock formations and probably some of the most beautiful beaches in Spain? 'Yes, sounds good.'

She crossed the bay of San José, with its several sandy beaches: the village one for the large family groups; a couple of smaller ones favoured by teenagers – with rocks to make out behind and a little bamboo bar; and then the one at the end, with lots of snorkel pipes protruding from the sea near the rocky end to the bay.

'Good snorkelling there – but you'd need fins,' Mati said, which probably meant it was deep water.

Then it was round the mountain to the first of the wild beaches... Playa Genoveses. A wide curve of sand guarded by the mountain one side, a climbable rocky hill, by the look of it, the other side – and a film-set unreal backdrop of orange-earth rounded hills and a distant range of mountains. Here, beach trippers were scattered apart, even in August, with so much beach to go round. 'Oh *wow*.'

'You remember this?' he asked.

She nodded, remembering her father building a huge

Venice-like sand town for Teddy. Ted, who'd WhatsApped her today, as he always did on the ninth of August, to say he was thinking of Theo and hoping she was having a nice time. *Theo?* Not *Dad?* But then, having been only six at the time, Ted had soon been happy to call Guido 'Papà'. She suspected he was always reminded about the anniversary by Mum, after Marina had given him hell some years ago when he'd clearly forgotten. It always felt like Dad was only really missed by her and a few of his old friends from the RNLI who still sent her Christmas cards.

'So, your father must have been keen to get out on a boat here.'

Jesus. 'Yes, he was.'

'He would have had a good licence and been able to take anything out.'

She nodded. Most people quite quickly sensed she didn't want to talk about him.

'You don't seem to want to talk about him.'

They didn't usually say that. What a persistent little sod Mati was. 'Well, it was a long time ago.'

'Oh? How old were you when he—'

'Ten.' That should shut him up.

'*Ten?*' he asked, wide-eyed with dismay. 'Oh *no*. I'm so sorry, Marina. That must have been very hard.'

'Yes.'

And what's the name of the next beach? she could hear Daddy say, as if he was changing the subject, stopping her going into one of those moments where his death seemed to make the whole world fade.

'Mónsul,' she said. 'That's the next one, isn't it?'

'Yes. You remembered that? Well done!'

And round the next mountain, there it was, with its gloriously massive soft sand dune and its lump of volcano rock that looked like a wave turned to stone... Then came the smaller beaches, Mati naming them and saying something about the volcanic process and the colours of the rocks that she couldn't seem to follow, too busy looking at the tiny coves and trying to find the one where she and Daddy had had their last swim...

She dropped the speed. Smaller than she remembered of course, but the 'bird village' rock face, the clump of baby palms, that array of coloured stones piled up after the sand, the rock from where Daddy dived...

'Good choice!' Mati said.

'What?'

'For a swim! Look, just drift forward a bit and we can drop the anchor.'

He took over, seeing she'd gone into a daze. 'I think you need some shade and a drink,' he said, pointing to the little palms. 'After the swim, that is!'

With the boat anchored, they jumped down onto the sandy bottom, the tepid water up to their thighs, and carried bags to the shore.

What happened to the pretty stones you collected? I'm sorry about that, Daddy seemed to be saying.

She sat down on the towel and started picking out a special little stone in each colour.

'You're not coming in?' Mati asked.

'In a minute.'

Then she looked up and couldn't believe it – Mati, now in just his bright blue swimming trunks, was off climbing along to the rock from where Daddy had dived.

'No!' she found herself screaming at him.

He turned round to her. 'It's *fine*, Marinita, don't worry.'

'Don't dive off there, *no!*' Because somehow if he did, this ninth of August day would go the same way.

He turned again and looked at her.

She stared back.

Marinita, she could hear her father say, as clear as if he was sitting beside her. Maybe he *was* sitting beside her. She turned to the somehow not-quite-empty space next to her, then back to Mati, who was coming back along the rocks. She should have let him dive, because unless she did something quickly, he was now going to see what a state she was in.

She stood up and ran into the sea – forgetting to take off her shorts and T-shirt, and that she'd have to go some way to get her face in the water.

'What are you *doing?*' he said, laughing uncertainly.

'Just...' In a daze, she could almost see *La Mari* instead of the RIB, waiting for them.

He came round in front of her and gently held her shoulders. 'What's the matter? Did you come to this cove with your father? Did... something happen here?'

She nodded. 'Well... not here, but... later.'

He took her arm and led her back to the towel. 'Come and have a drink.'

They sat down on the towel and he handed her a lemon tea. 'So, your family came here in a boat? It was one of your favourite places?'

'Just me and my father. It was wonderful.'

'But something happened?'

He wasn't going to let this go. Persistent as ever. 'Then

we got back on the boat and he hit his head on it and died. Today, ninth of August. I'm sorry, I should have stayed at the house today. This is—'

'Oh my God. And then...'

'I started the engine, which is how I injured my shoulder, and I drove back... There, you know it all now.' Well, not quite.

He put his arm round her and pulled her over until their heads were together. 'Oh, Marina... why didn't you tell me all this before?' he asked, gently. 'I don't know why my *aunt* didn't tell me. We've been so bad, trying to drag you into deep water, making fun of you... Then there's me forcing you to have lessons in loving the sea... I'm *so* sorry.'

'Yes, I don't know why Francisca didn't say anything to you about it. But please don't feel bad; it's not your fault. I'm just no good at talking about it.'

'Tell me what I can do to help.'

'Carry on just the same. Apart from this wobble, I'm really enjoying your help with revisiting my love of the sea.'

The sun was low now, but the evening had an unusually heavy warmth to it; Polly, Ewan and Marina had decided that floating on their inflatables on the sea was the only place to be.

'It's *great* that you told him, cleared the air,' Polly said in English.

'And he'll now understand about your family selling the house,' Ewan said. Polly had already mentioned to Marina that she'd told Ewan about her father.

'Well, I'm not sure about *that*,' Marina said, twirling

around in her orange segment. 'Knowing him, he'll probably twist things round to make it another reason why we *shouldn't* sell it.'

Polly tutted and shook her head. 'At least that can't start tonight! Where did you say the boys were going?'

'They're going off in the car from San José to spend the night with an old friend who's just moved to the city with his wife and baby. They invited me to tag along, but that would be weird.'

'Well, we could keep you company—' Ewan started.

'No, no. I really don't mind being on my own in the house.'

'I suppose you… Ha!' Water had splashed over Polly's head. 'Where have these waves come from? It's been like a lake all day.'

Marina spotted another one advancing towards them and got her rubber-ringed self into position for riding it in towards the shore. 'Yay!'

Ewan had done the same with his lilo, but had fallen off, all long limbs everywhere – much to Polly and Marina's amusement.

'You two are *so* cruel,' he said, then he got on his lilo again, paddled up to Polly, and tipped her over. When she'd recovered and splashed him, they put their lilos one on top of the other and both clambered aboard.

Marina laughed. 'That's just *too* tempting!' Inflatable wars commenced, with lots of laughter and spluttering as the sea joined in the fun.

'I'm going to go mad after swallowing all this sea water!' Polly said. 'Might be time to go up.'

Marina looked at the beach, now in the shade as the sun dropped down behind the mountain. 'Where is everybody?

Do the *turquitos* usually go off to their... dwellings this early?'

'No. But tonight they're getting ready for the community meeting at sundown,' Ewan explained. 'Why don't you come with us?'

'You kidding?' Marina said. 'They'd string me up – I'm the evil hotel-building developer's moll, remember!'

Polly and Ewan laughed then looked at each other. 'Well, we're working on that,' Polly said. 'And of course, now they've seen you spending so much time with Mati...'

'I'll be getting questions about two-timing, as well!' Marina said. 'No, I think I'm too tired to socialise. Maybe another time. I'll be fine, maybe a bit of cupboard and then just chilling out with some music.'

'Well, if you change your mind, the meeting's at Vivi and Edu's,' Ewan said. 'The couple who run the bar,' he added, and Marina felt bad she hadn't bothered to learn their names.

'They live in the higher of the two taken-over abandoned houses,' Polly said.

'Ah, okay.'

A wave slapped Polly on the back of the head. '*Uf...* Right, I'm out of here!'

The three of them walked out of the sea, making for the path, but Marina looked behind her at the deserted beach, the water now taking on the orange glow of the setting sun – and didn't want to leave quite yet. 'I'll let you two get ready, I fancy sitting here a bit.'

Polly put an arm round her. 'Really? Don't sit here and get too sad, please. Your dad would be so happy, seeing you drive the boat.'

'True. If you can have a good death anniversary, he probably did. I'll see you later.'

She watched them walk arm in arm towards the path. How was this relationship going to translate to Shoreham beach, where, even in mid-summer, by five o'clock you'd probably be wrapped in a hoody and holding a hot chocolate? She hoped Polly was right about how they'd keep each other warm; especially as, by the time Ewan had renewed his passport, it might be winter.

She took off the rubber ring, towelled herself dry, and put on her loose cover-up – even though she wasn't cold, and there was nobody there to see her. With her beach bag over her shoulder, she started strolling along the edge of the sea to the end of the bay she never went to – especially as nowadays it involved walking past Dani and his wife and friends who sat chatting next to the floaty cloth shop.

Winter. Where would she be in winter? In Shoreham hopefully, exchanging Christmas messages with each of the boys, in which they'd look forward to next summer's reunion, suggest new songs they could work out. Possibly, in Mati's case, talking about a little more – asking each other how life was going in Madrid and Shoreham. Unbelievably, this man she'd found so annoying was now becoming a *friend*. One she found distractingly attractive, with whom most girls she knew would be having... *benefits*. Or even, some kind of attempted long-distance thing. But Easter, summer, maybe the odd weekend... you couldn't have a *relationship* like that. What would happen in all those months in between being able to see each other? He'd soon be Faithless Number Five, the most painful one of all – and she'd never want to come back here again.

Not all men are faithless.

'Yes they are. *Even* you,' she answered her father's voice in her head. 'With that boat woman... who's maybe still living here somewhere, trying to break up other families – or distract the man so much that he...'

What was she doing, thinking of this now? On a moonlit beach walk, the best August the ninth for a long time. She passed the floaty cloth shop and sat on a rock she remembered sitting on twenty years ago, talking to Daddy about her jelly fish sting as he put something on it.

'But how often is this going to happen?' she'd asked.

'Not often.'

'Not for at least this holiday?'

He'd laughed. 'It's unlikely, but I can't guarantee that! Even though this cove must be the safest bit of sea ever, you can never be a hundred per cent sure what creatures you're sharing it with. But what do we do? We can't keep out of the sea, when it's the most irresistibly wonderful thing on the planet.'

She walked on. There was a smaller rock up ahead that looked like a low but comfortably rounded seat, beautifully positioned for enjoying the foam of the waves swirling round her feet. She'd sit there for a bit, then go up the path to the house and have a shower.

She made her way towards it. She looked around when she heard a sandy scraping sound, but there was nobody about. Except... something by the rock. Then the rock seemed to wave... and *move*. It wasn't a rock it was a...

She gasped. Went a little nearer. Up to a couple of metres from it... until the creature turned its head and its googly wide-apart eyes glinted in the moonlight. A sea turtle. A big one. Marina stepped back a few paces, not wanting to frighten him or her. Only one of its flippers scraped at the sand, the other hung in the water motionless; it must have been hurt.

What was that number you had to call? Juanjo mentioned it once, and how people often tried to shove stranded sea creatures back to sea, sending them to their death. She stepped back further and took out her phone, called Mati's number. No reply. She burbled something – in English by mistake – on the voicemail. She googled Equipo... what was the turtle rescue place called? Team something... *Equipo... Rescate... de Tortugas. De Tortugas Marinas.* ERTM. She found them and called the 112 number.

A man answered.

'I've got a turtle... on a beach... Cala Turquesa, near—'

He asked if it was alive, whether it seemed wounded.

'Yes. I think one its... arms has hurt,' she said, her Spanish failing her.

There was something about whether the creature's nose was clear.

She went a little nearer. 'Seems okay. Ah, it looks like there's something wound round the arm that doesn't move.'

He spoke quickly, said they would bring a boat... something about taking an hour, and how she should stay there, keep the turtle wet with water from the sea if she could, keep her distance and stop anyone from touching the creature. Then he was gone.

It was just her and the turtle again, in the moonlight – 21:35, her phone said. An hour. She was just beginning to get a bit cold, in her wet costume and cover-up.

She rang Polly and told her what had happened.

'Oh my God! I'll come and wait with you. Hang on...'
She heard her talking in rapid Spanish, several voices
exclaiming in excitement. 'We're all coming down. I'll bring
a flask of something hot and a dry T-shirt.'

'And a bucket, we have to keep her wet... *All?* Isn't that
too many? I don't want to scare her,' she said, realising she
was whispering. 'They said nobody should go—'

'Don't worry, they know that. There was one a few years
ago, and they called *Equipo*. See you in a minute.'

She – because somehow she'd decided the turtle was a
girl – had turned her head back to looking inland, resting
it on the sand.

'Don't stop moving, please keep alive!' she said, and
continued to talk to her, until a little group quietly came
towards her, led by Polly and Ewan.

They stood in a little awed semicircle. After Marina had
told them what she knew, Ewan's friend, jewellery-making
Lala, stepped forward and checked Marina knew everyone
by name – all twelve of the full-time *turquitos*, including
Dani and his wife and their two small girls. They all nodded
and smiled hesitantly, and there was talk of the previous
turtle, a smaller one, who the team saved and nursed at their
centre further up the coast – but was too sick to survive.

Sooner than expected, two RIBs, one much larger than the
other, came round into the cove, speeding quickly towards
Marina's waving hands and then much more slowly as
they neared the beach. Out jumped three women and an
older man from the first boat... and Mati from the second,
coming forward and giving Marina a quick hug while the
others examined the turtle.

'I got your message, just as *Equipo* called me and asked

if I wanted to come,' Mati said. 'Well done! What a beauty she is.'

'She?'

'Tail too short to be a male.'

He and the team surrounded the turtle, and then, after some discussion, lifted her onto a stretcher with straps and – with some difficulty – into the team's RIB.

'Will she be okay?' Marina asked, along with others.

'It could be just that right flipper – but she looks slow, she may also have an infection,' Mati said. 'Anyway, she's now in the best hands.'

The older man said something to him. 'Ah yes...' Mati said, smiling at her. 'It's a tradition that they always name the turtle after the person who found her. "Marina" is a bit confusing, being part of the team's name, so I'm suggesting La Mari.'

13

La Mari. It had been a long time since she'd heard someone say those two words. On the rare occasions Mum or Ted mentioned her, she was 'the boat'. Polly knew the sound of it cut like a knife and had barely ever said it. Then there was Mati saying it with a proud-on-her-behalf smile, because of course, he didn't know. But this was La Mari, *the loggerhead turtle*. Now having had the whole night to get over the shock, she was smiling too. She just had to hope the beautiful creature survived.

She got back onto the bed with her breakfast tea, looked out at the swirling grey clouds and sent up a silent prayer to the God of Turtles, if there was one. Well, apparently there was a Greek *tortoise* god, so he'd have to do. She'd been reading all about turtles on her phone last night and since she woke up – turtle life, turtle rescues, but also about how they'd forever been loved emblems of tranquillity, stability and fertility.

She'd spent the night in the house on her own, as Mati had gone back with the *Equipo* people to see if he could help. The wind had howled, and there'd even been a thundering of rain at one point, but she hadn't minded. It was cosy, and, feeling wired by the long and emotional day she'd had, she'd stayed up late, turned her music up, and finally finished the cupboard. Well, cheating a bit by flinging Dad's shoebox of faded Polaroids of the family, the scenery and *La Mari* into the suitcase after going through just a few of them. She didn't need to look at them all now; if he was having a secret thing with this woman, he wasn't likely to have left around a snap of her, was he?

All she needed to do now was to take the bag of Mum's more useful clothes around to see if anyone wanted any of them – although it might not be the best day to do this, with this gusty wind.

She got up and went to the terrace doors, which she'd had to wedge with stones to stop them banging. The sea had white horses further out, and big rolling and curling waves could be heard smashing and sucking at the sand even from here.

She grabbed her ringing phone from the bedside table. 'Mati! How's she doing?'

'Well, there *is* some infection, she's a poorly girl, but it looks like her flipper can be saved. We'll know more in the next few days,' he said in Spanish. 'How are you and Polly? Is the house still in one piece?'

'It is! Polly stayed with Ewan.'

'What? They could have slept in the house!'

'They like it at Ewan's – and they're only a few minutes' away. Anyway, it was fine, and I finished the cupboard!'

'*That* needs a celebration. Although it won't be today – and probably not tomorrow; we can't get back in this sea.'

'God, I should think not. How long is this going on?' she asked. She didn't want to miss the piano lesson, expat bar and amphitheatre concert on Friday.

'Should be okay by Thursday. Have you everything you need?'

'Well, too bad if I haven't!'

'The *turquitos* club together when the weather is bad – don't hesitate to ask for help.'

She'd have to be desperate to do that. 'Okay.'

'Don't worry, we'll soon be continuing our sea adventures.'

'Yes! Look, did I tell you my father had a boat called *La Mari?* Just a little dayboat with a cabin.' It's just possible she did, in her dazed state yesterday.

'No! So, also named after you! How lovely. You must tell me more about her another time… if you want to. But right now I've got to go and see to the other La Mari! Would you prefer that we just call her Mari?'

'Yes, I think so.'

'Okay. Take care of yourself, Marinita.'

She put the phone down and smiled. Would she tell him more about *La Mari?* Maybe. He had a way of getting things out of her, with that wide smile, stubborn persistence, and ready consoling arm.

'Hel-loo! Where's the turtle woman?' Polly and Ewan were coming into the house. 'Oh, we better shut this…!' A door slammed in the wind, and there was laughter.

'Here! Holed up in my shell!' Marina called out.

As usual, Polly and Ewan looked full of the joys of a new day – even one as windy as this.

'Any news?' they both asked in chorus.

Marina told them all she knew.

'The poor darling, fingers crossed,' Polly said.

'D'you fancy pancakes?' Ewan asked, with that toothy Bowie smile he had.

'Oh! Well I'm not sure I've got—'

'Everything we need is in here.' He was holding a cardboard box. Of course, the *turquitos* were used to being cut off occasionally, and produced as much food as they could themselves.

'And he's the best pancake maker *ever* – with his own chickens' eggs!' Polly said.

Ewan got to work, while the girls cleared the table in the living room. He turned to them for a moment. 'Wow, the luxury of a choice of *two* indoor tables!' he said, pointing to a smaller, battered little one used as a side table for putting things on when you came in. 'Do you need that? Nina and Bernardo's table blew over and fell down the hill in bits yesterday. I said I'd make them a new one, but if they could borrow—'

'Oh heavens, they can *have* it!' Marina said. 'Sorry, is that the older couple? Still haven't quite got everyone's names in my head.'

'Yes, the couple we arrived with in the boat,' Polly said.

'Right. In threadbare clothes… I wonder if Nina might be interested in the clothes my mum left here.'

'I'm sure she'd love to have a look,' Polly said. She looked out of the window. 'Maybe the three of us could brave it and go there after breakfast.'

'Theirs is the ruined old shepherd hut with a sort of wooden awning?' Marina asked. On a little path coming off the one going down to the beach. 'At least it's downhill.'

'Sounds a good plan,' Ewan said. 'Right, coming up.'

They sat down to lemon, honey and almond pancakes almost entirely sourced from Cala Turquesa.

'Oh… this is wonderful,' Marina said. 'Times like this,

I wish I didn't have to sell the house. Cala Turquesa? Cala *Eden*.'

'I know,' Ewan said, squeezing a fresh lemon. 'I think we all wish that.' He put up his hand. 'But don't worry, I understand.'

'Polly tells me you're coming over to England in a few months.'

'Yes. I think I'm going to become one of those seasonal *turquitos*, just come here for July and August.'

'And carry on with the expat magazine?' Marina said. 'I suppose you can do that from anywhere...' Although it would be a bit odd to be writing about the San José pirate festival from Shoreham.

'Well, I'm doing less and less writing... I'm thinking of attending this jewellery-making school in the Lanes in Brighton and trying to get into the scene there.'

'Even though he's already brilliant at it,' Polly said.

Marina looked at the growing collection of colourful and intricate bracelets round Polly's wrists. 'That's for sure. Sounds wonderful – as long as someone keeps feeding your chickens here!'

'I share them with Lala. My girls will be fine.'

'*Madre mía*,' Polly said, leaning back in her chair. 'Think I might have had one too many... just as well I'm not giving a yoga class today.'

'What? You promised me a private class!' Ewan said.

'Maybe later.' Polly got up and went to the window, looking up at the trees. 'It's definitely died down a bit. How about Marina and I wash up and then we take the things to Nina and Bernardo?'

'Okay, I'll give Nardo a ring,' Ewan said, getting out his ancient Nokia.

Marina looked out and saw the eucalyptus trees still shaking about. 'I don't know. Aren't these the trees they call "widow makers", for dropping massive branches on people's heads? Maybe we should leave it for another day.'

'Marina!' Polly exclaimed. 'They're probably talking about massive old ones.'

'It's not far – we'll be fine. But if you're worried, we can keep looking up, ready to dodge!' Ewan said. 'Anyway, if it freaks you out, you don't have to come; we can manage.'

'What? No, she *should* come,' Polly said. 'It's a good opportunity for her to get to know them a bit.' She turned to Marina. 'They keep to themselves, but they're really sweet.'

Ewan spoke on the phone and then closed it. 'They said brilliant timing. Nina's just been doing some baking! And Nina's Belgian, by the way, so need I say more!'

'But how does she bake… *there?*' Marina asked.

'She and Bernardo are *masters* of the stone oven. So that'll probably be our lunch sorted for later!'

'Hm. Okay, I'm in!'

They had a coffee and talked about Shoreham; Ewan had been there once, many years ago on one of his weekend trips down to Brighton from Clapham, and thought it a perfect base for trying to 'go back into the world' – for most of the year, anyway. It sounded like it could work out. Certainly she'd never seen Polly so relaxed, and seeing the two of them – perfectly in tune, laughing and smiling together – made her very happy for her friend.

They set off, Ewan and Polly with the table, Marina with the two bags of clothes.

'Bit slippery here, after that deluge last night. Careful, people,' Ewan said, as they went down the path.

They reached the beach path, and Polly looked up. 'Aha, now we've reached the pines, the widow makers can't get to us!'

'I should have tied my hair back,' Marina moaned, as it blew in front of her eyes and into her mouth.

Vivi and Edu, the bar couple, were coming back up from the beach. They all said good morning, and Vivi said they'd just been checking their boat was pulled up far enough away from the monster waves. The table was taking up most of the narrow path between the trees, but the couple managed to squeeze round the safer side – the one that didn't have the slope down to the stony little stream bed a couple of metres below.

Once they'd passed, Polly and Ewan picked up the table again, Ewan deciding it was easier to hold it walking backwards. But then, maybe he tripped on a tree root, because he dropped the table and had to grab a eucalyptus branch to stop himself falling.

'Careful!' Polly said.

'It's fine, I just—' The branch snapped. He started sliding down the wet bank, Polly trying to grab him... and then he fell, for what seemed like ages, landing heavily on rocks below.

'Ewan!' Polly screamed, scrambling down to where he lay. Awkwardly. Like Marina had seen before... 'Marina! Get Edu, quick!'

Marina shouted after them, but they were too far; she dropped the bags and ran as fast as she could towards their house... where they were just closing the door.

'Come! Quick! How we do... ambulance!' she shouted at them, her Spanish failing. 'Ewan fell!'

The three of them dashed back to the path and looked down. Polly had her face by Ewan's, whispering to him. His eyes were half open now, thank God, blinking. But there was blood, a *lot* of blood... from his head.

There was lots of rapid Spanish, something about the boat being quicker. Edu shouted into his phone about an ambulance for San José port. Marina pulled a long cotton dress out of one of the bags, then climbed down the bank and gave it to Polly for putting round Ewan's head. Edu and Vivi came down with a hammock, and the four of them managed to lift Ewan's light but lengthy form into the makeshift stretcher. They rushed along the stream bed until the bank wasn't quite as high, and then heaved him up the slope and onto the path.

Dani and Bernardo were there; they must have heard the commotion. They wordlessly took over from Edu and Vivi, who rushed on down to the beach to get the boat ready.

Ewan was mumbling something, which reminded Marina of her father... they had to be quick, there was nothing for it... but now they were on the beach... how could they get Ewan past these walls of waves? Marina started asking about helicopter rescue, but somebody told her no, they'd done this before, it was all about timing...

Polly was getting into the boat, kneeling down next to Ewan, holding his hand. Marina wanted to stop her, but knew it was useless to try. Instead, she found herself helping to push the boat near to the edge of the sea, the waves crashing and covering them with spray. One of the others threw some yellow life jackets in. Edu and Vivi looked calm, studying the sea, like they'd done this before... and then, when Edu suddenly called out, they leapt aboard, started the engine, and roared off, bumping over the swell.

An arm came round Marina – Bernardo, saying something she couldn't understand – and the three of them watched the boat, not much bigger than Mati's RIB, bob up and down on the wispy swell... until it went round the mountain and was gone.

'Maybe the Guardia Civil can help. They should know...' Marina said. 'I'm going to ring Mati – he might be in San José now.'

Dani and Bernardo nodded, and went back with her to the house.

He answered immediately. 'Mati! Ewan hit his head badly. Polly went with him in the boat!' she gabbled in English, her heart racing. He told her to calm down and explain more slowly.

'Okay, I'm near the port right now,' he said. 'The Guardia Civil boat is here. I'll call you, okay, *cariño?*'

There were six of them now, Marina's house for once becoming the community centre. Bernardo's wife Nina had brought round all her baking and kept saying it was as if she'd known a group of shocked and worried people would need feeding. Neither she nor Bernardo could face collecting the table and bags of clothes – partly because they were the 'cause' of the accident, but also because they didn't want to miss any news when it came in. The two young girls couldn't cope with the hanging around and wanted to keep busy – so they took the things to Nina and Bernardo's house, and then, because it was such an upsetting sight for everyone, somehow cleaned away the blood on the rock.

Lala, Ewan's jewellery-making mentor and best friend in the cove, was distraught, and sobbing with relief when Mati called to say that the Guardia Civil boat had towed them in, and Ewan was conscious and talking when he'd gone off in the ambulance with Polly. In fact, they were all overcome when they heard this, Dani relaying the news to his anxious wife at home with the kids; it seemed the dorky Englishman was a much-loved member of the community.

Marina wouldn't be able to relax until the hospital could confirm Ewan didn't have the slow bleeding between the skull and the brain 'talk and die' syndrome that had killed her father... but an hour or so later, after Nina had mothered them all with pizza, biscuits and herbal teas, Marina's phone rang.

It was a video call, with Mati and Polly. Her friend looked exhausted but was smiling, leaving the talking to Mati.

'His scan is clear. Mild concussion, a bruise and several stitches needed, but he'll be fine. Obviously, they have to keep him in for twenty-four hours, but there's nothing to worry about.'

Everybody cheered on hearing this.

'He's already demanding tea and complaining about their suggestion that he stays in San José until his stitches come out in two weeks. My aunt will visit tomorrow and see if she can persuade him. But I think, really, it's very simple: he will go wherever Polly goes!'

Later, when everyone had left, there was a slow Spanish voice message from Mati. *'I can imagine how difficult this was for you, after what happened to your father. Please don't* worry anymore. I've just picked Polly up from the hospital and she says Ewan's doing well. She was going to use my phone to message you, but she's fallen asleep on the sofa! One more thing, Marina. You are right about the house: we need to let something happen there; it's dangerous having no road to Cala Turquesa.'

14

Waking early to a pleasantly breezy and semi-clouded day, Marina finally got round to walking up the old road, past the three old houses, steeply onwards to the top of the valley and… the giant jagged rocks, chunks of orange earth and a huge, upended eucalyptus that blocked the road. The end of the road – but also the *beginning* of the road, if she sold the house.

If? It was never an *if*; it was what she'd come out to do. Yet here she was, feeling tearful. She had to admit that maybe part of her had always hoped Mati would persuade her not to do it – but even he, now, was accepting the inevitable. And last night, Mum had once again encouraged her to go ahead.

She looked down over the valley, starting with the turquoise sea that was still fighting, despite the drop in the wind. Then there were the *turquito* shacks – with their odd mixture of clever carpentry, metal repurposing and hideous plastic sheets. Agustín had said something about giving them wooden dwellings up one end of the beach to 'minimise visual impact'. Much as – especially from here – she understood what he meant, he shouldn't just 'tidy up' these human beings. *Very* human beings. He needed to talk to them – or rather, as the Spanish would say, talk *with* them.

She looked over towards the old ruined fortress, overlooking the beach on one side. Ewan had told her that some of the community had wondered about using it to live in – but making steps up to it had been judged too hard and too hazardous. What plans did Agustín have for it? It worried her that it hadn't been mentioned, because surely, with an existing building there, it would be easy to get permission to build something. Maybe this was where the *turquitos'* worries about a hotel had started. There was a lot she needed to ask Agustín – even though of course, once she'd sold him the house, there was no guarantee he wouldn't change his plans.

She walked back down, exchanging a wave with Dani and his wife having breakfast on their crumbly terrace. Perhaps they knew why she'd gone up there, what she was thinking – but after the horror of trying to urgently get Ewan to hospital yesterday, surely they wouldn't blame her for turning her mind to the future of the cove.

Now she was on the road above Casa Palmito – and good God, did she really think she could fool potential buyers with her painting and clipping of the pretty front and side? Agustín, of course, was only interested in the setting, but anyone else would only have had to come up the road a bit to see the sorry state of the roof, the worrying crack along the back wall, and a large green stain suggesting some kind of leaking pipe issue currently masked by the semi-desert summer. Nobody was going to take all that on, just for a two-bedroom house with no road access. No, Agustín would have his glassy-eyed houses here, and she would have a little place in Shoreham, occasionally visiting Cala Turquesa from Agustín's rented ground floor apartment, minutes from a carton of soya milk or a prescription for eczema.

She'd just come into the house and, as if waiting for her to get back – as well as come round to his way of thinking – Agustín's name flashed up on her phone. 'Hello, how—'

'How are *you*, Marina?' he asked in English. 'It must be bad, trapped there by this sea. At least you're not alone.'

'Well, I *am* alone, actually. Two of the boys are stuck in Almería, one's in San José, and Polly's... there too.' She couldn't face recounting what had happened to Ewan and hearing all the *told you so*'s.

'Oh no, *pobrecita!*'

Poor little thing. 'Well not really, the *turquito* community are fantastic. I don't feel isolated. And I'm keeping busy.'

'Ah good. At least it will be calm again Friday; it would be a shame if you had to miss our concert. Oh, and our ice cream on your arrival at the port! I have a fabulous place to take you for that.'

'I'm looking forward to it. Look, I was going to call you, there are a few things I want to ask.'

'Of course. If it's about renting the new houses for holidays once they're ready, you know I will always give you a special deal.'

'Yes, that was one of the things.' She sat down on the sofa and tried to concentrate. '*You?* D'you mean... you're not just going to organise the development, you're going to *own* it?'

'Well, *yes!* Have I not always made that clear? Absolutely.'

'Oh... maybe you have. I'm sorry. That's great.'

'What more do you want to ask?'

'What are you going to do with the ruined fortress? The *turquitos* think you're going to build a hotel there.'

'What? No! We'll make it safe so it can become an attractive look-out point. It will look beautiful in the brochure. What more?'

'The *turquitos*. They're remarkably self-sufficient and resourceful. Okay, there are sheets of plastic around and it doesn't look nice – but they live in harmony with nature, and with each other, and—'

'Believe me, they will be very happy with what I—'

'No, no, you have to *meet* and find out what would work for them – as well as you. You can't just put them in wooden hutches.'

'Hu-ches?'

'They're what you keep pet rabbits in. The *turquitos* aren't pets… or natives to be put in a reservation!'

He laughed. 'Marina! What you think I am? What woman you are, the way you say things with such… *brutalidad!*' He laughed some more. 'Of *course* I will meet them – when I know the project goes ahead. I've had confirmation about the planning permission in principle, and that the road would be restored. I'm just waiting for your decision.'

'Well… my decision – or rather, my mother's, for whom I have power of attorney – is *yes!* I'm accepting your offer.'

'Marina! This is wonderful news! You must give me the name of your Spanish lawyer. You do have one, don't you?'

'Of course, same company my mother's always used, for dealing with that money she has to pay every year, the house tax or whatever. I'll send you the details.'

'And we must celebrate – ice cream isn't enough! I know

you have the piano lesson and expat group on Friday before the concert, but maybe dinner the next weekend, after I am back from a conference in Granada? I could do the Sunday.'

'Oh, Polly and I are going to be joining in with the boys' next gig at the campsite that night.'

'Really? I don't want to miss that!'

Oh heavens, he could be there for her singing 'Kiss Me More', she realised. 'How about we have lunch after we've signed?'

'Probably that week, yes. Oh, this is splendid. When is it you go back to England? End of the month, before you start teaching again?'

'Well, it was going to be the 23rd, but I've been wondering about extending.'

'Good idea! Look, I have an appointment. I have to leave you now, but I will see you on Friday, for the first of our celebrations!'

'Yes!' Marina said.

She sat on the sofa, staring out at the table on the front terrace. So that was it; she'd done it. He was obviously very pleased, but *several* celebrations? What was that about? She'd just have to make any celebrations daytime things. Or, if Polly was right about him having plans to 'develop' their friendship, as it were, she should somehow make it clear, sooner rather than later, that that wasn't in *her* plans.

She looked around the room that had been her family's holiday living room for what seemed like forever, at the time, but was in fact only five years. Now that it was soon to be not theirs, she could see past the clutter of the boys' shoes, shorts and guitar tuners to how it had been when it *was* theirs.

Everything was newer and shinier, of course – even if, as her mum was always pointing out, rather shoddily put together. She could picture her father smiling, golden-tanned and enthusiastic about the day's plans. Her mother, on the other hand, unless doing something with her darling Teddy, she could only see… complaining. About ants, sand and buckling skirting tiles. Too much heat, too much boating. Not enough shopping, not enough restaurants. Probably, underlying most of these complaints, not enough money; they'd bought Casa Palmito as a second home when her father was still working for Shell, and had then had to manage it on a lifeboat coxswain's salary. Also, possibly, not enough *attention*; she saw for a moment that her adored father, in his last four or five years, had very much had his own way and his own life. Possibly, even, a *secret* life…

Nowadays, on the rare occasions she talked about him, Mum was happy he'd had his dream job, Spanish house and boat for his last few years in the world. At the time, however, Marina suspected her mum had felt very differently, having been pulled away from her comfortable Surrey life of socialising and London art exhibitions for… well, what she must have thought was going to be a lifetime of money struggles and his being out on the sea.

She decided to look through some more of those Polaroids she'd stuffed back in their box and put in her case, if only to see a happier Mum than she remembered. Besides, she was not going to feel like looking at them when she got back. She got up and went through to the bedroom.

When she got back. It was the 11th, so… twelve days. Polly had to go back on the 16th, and then the boys were off on the 19th – Yasiel and Juanjo to Madrid; Mati to his aunt and uncle in San José, for about another week, she thought she'd heard. If she extended her trip for a week, it would look like... oh, to hell with what it would look like; she was selling a house, had things to do. She went into the EasyJet app on her phone, and with a couple of clicks and a not too hefty extra payment, it was done.

She pulled the box out of her bag and sat down with it on the bed. Hesitated a moment, said, 'Why don't you join me?' and went through to the boys' bedroom, where... yes, there it was. The pale blue T-shirt – faintly salty and sweaty, but all the better. She went back to the bed with it, draping it on the pillow next to her, and opened the box.

First, the Polaroids she'd already seen of her and Teddy playing in the sand, Genoveses beach and *La Mari* anchored there, the blue of her stripe the same colour as the sky. Several of Mum, smiling and glamorous in a green bikini and matching headscarf. And then it seemed that, as usual, the boat trip had been tolerated because they'd been making for a smart seafront restaurant somewhere. They were with two other couples – one sunburnt and English-looking with a little girl she vaguely remembered, and the other darkly Spanish and apparently child-free.

Another picture of them all, whoever they were, the Spanish man now closer to camera and revealed as strikingly good-looking. She studied two more pictures of them all – taken later in the afternoon, maybe, because they were all now sitting in front of puddings and half-empty glasses, and she and Daddy, whose lap she was now on, looked like they'd had enough of it all.

'Who were they? I hope the Spanish couple spoke English, because Mum's Spanish was never great.'

Your mum managed just fine. As you can see, she was having a wonderful time, she heard her father say. Ha! As if he was jealous of the handsome *señor* who seemed to have everyone but her dad's and Marina's attention.

She flicked on through the photos: her and Teddy in helicopter funfair rides, then mucky with chocolate churros; Mum laughing as she posed with a cowboy at that old film studios amusement park; the four of them waiting for an outdoor concert to start, in front of what was probably the cathedral in Almería. A happy family.

Then there was a photo in an envelope. Not as good quality, maybe taken with a different camera. The woman from the Spanish couple, pointing at a rock, looking serious, as if explaining its volcanic geology. It looked like she'd taken the picture herself. Marina held it closer. The mass of shiny curls, the dark, wide-apart eyes... she could be a young Francisca – ah, except there was no way the handsome husband was Diego, bless him, so probably not. She put it back in the envelope.

'Weird. Well, that's it. Strange there aren't more of *La Mari*.'

Perhaps these are just some odd ones that got left behind. Mum will have the rest somewhere in a drawer. Anyway, well done, I told you it would be okay, no need to get upset.

'No,' she said, putting them all back and closing the shoebox. Then she put the T-shirt on the pillow and lay her head down on it. 'And it's good to see Mum looking happy, not always sitting there with a miserable Teddy on the boat.'

Pictures don't tell the whole story.

'No, they don't. But we won't get into that... D'you

know what? I'm not going to shove Mum's painting of *La Mari* in a drawer or give it back to her; I'm going to hang it in my Shoreham apartment.'

That's my girl.

Her phone pealed, making her jump. A WhatsApp video call.

'Hello!' A smiling Mati filled the screen, but then he moved back and there was Polly waving too. 'How are you doing there, all on your own?' he asked in Spanish.

'Fine, really! Any news of Ewan this morning?'

'Well…'

The view swung to one side… and Ewan was there, a dressing on his head but with his toothy grin and holding up a thumb.

'Ewan! How's the head? My God, you had the whole cove worried sick!'

'I'm sorry about that. Really just a scratch—'

'A very *big* scratch,' Polly interrupted.

'And I can't wait to get back,' Ewan continued.

'But he's not going anywhere until the stitches come out in two weeks' time,' Polly said, firmly. 'Francisca and Diego have offered to have us here, but we said no, they've been far too good to us already – we're even wearing their clothes! So she talked to a friend with an apartment hotel who's got a little self-catering room she normally keeps for her sister. We can move in this afternoon.'

'Oh! That sounds good! If the boat's running tomorrow, I'll bring your things over. Yours too, Ewan, if you—'

'What?' Mati said. '*My* boat will be running! We'll all be back in time to make a fabulous lunch! I can then bring you here to see them, no problem.'

'Oh, that'll be lovely.'

'In fact—' he scratched his chin '—you're probably going to want to come to the port as soon as possible. I decided to ask my uncle about your dad's boat, and you're not going to believe it… she's still *here!* Just repainted and renamed, because she does the tourist boat trips along to the lighthouse and back. And weirdest of all, the owner who rents her to the boat tour lady is none other than my aunt!'

Marina was speechless, her heart patting fast.

'D'you want to see her?' Mati asked, looking concerned. 'We could even take her out for a spin, between the boat trip times. If not tomorrow, another day.'

Marina nodded enthusiastically, her throat tightening.

Polly took Mati's arm. 'That's *so* amazing. A bit of a shock, but wonderful.' There was something else about how Polly would meet them at the port to collect their things, so Mati could take Marina straight to *La Mari*.

Marina collected herself. 'Thank you so much, Mati… I can't believe it!'

15

Mati had called to say he and the other two boys were just about to leave the port. Was it a bit too much to be watching out for him – *them* – on the beach? She could have been swimming, of course, but... she'd just washed her hair and put on her turquoise palm trees floaty market dress for their lunch together. Good grief, she was behaving like they were about to have a reunion after he'd been away three *months*, not three days.

At least she could hang out at the jewellery shack with Ewan's friend Lala – although, bless her, she wasn't helping.

'You must have missed him,' Lala was saying now, her face creasing into a smile. Lala herself, in her mid-forties, had a husband who went back and forth between Cala Turquesa and Granada, torn between his brother's ceramics business and the hippie life.

'Sorry?' Marina said. Making out you hadn't followed someone's Spanish was a great way of stalling.

'*Mati*, Marina! Everybody knows there's something between you.'

'What, like "everybody knew" I was with Agustín? We're just *friends*, Lala. Ah, here they are now.'

The boat was racing into the cove, Mati at the helm, his

wild hair floating in the wind. Doing his usual last-minute slowing down, the show-off, then throwing the anchor and leaping into the water like a pirate. Yasiel following him with a stumble, while Juanjo edged himself over the RIB's side.

She found herself rushing over, sharing a hug with Yasiel and then Juanjo, followed by a more awkward one with Mati – but he held her shoulders as they looked at each other with unstoppable grins. 'We're back!' he said.

'You're back!' she replied, like an idiot.

'Are you two going to help with these bags?' Yasiel asked with a laugh. As well as their rucksacks, there was a cool box Mati's aunt must have lent him, and a lot of supermarket bags.

They grabbed all their things and went up the beach path, Juanjo telling Yasiel off for having a little too much gruesome interest in exactly where and how Ewan fell. They were all impressed by the rugged post and rail fence Dani and Bernardo had put up to stop anyone else tumbling into the dry riverbed.

'And he's really doing all right, poor guy?' Yasiel asked.

'Yes. Although God... it really looked terrible at the time,' Marina said.

'I can imagine. What a shock, and poor Polly.'

They came out of the trees and turned towards Casa Palmito.

'Little house! Have you missed us?' Juanjo called out.

Mati looked at Marina, who, as he'd guessed, looked a little saddened by this exclamation. 'Have you said yes, yet?' he asked her quietly.

'I have.' The other two turned to her with resigned looks

on their faces. 'I'll tell you all about it. Most importantly, I'll get a special rental deal, which I'm sure I could extend to you three!'

Yasiel and Juanjo looked happier, saying that was okay then, but Mati still looked pensive.

'And he called this morning and told me he wants to try and reuse the odd quirky feature from the original houses in each one. So I like to think that will make Casa Palmito sort of... reincarnated.'

Mati managed a half-smile.

'Anyway, what's for lunch?' she asked, tapping the cool box.

'Aha,' Mati said. 'Surprise. And part of your maritime introduction course.'

Marina laughed at Yasiel's hand squiggling octopus fingers.

'You think I haven't had octopus before? I love it! Well, *most* of it.'

'Yasiel and I thought we'd get that old barbecue going – octopus and sardines, aubergine, halloumi, something else, can't remember... and meanwhile Juanjo's going to do his incredible Padrón peppers.'

'Oh my God, I *love* all that! Especially after a few days of tinned baked beans. And what shall I do?' she asked, as the boys went into the house and started rushing around getting things done, and was given a salad to make.

They were soon sitting down to a feast, and after Marina had told them all she knew about the development plans, she said she'd found a very reasonable little apartment in San José that she could rent for short trips.

'Maybe you'll come out more and more and one day find

you want to stay!' Juanjo said. 'You could live anywhere, teaching online.'

'You said you hated cold weather,' Mati said. 'Escape the miserable British January and February! It's quiet here, sunny, there are flowers… and a good time to do things it's too hot for in the summer – horse riding, walking, exploring places.'

'Well… a couple of weeks maybe! It'll be interesting chatting in the expat bar tomorrow.' She took another little salty-sweet fried Padrón green pepper. 'Oh my God, Juanjo, these are amazing. I swear I've eaten half of them already.'

He smiled and took one himself. 'Just don't forget what they say: "some bite, others don't".'

'I've never had one bite *me*.'

'You are playing pepper roulette, girl!' Yasiel said.

'It's part of the fun of them. Seeing if you'll be blown away!' Juanjo said.

'So, when do you sign on the house sale?' Mati asked, looking serious again.

'I'm not sure. I've got to see the lawyer. But I've got plenty of time, as I'm not going back until the 3*oth* now.' It seemed like a good time to mention it, linking it with property issues rather than her need to maximise her time with Mati, but he was looking down with a closed smile, and the other two were exchanging a look she couldn't read. 'What?'

'Just that…' Most unusually, Mati looked awkward for a moment. 'I've been thinking of staying on in San José – to have more time with my aunt and uncle. I've still got time before the university teaching restarts, and I could write up the papers I'm doing from here. It would leave me a lot to do in a hurry when I get back, but…'

'Oh come on, Mati, you know you're going to do it!' Yasiel said. 'This happens every year,' he said to Marina. 'Mati *always* ends up changing his flight!'

'Well, it's a hard place to leave,' Marina said.

Mati shrugged. 'It's true. Why I don't block the whole month in advance, I don't know.'

'Because once you're here, you're a different person,' Juanjo said.

'Looks like the Maritime Marina lessons will be continuing!' Yasiel said. 'How come you got called *Marina*? I suppose your parents didn't know you'd be scared of deep water.'

'My boat-mad father's choice.'

'And you're off to see his old boat, I gather?' Juanjo said, looking at her attentively, like one of his counselling patients. It looked like Mati had told the boys about her father's death, as she said he could.

'We are. But first, Mati, tell us about my turtle! Is she getting better?'

'I've heard she is. But they're still not sure when she can be released back into the sea. Of course, she's another reason for staying, in case I can be here for that. And when she's a bit better, I'll be able to take you to see her.'

'Oh! That would be wonderful!'

Marina bit into another juicy pepper and squeaked as her mouth filled with heat. The boys laughed and quickly filled up her glass of water.

'Told you!' Juanjo said. 'You never know, you're just chomping away, and then one strikes you! It's good luck, you know!'

'Is it? Doesn't *look* like it!' Yasiel said, laughing as Mati fanned Marina's red cheeks with one of their snorkelling flippers.

Marina swallowed some water, in danger of choking with laughter. 'Certainly deserve some, after that!'

On their way to the San José harbour, Mati must have seen Marina looking anxious, and patted her back. She'd turned down taking the wheel.

'I know, how can I be nervous about meeting a boat?' she said, above the noise of the engine.

'Ah, but not just *any* boat. One that saw such happiness and such sadness,' he said in gentle Spanish.

She nodded. 'That's right, the best and worst times of my life. But mostly I feel positive about this.'

'As I'm sure your father would want you to.'

She nodded, the threat of tears stinging her eyes. He seemed to totally understand, and was also driving slowly for once, as if he knew she needed time to get herself together.

'Just don't expect her to look quite as she did. She's a working boat. A hard worker! She has extra seats that wouldn't have been there, and well, she's...'

'Not as young as she was! I know. Quite an old girl really.'

'But she's lovely, and there's plenty of life in her yet.'

They were going round the mountain, past the entrance to the cave where they'd sat with their legs in the turquoise water. The wind had totally disappeared, but the sea was still slightly choppy, as if it couldn't quite forget the battering the wind had given it.

As they came into the port, he touched her arm and

pointed up ahead... where she could just see old *La Mari*'s pointy nose.

'Oh! That's her!'

Mati moored up with the other tiny boats, and Polly was waiting for them on the dock... with Ewan beside her.

'Ewan! How are you doing? Aren't you meant to be resting?' Marina asked, as she got up onto the dock. They exchanged awkward English arm pats.

'Honestly, I'm fine,' he said. 'Hardly any headache now. But never mind that – I understand you've got a special boat to say hello to!'

Mati handed Ewan a rucksack. 'I know you said not to bother, but Juanjo picked up a few things at your place. And here's your bag, Polly, although Marina says she'll have to put some of your things in her suitcase.'

'I know, too much stuff from the floaty cloth shop! Thanks,' Polly said. 'Now off you go! See you later.' Polly squeezed Marina's shoulder and then walked off arm in arm with Ewan.

A gruff, happy voice hailed Mati.

Marina turned and it was Diego – the smiley boat man, but unbelievably also Mati's uncle. Rather heavier set these days, much less hair, but the weathered face still had that same big grin that made his eyes almost disappear.

'Marinita! At last! How lovely to see you again, gorgeous.' There was the Spanish double kiss and then he looked her up and down and nodded. 'Look at you, all grown up, but just the same! Do you still refuse to wear a cap in the sun?' he said, miming in case she didn't understand.

'Yes! You've got a good memory! It's lovely to see you too.'

'But come, your *La Mari* is waiting to see you!' he said, beckoning with his hand for them to follow him... and then, as they walked along the dock, the boat next to *La Mari* pulled out, giving them a full, perfect view of her.

There she was, that same cheeky 'nose', the stripe that Marina used to think of as like a hairband, the boxy little cabin, the clapping of the little waves round her as if she couldn't wait to get out.

'Ha! She's beautiful. Smaller... but then I'm bigger now! God, I feel ten again, itching to get on!'

Diego and Mati laughed and touched an arm either side of her.

Nearer, she could see the little seats they'd added for the tours. There was scratching here and there, but someone had given her a good clean. Mati went aboard and held out a hand, and then she was on the deck, near the wheel. And there was a moment where she was back pulling the cord of the engine and looking over to her father slumped on the deck... but when she looked over at that place, as she had to, there were seats there now. Where her sea-loving father died, people sat and enjoyed the view of the coast, the ride over the sea. He'd like that, she thought, smiling to herself.

'Ah, Carla!' Mati said, as a woman a little older than them in sun-protective clothing and a long plait came over to them on the dock. He introduced the boat tour lady and Marina to each other.

'Look, by chance, a couple cancelled, so there's room for you two on the tour if you like, if Marina would like to see her in action!' Carla said. 'Or you could just wait and take her out yourselves in a few hours' time, between tours.'

'I'd love to do the tour, thanks!' Marina said.

'Mati, did Diego ask you about the end of August?'

Diego held up his hands. 'I'm sorry, Carla, I forgot, with the excitement of reuniting Marina and *La Mari!*'

'Ha! I can imagine.'

'What's this?' Mati asked.

'Well, I'm away five days in the last week of August, to help with my sister's wedding in Valladolid. A friend of mine had agreed to do it, but there's illness in her family and she can't do it now. Anyway, *you'd* be much better! We could cut it to just two trips a day. What d'you think?'

'How strange, I was just saying earlier I was thinking of staying longer! I'd love to do it. I better come along now and start to get to know what I'll have to say!'

'Fantastic!' Carla came aboard and unlocked the cabin. 'You'll be wanting to see in here, Marina. Nowadays mostly used for seasick children.'

'It always was! Well, for my brother. And on whole-day trips I had to have a siesta, but I loved it; it was so cosy.' The bench seat covers and the little curtains at the narrow windows had been changed to a more durable dark blue material, but she could still see herself lying down there with Mog Cat, Dad reading her an Enid Blyton adventure... She smiled and felt like he was watching over her shoulder saying: *Remember this? What happy times we had.*

Mati and Marina waited while the people who'd booked a trip assembled: a middle-aged English couple; a cute Spanish boy of about ten and his parents; and three young French girls in nothing but thong bikinis who looked like they were already exchanging looks and giggles about Mati.

Once everybody was aboard, introduced to each other and sorted out with life jackets, Carla started the engine.

She'd encouraged Mati to stand next to her at the wheel and put Marina on the other helm chair – meaning it was impossible for her legs not to be in frequent tingling contact with Mati's.

Oh that chug-chug sound as they pulled out of the harbour! Mati seemed to read her mind, bending down and giving her a quick hug. Jesus, he was so tactile today – a pat here, a squeeze there, and so close when sorting out her barbecued banana for her that she could have just leant forward a few inches and kissed his cheek. But then, people were more touchy-feely here; it probably didn't mean anything – and he probably had no idea what effect he was having on her. Any more than he seemed to notice the obvious effect he was having on the pretty and practically nude French girls.

They were coming out of the San José bay now. The life-jacketed little Spanish boy had persuaded his mum to let him sit up front, just like Marina used to do. Carla had agreed, as long as one of his parents went with him. This meant more room for the French girls to spread out, which they did without hesitation, much to the embarrassment of the Spanish father and the English couple. There were sighs of delight as they passed the beautiful Genoveses and Mónsul beaches, and then Carla started explaining the colours of the volcanic rock formations they were going past. She repeated all this in very good English, but Marina, remembering some schoolgirl French, helped her a bit when one of the young girls asked a question.

Carla turned to Mati, who was saying he'd have to put a lot of practice into the English explanation – and the French would be beyond him.

Carla laughed. 'Or just bring your girlfriend with you each time – no problem!'

His girlfriend. *Novia*: that wasn't just a friend who was a girl. In fact, they used the same word for fiancée... and even *bride*. *Jesus*. Was he going to put Carla right about this, or should she?

But Carla was now in full trilingual flow about the charm of the little wild coves, asking the passengers to guess their names. Marina watched them as *La Mari* chugged past, just like she had on her father's last day... and then a woman standing by a rock on one of the nearly deserted little coves took her eye. It reminded her of that Polaroid of the woman pointing at something. Was this woman also pointing at something? It looked like it, even though the rock didn't seem unusual in any way. Unless there was a creature on it. Or... writing. Could something have been written on the stone? She must have a look at the photo again.

They were sitting on the edge of the village square with little pots of ice cream – coconut for Marina, coffee and walnut for Mati – probably from the place Agustín had in mind for tomorrow.

Mati picked at the shoulder of her dress. 'Why haven't you got a bikini under that dress?'

Because she'd stupidly wanted to look pretty at the 'reunion' lunch, rather than think about practicalities. 'Because I'm an idiot. But look, if you want to go in, go ahead.' He was in his black trunks with a simple white T-shirt.

He looked at his watch. 'Actually, if we want to take *La Mari* out for a bit, we haven't *that* much time before Carla does the early evening trip. Let's start heading back.'

'Okay.'

La Mari was being attended to by Diego. 'Aha, come on then – I'm sure Marinita wants to drive a little!'

'Oh... I don't know,' Marina said.

Mati took the boat out, and then beckoned her to the wheel. 'Bit heavier than the RIB, but not difficult.'

'I don't know...' she said again. Memories of that last time came back to her, the tears blinding her vision, the heart-racing panic...

He took her arm and pulled her closer. 'I think... you will regret it if you don't. You can give her back to me any moment.'

'Okay.' She took the wheel, felt *La Mari* in her control again... and, maybe with her father's influence over her shoulder, was surprised to find herself laughing tearfully. 'Wow! I never thought I'd be doing this! Which way shall I go?'

'Whatever way you like! Except...' He turned the wheel to one side. 'Not into the path of a sailing boat – they have priority, can't change their direction as quickly.'

'Oh God! Sorry. I'm still only really up to pointing a boat in one direction.'

'You could go on a course and learn. It's only a day... Where are you going?'

'Africa?' She'd picked up speed a bit, enjoying the hiss of the bow slicing through the little waves. 'Then I thought I'd go to Cala Turquesa and on from there.'

'Waves will be against you on the way back; there won't be time. Just a triumphant tour of Turquesa and then maybe I'll take over.'

'Okay.'

'Seriously, you could go on a course, learn how to moor the boat, what all the buoys mean, things about safety, and get your licence. I did mine as a teenager – a more advanced one, meaning I can take the boat out at night, but Yasiel and Juanjo did the basic one a few years ago so they can take the boat without me... Great, Marina! But inland a bit now please, Captain.'

She turned towards Cala Turquesa. 'Do they do it in English?'

'No! Well, maybe somewhere like Marbella. But you need to do it here. The boys went to Aguadulce.'

'Where's that?' It sounded familiar; she must have gone there when she was a child.

'Just on a bit from Almería.'

'You'd have to be my translator.'

'Well, in *advance*, I could be. I mean, if I taught you what all the terms and parts of the boat were in Spanish, went through a few things I know they'll cover, I'm sure you'd be fine.'

'D'you think? Oh, then I'd be able to take *La Mari* out, or hire a little RIB, whenever I come here!'

'Yes! Maybe if you were staying here, Polly or another friend with you, and I'm not around to take you wherever you want...'

'You've been amazing at that. I'm so grateful.'

'No problem, my pleasure.'

'I can't imagine ever being able to enter that cave like you did!'

'Anything's possible... I mean – ha! – that was a start!' She had just got out of the way of José's RIB.

'So... it'll be the next level of our maritime reorientation course then?' she asked with a grin.

He nodded and laughed, looking as happy as she felt about having a reason to share more hours together.

16

After a fun evening playing cards and laughing with the boys, she hadn't felt like reopening the box of Polaroids. As soon as she woke up, however, she wanted to use the bright morning light for peering at that photo.

She took it to the window, held it up close... yes, there *was* something there. Initials. Two pairs. Although try as she might, she couldn't make out what they were. She checked for her father's TM, but although one of the first initials could be a T, it could also be an E or an F; this was hopeless. Anyway, would the initials still be there after all this time, scratched onto rock? It seemed unlikely – but that woman she saw was definitely looking at something... The only thing for it was to visit the beach and have a look herself – but there were maybe fifteen or twenty of those tiny beaches. Would she remember which one it was? And did she really want to involve Mati in this, when there was a chance this handsome woman with wide-apart eyes and luscious dark curls really *could* be a young Francisca?

If it had been Francisca on that other boat, the day of the accident, that would explain why the woman seemed slightly familiar; she would have seen her in the property management office – and maybe she saw her parents socially. She didn't want to believe Mati's adored aunt could have been having an affair with her father, and it didn't feel likely when she and Diego sounded so happy together... But then, if Francisca was involved in Marina's father's last day, and felt terrible about it, that might explain why she hadn't wanted to tell Mati about her father's death – or that she now owned his boat. But wait, would you buy the boat that your secret ex-lover hit his head on and that killed him? Surely not.

She put the photo away and sat on the bed. She could hear the boys stretching, yawning and chatting next door. It was time to start the day, one she'd been looking forward to; she mustn't let these thoughts spoil it. And she needed to get that boat licence, so she could go out alone, find that cove, see that the initials TM *weren't* on the rock, and forget about this. Or as much as she was ever going to be able to.

Just past the turquoise water cave and within sight of the port, Mati went into neutral and gave her an instruction.

'What? I'm *not* driving in there yet.'

'Marina!' He repeated the instruction.

'Oh! *Anclote... fondear...* drop the anchor, I get it.' The stress of trying to learn all the nautical Spanish terms seemed to be pushing her into English for all her other words – and Mati was kindly going along with that.

Once anchored, he started pointing to parts of the boat and she was very pleased with herself for remembering the Spanish for port, starboard, bow, stern, hull and keel from the list they'd made on the terrace. Then he tested her on understanding what he was saying about things in the port, and it was a lot harder.

He looked at her.

She bit her lip. 'That's a *lot* of words. Can't you spread them out? You said this would be easy!'

'Yes, but then you arrange to do course in *thirty-six* hours! Come on, try again,' he said in English, then repeated the Spanish, pointing over towards the port.

'It doesn't help that quite often there are two words for the same thing. And other times, one word can have two completely different meanings. I mean, when you say *abordaje*, I've just realised, you could either be telling me about boarding the boat or crashing it!'

He laughed. 'I'm sorry, yes! But you take the *contexto*,' he said in English. 'You would not crash the boat in the port.'

'I think I would *absolutely* crash the boat in the port – before and after people had boarded!' She laughed and groaned. 'Oh dear.' She took a drink of water, looking at the dimple in his cheek as he laughed, and then looked down at the sheet of terms they'd made.

The truth was, she was feeling somewhat overwhelmed; by the Spanish boating language, the midday heat, and – not least – the proximity to the bossiest, but kindest and frankly most gorgeous guy she'd ever known. Today in particular, finding him magnetically attractive seemed to be affecting the electrical activity of her brain; concentration seemed to have an intermittent fault, and a random impulse had now thrown up the thought that she didn't actually know the Spanish terms for the contents of a Spanish man's swimming trunks, nor the activities that—

He touched her arm. 'Are you okay? Let's get out of the sun for a bit, let you cool down.'

'Yes, that would be good. Let's *virar!*' she said, a little manically. Change course. Something her heart definitely needed to do; they had just two weeks and wouldn't see each other until heaven knew when; *if* anything happened, it would be a holiday romance – and, when he became Faithless Number Five, a totally heart-breaking one.

He made a bowline – ha-ha, she knew that, *as de guía* – and tied the RIB up to a stone in front of the entrance to the turquoise cave. They got out and sat on the shady ledge again, legs swirling in the clear water.

'Oh… this is heaven,' she said, steadfastly gazing at the sand and some gently swaying seaweed near the rocks. He nudged her gently. She looked over and found he'd brought the rope they'd found in the shed. 'Oh no.'

'I'll show you again. It's the knot I just used.' He made a little loop in the rope and took the end of it in his other hand. 'So, the rabbit goes up the hole, round the tree, and back down the hole…' She watched those sensitive, dextrous fingers. 'There.'

He undid it and handed it to her. She made the loop, put the end in it, but… He took her hand and guided her through it. Then with sudden inspiration she managed it on her own. 'Oh! I've done it!'

'You have! Clever piano fingers,' he said, squeezing her hand.

She looked down at her freckled hand in his brown one.

'Clever vet hands that pick up turtles...' she whispered, her heart tapping. He still wasn't letting go.

'Animals are more easy than...' He put his arm round her. 'Oh, Marina, tell me what to do. You have me... well, all in knots!'

Her mouth opened in amazement. She looked up at him, tried to read his face – which looked amused... but a little worried.

'Why are you so surprised?' he said, laughing, then his face fell. 'Is this... bad?'

She shook her head. 'No! It's just... I thought *I* was the only one in knots!'

'Oh!' He broke into a huge smile and sighed with relief. 'I wasn't sure! Fantastic! So... we just tie the ropes together, like the flat knot I showed you!' He released her hand, put both arms round her, her head landing on his warm T-shirted shoulder. Then he let go and put a hand to her face, as she finally stroked that crazy mop of soft dark hair, both gazing at each other with amazed smiles. 'Oh, Marina... and we still have two weeks. Two weeks and a half!' He leant forward and put his lips on hers, tentatively, and said '*te quiero*'. Which could mean *I love you*, but more likely: *I want you*.

She pulled away gently. 'Wait.' Wait for what? Until they both lived in the same country? The same village? 'I'm sorry, I'm afraid I... can't have a holiday thing.' If only she could just live for the moment – the fortnight – like most girls she knew. If only she didn't have to protect her heart so fiercely – but she'd always been like this.

She was expecting him to be persistent, try and persuade her – like with the house – and it made her adore him even more when she saw him nod, look resigned, and say something about how he'd expected she would say that. Although, that smile… maybe he hadn't given up hope.

She put her arms under his for another hug, and he held her tightly and stroked her back – so deliciously that she wondered how on earth she was going to resist him. 'Oh… this is heaven,' she said again. 'I mean, even more heaven than before.'

'It is. But… what time were you going to be teaching the little girl?'

'Oh God!' She looked at her watch. 'And oh no, Agustín will be waiting.'

'Where?' he asked, looking puzzled. 'And… *why?*'

'At the port. He said he wanted to take me for a celebratory house-sale ice cream before Zara's lesson.'

He groaned.

'I know. I'd much rather spend the entire afternoon here with you, then go back and get the boys for the concert.'

'Well… quite. But we can come here again… and other beautiful places!' He briefly kissed her on the lips, then pulled the boat towards them so they could get on board. 'D'you want to drive?'

'Um…' She was sitting there in a daze, her lips tingling. 'I don't think so.'

He laughed. 'I'm not sure I'm up to it either, but someone's got to!' he said, back in Spanish. 'Come on.' Mati untied the boat and started the engine. 'Okay. *Reverse*,' he said to himself. 'We don't want to end up inside the mountain.'

She laughed and watched him settle back into driving the boat, more slowly than usual, even though they were going to be late.

Agustín was there, waiting – and bless him, without a trace of irritation.

'I'm sorry!' she called out, as Mati moored the boat. She wasn't up to thinking of an excuse. 'This is Mati... one of my housemates.'

Agustín and Mati acknowledged each other – slightly awkwardly, Marina thought. She wanted to hug Mati again, knowing she wouldn't see him for what felt like umpteen hours until the concert, but he gave her a heart-melting smile, patted her back and strode off to chat to his uncle and some co-workers standing outside the port office.

She turned to Agustín and went into an enthusiastic Spanish two-kiss thing; after all, thanks to him, there was going to be a little apartment she could afford to visit – just minutes from Mati's aunt and uncle. 'Still just time for an ice cream in the square!'

'Ah, so already you have discovered it?'

'I have. And I'm looking forward to discovering it again! There are at least three more flavours I have to try before I go.'

'Which is when?'

'The 30th.'

'Oh! I thought it was earlier. That's great; we'll definitely have time for that dinner then!'

'Well... lunch would be better for me. Easier to get back to the cove.'

He opened his mouth and closed it again. He clearly had the night driving type of licence and could have been thinking of offering a moonlit lift back... which was *not* going to happen.

They'd reached the ice cream parlour, and while he

selected a double dark chocolate one, she went for the cool calm of a lemon sorbet. They found a bench in the shade and sat down.

'I imagine your housemates, with their annual reunion, aren't too happy about the sale.'

'They weren't, but they've come round – particularly after the horror of getting one of our *turquito* friends to hospital during a wind storm.'

'Oh no, was he all right?'

'Yes, but... he might not have been. He's a lovely chap, and now my friend Polly's boyfriend.'

'Oh! Romance in Cala Turquesa! Wonderful. And for you?'

Yes, a whole sea of it... 'No, no. I'm not a holiday romance girl.'

'But it wouldn't necessarily be that.'

'Anyway, I'm not looking for romance at the moment.' *I've already found it.*

'Do people *look* for romance? In my experience, it finds *you* – usually when you don't expect it and it's the most inconvenient.'

'*That's* certainly true,' she said, rather too quickly.

He put down his ice cream tub and took her hand. 'You can also find *friendship* – and a piano teacher – when you don't expect it. Don't worry, Marina, I'd have to be blind not to see the... *chispa* between you and Mati.'

Sparks. 'Oh...'

'Does he work with boats?'

'No, animals. He's a vet researcher... in *Madrid*. So... it's a bit of a problem!' She looked at her watch. 'Oh, better get going. Thanks for this. Well, for everything, really.' She gave him a warm smile and a peck on the cheek.

Marina listened to Zara play 'O Waly, Waly' – or 'The Water is Wide', as the little girl had renamed it.

'Oh well done, Zara! That's really lovely. Your left hand turned itself into a beautiful singer, while your right hand just tapped away like a heartbeat.'

Zara beamed up at her. What a sweet-looking child she was, with her mother's black-brown eyes but a few freckles and brown rather than black hair suggesting a Caucasian daddy. 'The girl's song you sent is very, very nice. Mummy says it's a love song, but...' Her little brow furrowed. 'It's very sad.'

Zara still probably thought love could only bring happiness – like she herself had at her age. 'Well, there are those words about not being able to cross the wide water... Maybe the couple just live too far apart.' *Oh Jesus, Marina.*

'So... they need to get a better boat!' Zara said with a giggle, making Marina laugh.

'Yes!'

'I like that piece now. But this "Singing Sun" one... doesn't sound sunny at all!'

'Oh... that's your third exam piece?' Why had this teacher chosen *two* miserable modern ones for this perky little lady to play?

Zara played it, and, apart from needing to correct the pedal here and there, it was pretty much ready – as was the classical one. Then she asked Marina to play an alternative exam choice in her book, the modern rocky little 'Inter-city Stomp'.

'I love that!' Zara said. 'Will you teach me it?'

Shefali had come into the living room. 'Now, Zara, we said just half an hour – Marina's on holiday!'

'I can quickly show her this, don't worry,' Marina said. She explained each hand and put some fingering in, got Zara to try the right-hand melody while she did the pounding left-hand rock. Zara literally bounced on the piano stool with excitement and started hammering out some of the left hand as well.

'I'm sorry, you might be going to regret this lesson!' Marina said to Shefali.

Zara laughed, then looked pensive for a moment. 'My friend's big sister Izzy has online lessons with you. Can I do that?' She turned to Shefali. 'Mummy?'

'Well, we'd have to give notice to the school, but if Marina had time...'

'I'd love to teach you again, Zara. Perhaps we should try some online lessons this term and see how you get on with it?'

'Excellent idea!' Shefali said. 'Thank you *so* much, Marina. Here's your envelope... now let me take you off for a well-earned drink.'

Leaving Zara to show her daddy the new piece, Marina and Shefali walked down the road into the village centre, with its glimpses of delicious blue sea and sandy beach between the houses and restaurants. They stopped outside the brightly painted Blue Octopus bar.

'There aren't that many San José expats – or even half-expats like us, nipping over to our place here whenever we can. Brits all go to Mojácar an hour or so away,' Shefali said.

'Where they don't have to learn Spanish.'

'Exactly. So there only tends to be half a dozen of us at the most, including a few honorary Spanish members who use it as English practice.'

'Sounds great.'

They went up steps to a terrace overlooking the sea the other side of the road, ordered drinks from the bar, and then went over to a table of happy-looking people of mixed ages. Shefali introduced her to thirty-something language school owner Kim, originally from Leeds; May, another English teacher, younger and maybe half-Asian, who lived in Madrid; Jen and Phil, who'd just retired and sold their property management business; a blonde chap called Ben who worked in a nearby botanical garden; Spanish Mónica who worked as a photographer; and another very Spanish-looking girl called Juliana, about her own age, who surprised her by speaking perfect English.

Shefali told them how she'd bumped into Marina, who used to teach Zara the piano, and found she was staying in her family's house in Cala Turquesa for the month.

'Only reached by boat nowadays – how exciting!' Ben said.

'I *love* that place,' May said, with a dreamy look in her eyes.

'Well, yes, it's wonderful, but now unrentable and too isolated. I've just sold it to Agustín Méndez, who's going to rebuild the four houses there and then the road will be reopened.'

'Ah, the lovely Agustín,' Mónica said, with a strong Spanish accent. 'I used to work for his father – not a good man. Nobody understan' how he have son like this – and so handsome too! Agustín will do good for the *cala*, I am sure.'

'Hm, but he's bit of a slime ball,' Ben said. 'Walks around like he owns half the village. Mind, he probably will do, eventually. The village's most eligible bachelor. A couple of my girlfriend's friends have got their eye on him, but he seems to be very picky.'

'He's been a perfect gentleman,' Marina said. 'Actually, he'll be here before long. He's driving me to a concert in San Rafael, where I'm meeting friends.'

'Ooh-er!' Kim said, nudging her.

Marina smiled and shook her head. 'No, no, it's not like that!'

'Must be hard, letting that place go,' Ben said, May nodding in agreement.

'Yes, but I'm going to come back, rent a little apartment in San José now and again.'

'It's good you haven't had to deal with Agustín's father,' Phil said. 'Before we retired, we used to do some house sales, but he was forever pinching our clients.'

'In contrast,' Jen joined in, 'our main *rentals* competitor, Francisca León, was a delight – ringing up and warning us about difficult customers!'

'Francisca, yes!' Marina said. 'My mother's been dealing with her for years.'

'And how often are you going to visit, d'you think?' Kim asked.

'Hopefully whenever *we're* here, and you can give Zara a lesson in person!' Shefali said.

'Yes! Well, I'll have to see. But all my pupils are by Zoom, so if I kept a keyboard here, I could work.'

'Ha – you'll come more and more, and for longer… that's how many of us ended up living here!' Kim said. 'Sooner or later, you realise England has become a place to visit, rather than live in.'

'And it might look like a sparsely populated desert region, but the music scene is incredible!' the Spanish-looking Juliana said. 'I have such fun at the music and drama centre. It's expanding. They're always needing more music teachers there, if you wanted to do face-to-face teaching. And you could be in the big annual musical!'

'Oh wow, I *love* singing! When is it?'

'End of July. You've just missed it. Make sure you're here to start rehearsals next May!'

'Whoa, what are we doing here?' Phil said, laughing. 'Feels like nearly every year we're persuading a young lady to get out of Blighty and come and join us!'

They all laughed, and Ben patted Juliana on the back.

'No regrets, I've got to say,' Juliana said. 'Oh – except that, if you're a fan of Thai food, the nearest restaurant is an hour away!'

'Oh Jeez, that *would* be an adjustment,' Marina said, laughing.

'You'd have to join May, Juliana and me,' Kim said. 'It's English-run, up near Mojácar. The Spanish just don't seem to *get* Thai food. Although oddly, last time we went, Francisca and Diego were there, celebrating their anniversary!'

'Francisca is *such* a legend,' Ben said. 'Honestly, she and Diego are likely the cornerstones of the village. I'm surprised they didn't manage to persuade the restaurant to open a branch here.'

'Preferably before I'm next here!' Marina said. 'Oh... here's Agustín. Thanks for bringing me here, Shefali. Maybe

I'll make it here again and see you all before I go back to England.'

They all encouraged her to do that, said their goodbyes, and a few waved hello to Agustín, waiting outside.

She went out to him and then put a hand to her mouth. 'Oops, can you give me a few minutes?' She dashed back in, made her way to the loos, took the rolled-up floaty dress out of her handbag and changed out of her shorts and T-shirt to put it on.

She went back out and got a nod of approval.

'A bit crumpled, and there's nothing I can do about the salty-sandy Crocs. Also, not sure my bag will ever recover from the salty-sandy shorts I've just stuffed into it. Cala Turquesa living problems!'

'A problem of which you'll think with affection in the future,' he replied in English.

His white BMW was parked nearby. Inside, it was unnaturally immaculate for sandy and semi-desert dusty Almería. The car purred silently and carefully out of the village, skilfully dodging families still coming back from the beach, or on an early evening out. Then they were out among the rounded hills fuzzy with esparto grass and *palmito* baby palms, going past a few smaller coastal villages, until the hills started to become a mountain and their road clung to the edge of it, the glinting dark blue sea further and further below them.

'Oh wow, I remember this! Although I think the road wasn't as good. My mother hated it, and my brother used to cover his eyes – while my dad and I felt on top of the world!'

'Ha – I agree with you two; there is nowhere more beautiful. Except for the sight of the San Rafael valley as you come over this hill… '

They turned steeply inland for a few metres, with nothing but sky before them, until they reached the summit and there it was, laid out beneath them: a huge valley surrounded by terracotta rocky mountains, set into intense relief by the low sun; a band of dark blue at the far end that looked like the sea had been poured into the gap between two hills. The ex-goldmining village of San Rafael sat in the middle, with its white houses and ochre church glowing in the last sun.

'Oh my *God!*' Marina exclaimed.

'I know. I will never be tired of this view.'

They glided down across the valley and into the village, up the road going past the church and into a little car park near the botanical gardens where Ben worked. They joined a queue of chatty, excited people waiting to go into the amphitheatre. It was a small stone space surrounded by a higher tier, and rows of plastic chairs facing a wooden stage. Backing it, there were up-lit ruined small mining buildings and a dark hill silhouetted by the last rays of the sun.

'What a magical place!' Marina said.

'It is. Ah, we can go in – and speak Spanish now, Marina, to get in the mood for flamenco!'

Friendly organisers took down the barrier, checked tickets and beckoned the audience through. There were no seat numbers, but just as Marina started to wonder how they were going to find two seats and save five, she spotted tall Yasiel and the others coming in, Mati grinning and calling out: 'Yes – *there*, Marina!' and pointing to a line of chairs in the third row.

There was a confused milling about while they decided who should sit where, Mati eventually taking over and letting Agustín go on the end seat with Marina next to him, then making sure it was him rather than Polly the other side of her. Once they were all seated, Marina and Polly then took drinks orders for everyone and went off to the little bar.

'Well? Come on, how's your day been?' Polly asked, as they waited their turn. 'Most importantly, has Mati got you ready for tomorrow's navigation course? Or were you too busy navigating around your feelings for each other to be able to concentrate?' she asked with a laugh.

'Well…!' Marina smiled, breathed out heavily and raised her eyebrows.

'Oh! He made a move?' she asked excitedly.

'We both did! But I can't have a holiday romance with him – you know I can't; it would be too upsetting.'

'Oh, Marina… No romance comes with a guarantee. You've just had awful luck.'

'Yes but… Madrid and Shoreham – how's that going to work?'

'Perfectly, I'd say! You'll both enjoy both places! Who knows what will happen? Time to go with your heart. Or at least a mixture of heart and common sense.' She leant forward, aware a couple of Spanish guys next to them obviously understood English and were finding this conversation hilarious. 'Did he kiss you?' she whispered.

Marina hesitated, smiling. Then nodded.

Polly hugged her. 'Heart as well as head. Listen to both.'

They went back with a little tray of beers and Cokes, and sat down just in time before the lights dimmed. Marina was surprised to hear Agustín and Mati finishing off an enthusiastic chat about La Mari the turtle.

The guitarists walked in, to rapturous applause. The one with neatly combed hair sat down with his guitar and put his shiny shoe on a footstool, the other looked more relaxed and balanced his guitar by putting an ankle on his knee; it wasn't difficult to guess which one had the classical background, and which one was the *flamenco*. They'd been playing together for years, apparently – initially alternating their styles in the performance, and then finding a way to blend them in every piece they wrote together. A short introduction from the classicist, and they started with a ponderous scale-like piece Marina wasn't sure about... until the flamenco guitarist came out with a plaintive melody, which they then shared between them, supported by exquisitely warm rippling chords. The beauty of it, as the melody soared higher and higher, was almost too much to bear... her throat constricted... until she felt the warmth of Mati's hand as it found hers among the crumpled salty folds of her dress.

17

'Are you sure I can't drive you?' Mati asked. They were clearing up after another barbecue lunch on the terrace – that they'd had at an English hour, so Marina could enjoy it before going off to Aguadulce for her course.

'We could *all* go,' Yasiel said. 'Look at the boats, have a swim...'

'I'm up for that,' Juanjo said.

'Thanks but no, really.' She turned to Yasiel and Juanjo. 'And you two shouldn't be spending two hours in a car, when you've only got four days left here. Anyway, I'm looking forward to driving – it'll be good for me.'

'Leave that,' Mati said, taking a tea towel from her. 'Go and get ready.'

She went through to the bedroom and rechecked her bag, put the list of Spanish navigation terms in there, in case she had to wait at the place where she had to do the psychotechnics test.

'I think you should wear those shoes you have for beaches with stones,' Mati said behind her. 'We don't want Croc shoe fall in the sea as you board!' He'd started speaking to her in English a bit more.

'Ah, good point. I'll put them on when I arrive.' She placed them in their waterproof bag and packed them.

'Lots of sun cream?'

'Yes.'

'And take the satnav.'

'What? It's just straight along the coast. I can't miss it.'

'No, no, take it. Just after Almería the road divides.'

'Oh. Okay.' She took it from him. 'Honestly, you're as bossy as Polly.' Her phone pinged. She looked at it, laughed and showed it to Mati; it was Polly telling her to drive slowly, *please*.

'I was about to say the same! Are you ready now?' He was putting on his shoes; he'd persuaded her to at least let him take her to San José.

'Ready as I'm going to be!'

They went down to the beach, and got smiles and nods from Lala, Dani and even the usually self-involved girl couple; it seemed everyone had made up their own minds about whether she and Mati were a couple now. Even Yasiel and Juanjo were calling them 'you two' all the time, despite Mati still sharing the kids' room with Yasiel at night. Then there was the way they seemed to be unable to keep their arms off each other. It was lovely, this new level of closeness, this almost-relationship – but at the same time rather agonising.

She let him drive the boat, with four hours at sea ahead of her. Diego was there on the dock and wished her luck when he heard where she was going. Then he walked off to the office, as if he knew they'd want a few minutes together.

Mati put his arms round her. 'You will be *capitana fantástica*, I know it. Tell me when you arrive, no?'

'I will.'

She found a place to park at the Aguadulce port, turned off the engine, and breathed a sigh of relief. Sent Mati a photo of the boats and a smiling emoji, and got a string of congratulatory emojis back. It had been a beautiful if slightly nerve-racking drive – along the busy Almería seafront and then, after cutting through the mountain in a tunnel, enjoying a road hugging the mountain cliffs with the sea just below her until she dipped down to the large *puerto deportivo* of pleasure boats at Aguadulce.

She had a fortifying iced coffee in a boat-themed café just by the dock, and then made her way to the place for her navigation certificate's psychotechnics exam – where apparently her eyesight, colour vision and coordination would be tested.

She took out her phone, googled the address again and followed the blue blob along a few quiet roads to find it. It was just a modern block with entrance steps in the usual white-grey Almerian marble, nothing out of the ordinary, but something about it, as it looked down at her from the top of a steep street, seemed familiar. Like she'd been somewhere like this in a dream.

She forced herself up the incline and pressed the buzzer. She was let in and shown the waiting room... and then saw it: the simplistic painting of Mónsul beach that she'd gazed at through tears last time she was here. Twenty years ago.

★

'We are just tryin' to understan' what happen to your daddy, Marina,' said the lady who she'd been told was a specialist at talking to children. Or maybe at finding out if children were quite all right, because in the other room she'd been asked a lot of very silly questions, encouraged to play with some dolls on a boat, and then told to draw a picture of her family.

The Guardia Civil man with the big tummy and smiling face had just turned on something like a CD player. She watched its little red light flash on and off. 'Tell us again what happened. You were sleeping and then...'

'I woke up.'

'And where was Daddy?'

She looked back down at the red on-and-off light. There was one on *La Mari* like that. And she'd seen it on Mummy's camcorder... they were *recording what she said*. When Daddy told her not to tell anybody about that woman, he should have told her what to tell them instead. She needed to keep doing what she did before, snip the woman and boat bit out like with a pair of scissors, and make the rest the truth. But it didn't seem to be working, or they wouldn't keep asking her again and again.

'He was in the sea. Then he got onto the boat.'

'How did he get into the sea?'

'I don't know.'

'Why did you wake up?'

'It was hot.'

'Or maybe because you hear Daddy talking to the lady?'

On and on went the little red light, swallowing her lies. 'No.'

'But there *was* a lady.' He'd leant forward. He had even bigger eyes than her and Daddy, but they didn't quite smile when his mouth smiled.

'Marina. Do you understand how important it is to tell the truth when somebody has... had an accident?'

But it was also important to keep a promise. 'Yes.' She could hear Mummy blowing her nose in the waiting room, probably crying again. Mummy needed to get back to Teddy; she was better with him to hug. Like he was a teddy *bear*. And to get back to her *own* mummy, Granny, who had slept the side of the bed where Daddy goes. It wasn't fair to keep Mummy sitting here. 'But I don't know what you're *talking* about,' she said, 'and I want to go home now.'

The woman stroked her arm, which was annoying. 'You said "it wasn't her fault." Is that what the lady told you?'

At one point yesterday they'd said something about how boats could be dangerous, as if *La Mari* was to blame, and she'd felt the need to defend her. Perhaps if she hadn't said that, she wouldn't have had to come back today. Although they were also finding it hard to understand how Daddy had hurt himself so badly from jumping off to do snorkelling.

'I said it wasn't *La Mari's* fault.'

The man looked puzzled and looked through his papers, but the woman smiled and said of course it wasn't.

'What about the other boat? Maybe it was the fault of other boat?' he said, fixing her with those eyes like he could see inside her head. 'Marina, somebody thinks they saw another boat next to *La Mari*.'

Marina stared back. Blinked. Silently, she asked Daddy for help. Under the table, her hand gripped her other hand, instead of his. 'There was no other boat,' she said, slowly and clearly. 'It was just me, Daddy and *La Mari*.' As it always was. As it always would be.

'Marina Mey-er?'

'Oh... yes,' she said, forcing herself back into the present.

'Come through,' the white-uniformed woman said.

She followed the assistant into the examination room. Twenty years on, and those dreadful days could still come whizzing back to her when she least expected it; would there ever be an end to it? Perhaps if she understood what had really happened.

'Take a seat. Just a few health questions first,' the woman said. 'Don't look so worried! The tests aren't hard; we'll soon get you ready to sail!'

Marina broke into a smile. 'Great!' It was just a *building,* where she'd done well to keep her promise to Daddy. And where she'd now take the first steps towards getting a navigation licence – how pleased he'd be about that!

Half an hour later, certificate in her bag, she walked back down the hill towards the port. Now she just had to get the navigation one. Then she'd be able to take a boat out on her own – and look at the initials on that rock. What if Daddy's initials were there with Francisca's? What would she say to her? Mati's adored aunt. A woman so many thought well of. No, it couldn't be her; she just had to prove it *wasn't*.

She made her way to the dock opposite the sailing club, as she'd been told in the email. The instructor, Paco, was middle-aged, welcoming and had very Andalusian but mercifully not too rapid Spanish. She joined the others sitting on the artificial grass and listened to Paco go through the pre-departure checklist Mati had told her about. All five of her fellow students were male, and adamant they already knew all about boats but needed this 'piece of paper'. After looking her up and down and registering the skinny plait, small breasts and modest shorts, all five completely ignored her, even when Paco encouraged them to work as a group to answer questions; it looked like machismo was alive and well in the Aguadulce motor boat world.

It was a RIB a little larger than the one Mati was hiring – probably the six metres of boat length that this certificate allowed you to drive. Paco took the boat out, and then once in the open water, had each of them in turn drive it while he showed them different kinds of buoys and talked to them about coping with other boats. It was finally her turn. She mounted the horse-like seat, just the same as the one on Mati's boat, without a thought – until she heard sniggering behind her. Then there was more sniggering, and mention of her *culo*.

She looked around for other boats, pulled the gear into neutral and flipped round to the ones laughing at her. '*What?*'

The three of them, including the one in the official *Policia* T-shirt, shrugged and swivelled their eyes to each other.

'I understand Spanish, okay? Including the word for my backside. Just *shut up.*'

All five of her fellow students now looked surprised but even more amused. Paco started mumbling something about calming things down; they were here to learn navigation.

'Well, *I* am, but I'm not calming down until these three *backsides* apologise.'

Silence in the boat. Hands were going to faces, perhaps to cover further amusement, but she was having that apology even if it was just token.

'This is a lesson on the importance of crew cooperation,' Paco said, 'for both enjoyment and...' he stood up, put the engine in gear and turned the boat to keep out of the path of a madcap chap on a jet ski '...safety. Please apologise to the lady; we are a non-sexist boat!'

Apologies followed, and from the young policeman, it looked possibly genuine. The others didn't have much to say after that, and, maybe to make amends, let her do more boat handling than anyone else. Over coffees and croissants in the café, they practised tying the knots and were tested on safety procedures. She had to ask Paco to repeat a few things, but otherwise she was understanding nearly everything, thanks to Mati.

A few hours later, she WhatsApped a photo of her Basic Navigation certificate to Mati and got a video call of the three of them waving and cheering and putting thumbs up.

'It was great! I loved it!' she said, feeling elated.

'And you understood okay?' Mati asked.

'Yes! Thanks to you! And I got to do *so* much – including mooring in the busy Roquetas port!' There was no point in spoiling things by telling them why.

'Brilliant! Now have some cake and then drive back carefully,' Mati said. 'Tell me when you're near San José and I'll set off to pick you up.'

'Okay!'

She went back to the boat-themed café for a coffee and

piece of carrot cake and watched the three laughing *culos* from the boat going into a bar further along. She fought off some residual anger. This, she realised, was pretty much her usual feeling about men: anger, irritation and – occasionally when she thought she'd actually met a decent one – massive disappointment. Unlike Polly, she'd never had a platonic friendship with a member of the other sex; she'd tried a couple of times, but both men spoilt it by sooner or later suggesting being 'friends with benefits.'

She and Ted had always been too different to be close. Guido was a lovely man, but, like Mum, had little time in his life for her. Basically, she'd almost given up on men. But now, after the horror of finding she had to share Casa Palmito with three of them, she'd made three wonderful friends. Unbelievable. Surely she didn't want to ruin that by starting an impossible relationship with one of them, did she? And it would be even more impossible if she started accusing his adored aunt of an affair that indirectly caused her father's death. She remembered the feel of Mati's arms round her and sighed.

When she arrived back at San José, the sun was beginning to set – but she saw Diego talking to a colleague, obviously still on duty. It was the perfect opportunity to ask him about a boat.

Mati rang. 'Where are you?'

'Sorry, I was just about to call you. I'm at the port.'

'Oh no, Marina – now you'll have to wait! I'm coming now, *cariño*.'

'I'm fine. I'll just watch the boats!'

Diego saw her and came over. 'So? Is it Captain Marina now?' he asked with a wink.

'It is! And I wanted to ask you, is there a little boat I could hire?'

He looked puzzled. 'Mati has his until the end of the month – I'm sure he will share.'

No. She might need quite a lot of time to find this cove; it wouldn't be fair, and it would need explaining. 'His friends only have a few days left. I couldn't do that.'

'Maybe when they've gone.'

'Well... I'd really like one as soon as possible.'

'You two going to be having races or something?' he joked but was still looking rather baffled.

'Ha! I wouldn't stand a chance. No, I... I'd just like one for a week.'

He scratched his head. 'There's a RIB like the one Mati's using, but it goes out for rental on Wednesday; we'd need it back Tuesday evening. I'll have to check with the owner.'

Three days would have to be enough. 'Okay.'

'Come with me to the office,' he said, and they started walking towards the old white rendered building. 'Mati's coming to pick you up, is he?'

'Yes. He's been amazing, taking us all everywhere.'

'Ah, he won't mind. He's like his aunt – can't keep them out of boats, if they have the chance!'

18

Yasiel and Juanjo looked up from their *tostadas*.

'Why?' Juanjo asked.

'Well... I want to go off alone to a few coves I went to with my father. I know it sounds daft, but it's just something I want to do.'

Juanjo nodded. 'No, no, quite understandable.'

'For *three* days?' Yasiel asked.

'I didn't want to do it all in one go.'

'The weather's turning,' Mati said. 'You might only get today and tomorrow morning. But then I'm sure Diego told you that.'

'He said I'd probably be okay for the cove and San José, when the wind comes.'

'All the same, best to do most of your boating today.'

'I will, then I'll pick up Polly and Ewan to bring them back for lunch and Polly's rehearsing for tonight.'

'You'll have more time if you let me take you to the port now, rather than wait for José's first boat.'

They looked at each other. As she somehow guessed he would, he looked more than a bit put out. Shunning his offer would only make it worse.

'Well, if you don't mind, that would be great. I'll go and

get ready.' She got up from the table, aware that Yasiel and Juanjo were watching them with concern.

Mati followed her and came to her bedroom doorway as she was sorting out her rucksack – luckily she'd already packed the photo.

'I don't understand why you didn't mention this yesterday evening when you came back,' he said.

'Your uncle had to get confirmation from the owner. I only heard this morning,' she said, knowing this didn't fully answer the question. The four of them had had a lovely evening rehearsing the songs and deciding the order for tonight's second campsite gig; she hadn't wanted to spoil it. Especially as, when tiredness got the better of her and she said she was off to bed early, he'd given her a long, tight hug wishing her goodnight.

'Look… If you're also getting a boat because you want to distance yourself from me a bit, you only have to say,' he said, his face serious.

She looked up from her bag. 'What? I don't need any more distance; in a couple of weeks, we'll be a thousand miles apart.'

'But only a couple of hours in a plane.'

'Two hours and twenty-two minutes.'

He smiled and nodded. 'Did you look it up?'

'I've been there several times with Polly, remember.'

'Ah, yes.'

She zipped up her bag and put it over her shoulders. They walked out, the boys telling her to enjoy herself but not go crazy, and went down the path. Mati was very quiet.

She stopped a moment. 'I did look it up. You know, just

out of interest. Madrid flights are also surprisingly frequent and cheap.'

He broke into a smile.

'Maybe I'll come over with Polly and we can all meet up before next year. But, Mati… I can't have a long-distance relationship. I just can't do it. And I don't want to spoil our friendship trying.'

'I think is that you have no… trust,' he said in English.

Or she was a realist. They went down to the beach in silence, waded into the sea and got on board.

'So where are you going?' he asked, as they set off.

'The little coves after Mónsul beach.'

'Lovely. Remember, it'll take longer on the way back, the way the sea is today.'

It was just like after she passed her car driving test – she suddenly didn't feel up to handling a boat on her own, and yet at the same time knew she had to do some solo skippering to get the confidence. Genoveses and Mónsul beaches were easy enough, just straight across the slightly choppy sea in the bays, enjoying the views, but she'd now started on the little beaches.

She dropped the Danforth anchor into the sandy bottom of one, just for the practice. Not very elegant, but she managed – and got off to celebrate with a swim. She waved to two couples further along, who must have scaled the volcanic hill to get here. They waved back uncertainly; a girl in a boat on her own seemed to be an oddity.

She set off again, scanning each little beach for a rock of

the shoulder-height hulking size in the photo, meaning to count how many beaches she'd checked but becoming unsure when she got to five or six. Then she remembered that she'd discounted one of the earlier beaches because it was too wide – but it had loads of those kind of rocks on it. She turned the boat round and headed back to the rocky beach – and had to spend a sweaty, anxious half hour trying to anchor without risking collision with any of the rocks or a smart yacht enviably anchored in the sandier part of the beach.

Once ashore, she decided not to bother waving to the loud gaggle of yacht boys and girls who'd been laughing at her efforts. After all, she was about to look even more daft, as she started examining all the rocks. She took a slow, casual-looking walk down the beach and back again, and... no, there were rocks – shoulder-height sometimes, stunningly strewn against the pale sand like a giant game of Jacks – but none seemed to have been chosen to bear witness to a love affair twenty years ago.

Light-headed now, she sat down in the shade of one of the rocks and drank her water bottle and ate the biscuits she'd put in an ancient little green plastic container she'd found in the kitchen.

'Oh, where the hell is it?' she said out loud, to herself – and maybe to her father.

But her father was very quiet today; he seemed to have nothing to say about her quest, the photograph, or even her managing a boat on her own. Her head started to pound. She went for another swim, submerging herself in the clear, barely cool water, then using the floaty square so she could swim around without aggravating her shoulder. When she came out, rubbing herself dry to be able to wear her shorts and sun-protective T-shirt again, she noticed she needed to get going if she wasn't going to be late to pick up Polly and Ewan at the port.

They were waiting for her on the dock.

'Sorry, took a bit longer than I thought!' she called out.

'It's okay. Look at you! Where have you been then?' Polly asked, as she came aboard.

'Oh, just looking at the little beaches I used to go to as a kid.'

'I thought Mati already took you along there.'

'Well, just wanted time to... remember on my own, really.'

Polly smiled but still looked a bit puzzled.

'How's the head, Ewan?' Marina asked, looking at his now uncovered stitches.

'Absolutely fine. Bit itchy.'

'He's insisting on going back to the cove tomorrow,' Polly said. 'Says he'll be careful with it, but—'

'I'm *not* staying in the apartment after you've gone,' Ewan said firmly. 'I can keep the wound clean and keep using the antibiotic spray at home in the cove.'

They were sitting down next to each other now, but not quite their usual dream team selves; Polly was obviously worried about him, and they were probably both dreading saying goodbye tomorrow.

'I'm afraid I'll be taking over the checking of that head, Ewan,' Marina said. 'After all, it was my table that caused it, so it's sort of my right?'

They laughed, and Ewan put his arm round Polly.

'And obviously I'll drive you to the appointment for having your stitches out.'

'That's very kind, Marina,' Ewan said. 'So come on, let's see the new *Capitana* in action!'

'Well... I'm just going to wait until there are no boats moving around in here!' Marina said, looking around the port anxiously. Then she saw Diego up by the fuelling station near the entrance, gesticulating with a thumbs-up and a beckoning hand. She held her breath and set off between the boats, getting a cheer from Polly and Ewan and a wave from Diego as she went out through the red and green stubby lighthouses.

Ewan sighed as they came into the cove. 'Good to be home!'

Polly squeezed his arm, but she must have been wondering how Ewan was going to adjust to Shoreham, when he came over. *If* he came over, Marina thought, because how could Polly be absolutely sure he would?

As they came down the navigation lane between the buoys, Marina concentrating on keeping back from José's early three o'clock boat in front of her, Polly leant forward and tapped her arm. 'Marina – you've got a reception! Well... looks like *two*, actually!'

The three boys, who looked like they'd just been larking about in the medium-sized waves with Marina's rubber ring and lilo, were cheering and waving to her.

'Go away, you'll put me off!' Marina called out to them, grinning.

'Well that's nice, isn't it?' Yasiel said with a laugh. 'You want us to take the boat up onto the beach for you or not?'

'Ah – well okay, yes, that *would* be good!' she said, turning off the engine.

While the other two put the inflatables back on the beach,

Mati came over and took hold of the boat for her, just as José was laughing and bracing for a collision.

While Mati chatted to Polly and Ewan, Marina waved at her other reception committee: a group of people standing up in front of sunshades and towels and coming over... who turned out to be Kim, Shefali, and little Zara; and May... except the calmly angelic-looking half-Thai girl had just been barged into by Juanjo, rushing into the water to help with the boat. Bless him, he'd caught and stopped her fall, then apologised profusely.

Once they were all on the beach, Marina also said hello to her two friends' husbands and Kim's cute half-Spanish toddler son.

She introduced the three boys to her new expat friends, and reassured the shocked but gently laughing May that Juanjo wasn't usually a rough rugby-tackle kind of guy.

'Not at all – he's one of my best yoga students!' Polly put in.

'Really?' May said. 'I *love* yoga. Only thing I miss while I'm here.'

Polly, Ewan and Juanjo looked at each other and laughed.

'Then you are very lucky,' Juanjo said to May, in English, 'because unless she changed mind, Polly will give final Cala Turquesa yoga lesson in about a half hour!'

'Oh, that would be...' May's face lit up with a broad smile.

Polly told May she was very welcome, and Ewan and Juanjo recommended Polly as the best – although admittedly their first – yoga teacher in the world. Meanwhile, Mati and Yasiel had used the pulley and got Marina's little RIB up the beach for her.

CHERRY RADFORD

Mati, Yasiel and Marina went up to the house, Mati soon disappearing off to the terrace to return a work call, leaving the other two to make a start on lunch.

'Oh God, the two worst cooks have been left in the kitchen,' Yasiel said, nudging her.

'We'll just chop and slice a bit; it's all we're good for.'

'True,' he said, then sighed. 'Our last barbecue all together.'

'Yes. It's all gone so quickly.'

'And when Juanjo and I leave on Thursday, it's the end of the rental, so Mati goes to Diego and Francisca's. You'll be all on your own... unless he stays here, of course.'

'He's welcome to stay, but I don't think he'll want to. He'll just visit a lot.'

'Of course he'll want to! How can you say that?'

'Because... maybe it would be a bit awkward, I don't know.'

'You haven't *talked* about it?' he asked, seeming to have stopped all culinary activity to concentrate on this.

'No. We're sort of... following the plan.'

'Oh, Marina... It really doesn't have to be so awkward, you know! Well, unless you don't feel the same way about him.'

'I absolutely feel at *least* the same way about him! But I don't want to spoil our friendship with a romance that just isn't possible.'

'How d'you know it isn't possible?'

'Have you looked at a globe recently?'

'People change.'

'Well... *exactly*.'

238

'No. no. I mean... look, Mati gets a lot of attention from women, but he's always been a serial monogamist. And he's now getting even fussier... There's been nobody since he broke up with Sofía nearly a year ago – very civilised, they still work together. And now it's just work, work, water sports, work, work, music, work, work.' She must have been looking surprised. 'Didn't he tell you this?'

'No! Well sort of, but in my experience, guys saying, "There's been nobody," normally means about twenty girls that somehow don't count.'

'Ha, you're right! I think I said exactly this to my girlfriend when we started dating, having been truly appalling for a few years.'

'Well at least you're honest! A rare trait in men, I find,' Marina said, suddenly very aware that she was cutting up a courgette.

'This is the problem. You sound like you've been very unlucky. You would like to...' He took the knife from her and did some fast slicing to the end of it.

Marina laughed. 'Yes, some of them deserved that!'

They could hear Mati coming in from outside.

Yasiel rinsed his hands and dried them. Turned to her and patted her arm. 'Give him a chance.'

The three boys, along with Marina, Polly and Ewan, were sitting in the campsite bar, the boys tucking into a variety of *tapas* with their drinks, Marina and Polly – feeling slightly sick with nerves – sipping iced *mosto* grape juices.

'Why did we agree to do this, again?' Marina asked Polly.

'I have *no* idea,' Polly replied.

'What?' Juanjo said. 'I thought you two did karaoke all the time.'

'Not all the time – and anyway, there's very low expectation there,' Polly said.

'Yes, I mean look at this crowd here already, wanting a repeat of the last time you three were here. We can't mess it up!' Marina said.

Mati leant forward. 'You two were fantastic in the rehearsal. They are going to be mad for you, enjoy it!' he said in English.

'I'm certainly going to enjoy hearing it again!' Ewan had been bowled over by all of them that afternoon – but especially his Polly, of course.

It was soon time for the boys to take their places, and Polly and Marina – who weren't on until near the end – took their seats with Ewan at the reserved table near the front. Not far behind them there was a table with Kim, Shefali, May and Juliana the musicals girl; another with retired property services couple Phil and Jen with some friends; and standing behind them, gardener Ben with an English-looking red-haired girlfriend. Further back, Marina saw the tall figure of Agustín, with a couple she recognised from the bank. And then somebody put a gentle hand on her shoulder and Polly's, and somebody else had hands on Ewan's shoulders...

'Good luck, girls!' Francisca said. 'I hear you're joining in later – and are amazing!'

'The singing captain – who would think?' Diego said with a wink. 'Ooh, we need to sit down, *cariño*,' he said to Francisca as the lights dimmed.

Behind the tables and chairs, there was a big semicircle of standing audience; it felt like half the village was there.

The boys were on good form, sparking off each other, playing with an energy Marina hadn't seen before. A few songs in, they surprised Marina and Polly with a song they must have hastily got together while Polly was teaching and Marina was in the shower: that sweetly quirky 'Orange Coffee' song that had been a success the year before from a band in Thailand. Juanjo took the gentle lead vocal and blew a kiss to May, who smiled and blew several back.

Then finally Mati invited the girls up, but not before telling the audience how a miracle of an accommodation mistake had brought them these two fabulous housemate girls with gorgeous voices. Polly was stunning with her lead in *Rebelde*; the Eurovision '10 Years' song with Marina on her hand-held keyboard was very popular; and then it was time for the girls to sing their sweet but raunchy rap of 'Kiss Me More', which got lots of appreciative shouting and whistles – as well as a kiss for them from each of the boys. They ended with the audience joining in with the popular 'Me Maten'… and then 'Volver', about returning – which Mati said they hoped to be doing next year and for many more to come.

19

Marina tied up the boat and then put her arms round her friend. 'Oh, Pols.'

'I'll be... okay,' Polly said, hiccupping and taking out another tissue.

'Once you're busy looking for a lovely Shoreham flat for him to join you in.'

'That's what I keep telling myself.'

'And in just two weeks I'll be joining you, we'll be busy Shoreham-ing, and then the next thing you know you'll be picking him up from the airport.'

Polly nodded and managed a watery smile.

'Come on, let's get going,' Marina said. 'More chance of having time for a little ice cream stop on the way.'

'*Exactamente.*'

They got into the car and were soon driving through the undulations of stubbled orange hills occasionally dotted by a herd of white goats.

'Oh, I'm going to miss all this,' Polly said. 'I hope what Mati said about us all coming back every year really happens.'

'Absolutely. Why shouldn't it?'

'Although surely you're not going to wait until next summer to see Mati again?'

'Well, we might coincide at Easter.'

'*Might coincide...*' Polly tutted. 'Let's see how you feel after ten or eleven days alone with him!'

'We won't be alone. He'll be staying with his aunt and uncle, and then, in the last five days or so, busy doing Carla's boat trips. And I'll be busy signing documents and giving away furniture.'

'Not *all* the time.'

'Well, no, of course we'll meet up.'

Polly looked over at her, opened her mouth and closed it again. Shook her head.

'And I was thinking, maybe I'll come out to Madrid sometime this year—'

'Yes, come out with me when I visit my parents in October, and we could all meet up.'

'That would be great.'

'So, what are you going to be up to today? Aren't you supposed to be meeting your namesake turtle?' Polly asked.

'Mati's talking about the day after tomorrow. So looking forward to that!'

'Ah! I want footage on my WhatsApp. Meanwhile, you've still got the boat. Why don't you take all the boys somewhere? In the other direction, for example?'

Marina could have just said yes, she'd suggest that; but she couldn't lie to Polly.

'Well, it's going to kick up later, so I thought I'd look at some more of my dad's beaches while I can and then take the boat back to Cala Turquesa.'

There was a pause. 'Is this doing you any good, Marina?'

Marina stopped at a roundabout and gave it an exaggerated amount of concentration. Polly had already somehow sensed there was more to this beach viewing than she was letting on.

Polly put a hand on her arm. 'You should have taken me with you yesterday. I feel like I've deserted you.'

'Not at all! Don't be daft.'

'Well, take Mati with you, you said he was sweet about your dad.'

'I can't take anyone with me.' Oh no, that had come out much too harshly. Polly was looking over at her in surprise. Maybe sooner or later she would tell her about the woman on the boat that day, Marina thought. Just Polly, because surely there was no harm in that? But this wasn't the moment, when she needed to be radiating positives for Polly. 'For this. But yes, hopefully the sea will calm down tomorrow and I'll whisk them off somewhere. Oh, I wish you were staying longer. I'm going to miss you.'

Marina parked back at the port. God how she hated this heavy, inexplicable secret her father had given her. If the woman was Francisca, and they'd been having an affair, it was going to be very hard not to feel extremely angry with her for the burden of it. But it wouldn't be her. She would almost certainly never find out who the woman was, or what had been going on. She'd just need to accept that her father might not have been quite the perfect hero she thought he was and leave it at that.

She'd nearly reached the boat when she heard her name. 'Marina!'

Mati. He was standing further along the dock, with Carla and *La Mari*. If she hadn't been so involved in her thoughts, she would have seen them.

She went over and noticed a young Spanish-looking couple and a group of three English-looking middle-aged women waiting by the boat. 'Hello! Are you doing your first tour guiding today?'

'I am – with Carla on board to check my geology! Want to come with us and laugh at my efforts?' he asked in Spanish, as if saving his energy for the English he was about to cope with.

Carla kissed each of her cheeks. 'Yes, come and give feedback on his English!'

'Oh…' Less time on her own RIB boat, looking for the rock, before the sea kicked off this afternoon. On the other hand, it was from *La Mari* that she thought she'd spotted it. 'Well, why not? Thanks!'

While Mati and Carla got *La Mari* ready, Marina chatted with the other passengers and then got on board with them.

'Hate to tell you this,' she whispered to Mati, 'but the Spanish-looking couple are actually Croatians expecting English, and the English ladies include a geography teacher.'

'*Madre mía!*' He put a hand to his forehead and laughed.

All seated, they set off – with a heavily accented but warm English welcome chat from Mati that looked like it had won round all five passengers before they'd even started.

It wasn't easy, listening to Mati's adorable English, and twice correcting pronunciation when he wasn't being understood by passengers asking questions – while at the same time scanning the beaches for the rock his aunt might have written on.

She was beginning to think she'd missed it, when they'd gone past more beaches than she had yesterday, and the lighthouse was in sight... but then she saw it. A tall rock like a bear on its hind legs, with the striations in the cliff face behind it; it was definitely the one. And good God, it was at the end of that beach she went to with Mati – and with her father, for what turned out to be their last swim together. But why would Daddy have taken her there, where maybe he'd spent time with a lover, when there were so many other little beaches to choose from? It made no sense. As soon as she got back to the port, she'd take her little boat out, come back here and read those lovers' initials if they were still there.

Mati patted her shoulder, tilted his head towards the beach and smiled at her.

She nodded her head and smiled back. Aware she'd not been engaging for a while, she made more of an effort on the way back – joining in with the other passengers' enjoyment of Mati's beach and volcano chatter, while trying to put that particular bit of beachside volcano debris out of her mind.

By the time they got back to the port, it was clear that all the passengers were totally won over by the stunning volcanic scenery, Mati and *La Mari*. Carla insisted on taking them off to celebrate with iced coffees in a place by the entrance to the port.

'You were *amazing*,' Marina said, patting him on the back.

Carla nodded. 'Our only problem will be the confusion of multiple repeat bookings by enamoured ladies!'

Mati laughed and shook his head.

'Seriously, you knew enough – even for the geography lady – and if they want more than that they can read up about it later.' Carla relaxed back into her seat. 'And I'm so grateful, Mati, because instead of resenting my sister for picking a high-season date for the wedding, I can now go off and enjoy it, knowing I'm leaving the boat in not one but two sets of loving hands.'

'Well, I have to thank Marina for my improved English.'

'What?' Marina said, laughing, although it was true that he had started to speak to her in English more.

'Well, they say love is the best language teacher!' Carla said, making Mati break into a wide smile.

Jesus, why wasn't he telling her they were just friends? But then, feeling a warm glow coming over her at Carla's words, she wasn't going to say anything either.

Carla soon had to leave to go and relieve her assistant at the kiosk near the beach. Mati and Marina walked back to the port together.

'Have you left anything in your boat's locker?' he asked.

Oh. He was assuming she was going to leave her boat here and go back to Cala Turquesa with him.

'I was going to drive her to Cala Turquesa.'

'Why? It's going to be choppy later – you won't be taking her out.'

'Well... I was going to go out for a bit *now*.'

He looked over at the sea beyond the port – where sure enough, splashy little white horses had arrived even since their return journey in *La Mari* less than an hour ago. 'I wouldn't do that. You don't have experience of handling a boat in rougher sea.'

'I'm not going to be long. There's just one more little beach I want to look at.'

'If you really must, then I'll come with you. You shouldn't go on your own.'

'But... it's something I *have* to do on my own.'

He frowned and looked down at the ground. 'How far are you planning to go?'

'Oh, I'll be back at Cala Turquesa in half an hour,' she said, even though it was probably going to take that long to reach the beach, let alone get back against the sea.

He still didn't look happy, eyebrows pinched with concern. He gave her a hug, let her board her RIB, but held on to the rope. 'Kill switch.'

'Well of course,' she said, raising her eyes to the heavens and then attaching the key to her leg.

'Life jacket.'

'Oh, what? I thought these RIB boats were unsinkable. Too hot for that.'

He moved back, pulling on the rope.

'Oh all right!' she said with a laugh. She pulled one out of the locker and put it on. 'Can I go now?'

He hesitated. 'Just be careful. Only Genoveses or Mónsul, okay? Then straight back.'

The next two beaches; it was quite a bit on from there. She nodded and smiled. Then she pulled the cord and was off, waving to him as she went out of the port.

Once in the San José bay, she couldn't see what the fuss was about: a little swell taking the boat up and down in a lovely boaty way, the odd little cooling splash, a refreshing breeze. She pushed the speed to the maximum that felt right; she was definitely going to be more than half an hour, so she may as well save time where she could. It was a bit choppy going round the point to the next bay, but nothing to worry about; a little more so going round into Mónsul, but she just had to slow down a bit, that was all. Slow down and... make sure she took the swell at a diagonal; if it came sideways on, it felt a bit... capsizey. No, you can't capsize these RIBs, it would be fine. Wouldn't it?

But once she was out along the row of smaller beaches, there was a temperamental blustery wind, the swell started looking a bit scary, the little RIB rocking and thwacking into waves, soon covered in water... maybe it was time to turn back. Then a rogue wave towered above her and half-broke, showering her in water, leaving her heart pattering; it was *definitely* time to turn back.

As Mati had warned her, it was harder in the other direction, the wind and sea against her. Huge humps of water rolled towards her now, hissing and spraying her in the face. She glanced at the shore... she was barely moving forward. This was going to take ages. A knot formed in her stomach. She kept holding her breath. Her arms ached. The concentration was exhausting.

A fishing boat passed her, a man shouting something, waving, pointing ahead. What did that mean? *Of course* she was going ahead, back to the port. Taking her eyes of the waves for a moment to wave back, she was hit by a swell that tilted the boat on its side, her rucksack sliding over the floor and landing worryingly near to the rounded edge of the RIB.

'Damn.' Bloody man, putting her off. Could she leave her rucksack there? If there was another tilt like that, it might go over. She'd have no phone. *No photograph of the rock.*

Why in hell hadn't she clipped it to the bar? She waited for a gap between swells and stretched her arm over to it... but got nowhere near. Tried again, letting go of the wheel a moment, but keeping her right leg in place so the kill switch didn't activate... Jesus, without the motor going, the boat could quickly get swept towards the cliffs... She reached out and touched the rucksack's handle with the end of her fingers, but couldn't quite... She stretched one last time... and then a huge swell must have tipped the boat to one side, followed by a wave from the fishing boat's wake... and she was in the air, upside down... landing on her life-jacketed back on the water.

She quickly wiped the water out of her eyes as she bobbed up and down. The RIB was tipping and swaying, silent without its motor, but... already somehow several body lengths away from her. Handle of her rucksack just visible, her phone there, to ask for help... but how to swim against these pushing mounds of sea? She worked her legs and arms as hard as she could, but the boat was getting further away from her... She spun around in the water: the fishing boat was just a speck. Something else, far away, wouldn't see. Might be just a moored boat. God – *no beach on the shore.*

Maybe forget about the RIB. Swim, going with the diagonal waves, hoping they took her further along, to where they would fling her onto sand rather than these rocks. But they would also be taking her further from the port, further from the chance of other boats or people on the shore seeing her... She spun around again, one minute on top of a swell, looking for boats, trying to work out where she was; the next moment in a terrifying watery valley.

'Daddy!' she cried out. 'What do I do?'

A wave flipped her onto her back, floating, as if someone had pushed her there.

I'm here, Marinita, it's okay. You know what to do.

Save energy. Save these aching limbs. Calm the manic breathing... so she could try and cope with whatever happened when she reached the shore. The ringing in her ears intensified. She tried to *think*... the RIB, unlike her, seemed to be going along as well as in towards the shore. Would someone see it empty, and call for help? But would there be anybody clambering over rocky hills to reach those beaches today? Maybe nobody would see it until the Cabo de Gata houses, past the lighthouse... if it made it that far. Mati was her only hope. How late would he let her be before he'd ring the Guardia Civil? But she probably wasn't late yet. She had to wait, float, swim a little... concentrate on avoiding ending up on the rocks.

She'd moved along now, but it was worse... she was heading for the cliff face. Nowhere to climb onto. Nothing to hang on to. Those waves throwing themselves against it would take her with them... In about... how long did she have? Ten minutes? *Five?* She started swimming to the side, hoping for the tiny beach of small rocks, where she could at least crawl out of the waves, even if hurt... Her heart was pounding, it was difficult to breathe again, and there was that ringing in her ears... But... was it a ringing? She swivelled round, and for a moment on top of a swell, she saw it: a boat motoring towards her. Down she went into the watery valley. Up again, and the boat had grown... it was nearer!

She waved her arms. 'Help! *Ayuda!*' She was croaky with the sea water she'd swallowed; they'd never hear her. They just had to see her yellow life jacket. They *had* to, surely. Because at the moment... they were coming straight for her and could... Every time bigger and nearer... She shivered with fear... But was it the green of the Guardia Civil boat? Maybe... Yes! She waved her arms wildly, the effort making her faint, her vision darkening...

Somebody patted her face, saying something to her. She opened her eyes to a man next to her in the water, asking if she was hurt. Once she'd shaken her head, he grabbed her and they were quickly pulled back on a rope towards the boat, where he put her in a stretcher that had been lowered.

'No, I don't need this, I can go up the...' Up the ladder, like the one *La Mari* had, but nobody listened. They hoisted her up. She was soon on deck with a big green towel round her, being asked again if she was hurt. Like she'd been asked twenty years ago, when she last fell into the sea. She shook her head, her shivering making speech impossible, as the green uniforms, the stern concern and the sound of the powerful boat's engine brought it all back to her...

A Guardia Civil woman handed her some loo paper to blow her nose. 'Ingleesh?'

She nodded.

'We are going for your boat now, okay? Then you go back to port, where your friends are.'

'Fr-iends?' she croaked.

'Raúl and Ramón – the fishermen – who called first, and Matías, who asked us at the port, because he wait and you not come.'

So, Mati had waited at the port... She smiled, breathed a sigh of relief, the thought of his arms around her steadying her shaking body. Then she looked back up at the policewoman. 'I'm *so* sorry; I've been such an idiot.'

He'd settled her in a lounger in the shade of a sun umbrella on the terrace, given her plenty of hugs, encouraged her to drink gallons of water he'd flavoured with peach juice, and made her a comfort lunch of scrambled egg, cheese, tomato and toast – but Mati was still bristling with anger and disbelief. Not least, at her insistence on being taken straight home to Cala Turquesa, rather than first recovering at his aunt Francisca's.

'How are you feeling now?' he asked in English, sitting down next to her with yet another drink.

Glad not to be lying in a bloody heap on some rocks. Or worse. 'Okay. Grateful. Idiotic. Where are the others?'

'They are helping Ewan to be busy, creating a *torneo* de chess at the end of the beach; they have made pieces. Didn't you see them?'

'Think I was still in a bit of a blur.'

He put a hand over hers for a moment, then took it away and fixed her with his serious dark eyes. 'It's time you told me what's going on, Marina.'

'Going on?'

'What are you looking for, that is so important you risk your life?'

She shook her head. 'I didn't mean to… I didn't realise how the sea could change so much as you go further along.'

He looked at her steadily. Waiting for her answer. She was going to have to tell him something.

'I wanted to go to that beach again. Remember things.'

'From your father's last day?'

'Yes. I couldn't find it yesterday. I… took one of my parents' photos with me this time. Actually, it's got a woman in it who… looks a bit like your Aunt Francisca.'

'Really? Let me see.'

She reached over and fished it out of her rucksack, which was drying out in the sun next to her. She took the Polaroid out of its protective folder and gave it to him, her hand starting to shake again.

He smiled at the picture. 'What a beauty she was!'

So it *was* Francisca. Her heart thudded. 'It's… not very clear,' she managed, hoping he was wrong. 'How can you be sure it's her?'

'I am sure. Anyway…' He put it closer to his face. 'Yes, I can see the scar on her neck. She was in a accident – her husband was dreadful driver of cars.'

'Diego?'

'No, no, her *first* husband. Lucky she wasn't in the car when he went off the cliff going up to San Rafael.'

Marina winced. 'He died?'

'Well, he wasn't very well after that, was he? Yes. Poor Uncle Fernando. I never liked him, but that is horrible way to die.'

'When was that then? Have she and Uncle Diego been together long?'

'Oh, let's see… A couple of years before I started staying here in the summer, when I was thirteen, so… 2002.'

So Francisca was married to this Fernando at the time she gave her father this photo. It suddenly felt a lot more likely that she could have been the woman in that other boat. Marina's heart started to tap away, making her faint again... What should she do? She couldn't think straight... Oh *why* did it have to be Francisca?

Mati's phone rang. He listened and then smiled over at Marina. 'She's okay, although I'm going to insist she has a siesta,' he said into the phone. 'Oh no, tell him not to worry, she understood. Hang on.' He looked over at Marina. 'Diego thinks you'll hate him for being so cross with you when you got back. He says really he's just cross with himself for not stopping you go out.'

So he was talking to Francisca. 'Tell him he had every right; I was an idiot.'

He repeated this and nodded at the reply. 'Oh, yes that would be lovely... Absolutely! Okay... Mainly vegetarian, but she eats fish... Sounds brilliant. I'll just check with her, hang on.' He patted Marina's arm and beamed. 'Paella lunch at my uncle and aunt's tomorrow? You could bring the photo!'

20

'I'm fine, really,' Marina said, taking T-shirts and vests off the washing line.

'No, you're not. Your hands are red, itchy and desperate for aloe vera. Sit down here and I'll sort them out,' Mati said, back in bossy Spanish, taking her arm and pointing to the patio chair in the shade.

'After I've—'

'I'll do it,' Juanjo said, taking the pile of T-shirts from her shoulder and then unpegging the rest of the washing. When Yasiel finished his call to his girlfriend Isa, he came and joined him.

Mati prepared the aloe and took his hands in hers, stroking them with the cool gel. She sighed with relief, and then blushed at the sensuality of it.

He finished, and then put an arm round her and squeezed. 'There's nothing to be nervous about; my uncle isn't going to tell you off anymore! Just brace yourself for my aunt making... comments about us.'

'Comments?'

'Well, you know... *assumptions*. She won't listen, even though I've explained.'

'Ah.'

She saw Yasiel and Juanjo exchanging a look.

'Or is it the boat that's stressing you? Trust me, the sea will be okay today.' Mati was clearly convinced her eczema was a sign of nerves, even though she'd said it was probably a delayed reaction to the shock she'd had the day before.

'No, no, I'm fine.'

'Right,' he said, 'I just need to put a T-shirt on and I'm… aha.' He pulled her dad's pale blue one off Juanjo's arm. 'Can I wear this?'

'Of course!' she said.

They were soon all in Mati's RIB heading for San José, where Juanjo and Yasiel had booked kayaks followed by lunch at the fish place at the port.

For some reason, Marina had assumed Francisca and Diego lived near the office on the main street, but as soon as they were out of the port, Mati took her up a flight of steps to a little road that ran along the hill above the port.

'Oh! So they can see *La Mari* from a balcony, and Francisca can wave to Diego at work. How lovely.'

'If she's not in the office, yes!'

They went up the road a little way then stopped outside what at first looked like a small single-storey house with a little shady garden of fig and pine trees – but in fact the house also had a lower level, which explained how Francisca and Diego had managed to put up Polly and Ewan. The house had the gorgeous bright blue paint that was so popular for woodwork here and was adorned with plants in pots of all different colours and sizes.

'Oh… what a gorgeous place!' Marina said.

'Wait until you see the view.'

He didn't have to knock; they must have been looking

out for them. The door opened, and Francisca and Diego kissed each of Marina's cheeks and then each held on to one of her arms and asked how she was.

'I'm fine, not a mistake I'll make again!'

Diego started apologising for shouting at her the day before.

'No, no, I deserved it – don't worry.'

A waggy little brown and white dog called Beti came bounding through to say hello with a couple of excited little barks – mostly to an adoring Mati, who patted her and stroked her ears.

'Come through, you two, come through,' Francisca said.

Inside, there was a delicious scent of paella. They followed her into an airy living room with rug-covered chairs and a lifetime of knick-knacks – and through to a wide balcony terrace shaded by a yellow-striped awning.

'Oh! Wow!' Marina said, as she went to the edge and looked down at the port, the curve of the sandy San José bay and the mountains beyond.

'Yes, we're very lucky,' Francisca said. 'We also get the best of the sun all day, which means fans on maximum for August lunchtime, but lovely sunsets and, in winter, the house tends to stay warm into the evening. Something to keep in mind if you ever want to buy another place here, Marina! How's the house sale going?'

'Good, I sign in Almería next week. The same day I take Ewan to have his stitches removed.'

'Fantastic.' Diego handed Marina a grape juice, and the four of them sat down in the squishy outdoor sofas on the terrace.

'And how's poor Ewan doing? Must be missing his Polly,' Francisca asked.

'Juanjo and Yasiel said he was a bit blue, but he's looking forward to his Shoreham adventure.'

'Ah. We thought they were a lovely couple, didn't we,' Francisca said, looking over at her husband.

Diego nodded. 'I worry how his slim frame will cope with going back to that cold weather, but yes, there is a magic in the air around those two.'

'Diego! Marina manages it! He can buy a coat! And they'll be back for lots of visits. As I'm sure Marina will.' She turned to Marina. 'Mati tells me you've found a very reasonable little apartment you'll be able to rent now and then. Where's that?'

'Oh... not far from the promenade.'

'Really? This end? Which road?'

She had no idea. 'Um... d'you know, I can't remember the name of it now!'

All three looked at her. Of course, rentals were her business – Francisca was obviously going to be interested.

'The road with the white houses coming up from the Neptuno restaurant,' Marina said, hoping they didn't know where Agustín lived.

'Really? I thought most of those were whole houses these days.'

'Well I'll have the ground floor of this one.'

'Oh – isn't that where Agustín... Is it he who's—' Francisca started.

'*What?*' Mati said, frowning. 'Does this man never give up?'

Marina turned to him. 'Give up *what*? I've had that conversation with him; it's all good.'

'When?'

'Last Friday.'

Mati looked indignant, as if he should have been informed.

'And I'm sure he'll be the perfect landlord,' Francisca said. 'Don't be such a grump, Mati.'

Marina elbowed Mati in the ribs, making him smile.

A white cat with marmalade and tabby splodges jumped up onto Marina's lap. 'Oh, hello! Who are you?'

'Blanquita,' Mati said, next to her, and the cat immediately moved on to him, turned itself round and landed on his lap cosily wound up like a Danish pastry.

Beti, meanwhile, came over and rested her head on his leg.

'Are you an animal magnet, or what?' Marina asked Mati, with a laugh.

'Exactly that!' Francisca said. 'You will have to learn to share him, I'm afraid.'

'Tomorrow I'll be sharing him with a turtle!' Marina said.

'Really?' Diego said. 'How's she doing?'

'Yes, I'd love to meet her!' Francisca said.

'Well, it looks like you all will, in two days' time!' Mati said. 'Her release is planned for this Thursday, if all goes well.'

'Ooh, you didn't tell me this!' Marina said.

'I got a message on my phone this morning,' Mati replied. 'But the final decision will be today, after some test results are in.'

'And it'll be Cala Turquesa?' Marina asked.

'Well of course! The usual thing is that they make a little early evening public party of it on the beach, as a way of raising funds for the charity.'

'Oh!' Marina said. 'Just such a shame that Polly and the boys won't be here for it. But I'm sure some of my expat friends will come.'

'We'll *certainly* be there!' Francisca said. 'Right, I better get the paella served up, as Diego needs to get back to the port before long.' She got up and floated out of the room in her elegant loose dress of swirling blues.

'So you won't be coming to stay on Thursday, after the boys have gone?' Diego asked Mati.

'Well... I'll be busy, I've got to prepare the beach...'

'Lovely as it is to have you here, we don't want to take you away from the cove, the turtle preparations and, most importantly, Marina,' Diego said, patting her arm.

Before they could answer, Diego got up to go and give Francisca a hand, leaving Marina and Mati looking at each other.

'You're very—' Marina started.

'I don't know—' Mati started at the same time.

They laughed.

'Ladies first!' Mati said in English.

'Well, I know your rental ends on Thursday, but obviously you're very welcome to stay as long as you like.'

He smiled. 'I wasn't sure how you'd feel about that.'

'It's... fine,' she said, nodding.

He leant over and kissed her cheek, reminding her that it probably wouldn't be completely fine. They seemed to be getting closer and closer; how on earth was she going to resist him for another thirteen days?

Francisca and Diego brought in a massive pan of paella, a bowl of salad and freshly baked bread. They got up and sat round the table to eat, Mati and Marina on one side, his aunt and uncle on the other. There were stories about the younger Mati and his first encounter with a turtle; a gecko that lived in his room all one summer, despite the horrendously loud music he would play in there. This led to his aunt and uncle praising the recent concert and Polly and Marina's musical input – and questions about her online piano teaching in England.

The paella was delicious, the view was breathtaking, the company warm and natural like they'd known each other forever; even the background music was perfect, with the singer 'La Mari' from Chambao singing the divine 'Duende del Sur' – Spirit of the South. But for Marina, the butterflies flapping inside her since this morning were still there, because in her rucksack by the chair there was the photo that she had to show Francisca – and she had a feeling that as soon as she did, she would know the truth about this lovely lady and her part in her father's final hour.

Pudding arrived – apparently Thai-inspired mango, little pieces of *bizcocho* cake and a homemade coconut ice cream.

'Now look, Marina,' Francisca said, 'once Mati is doing his five days of boat tours for Carla, it'll be easier if he's staying here – so you're very welcome to come and join him rather than be in the house on your own.'

'Oh, that's a very kind offer!' Although, were they assuming they'd be sharing a room? 'Can I let you know?'

'Of course!'

Diego looked at his watch. 'Oh, I have to go. Marina, it's been delightful to chat with you about more than boats! Not that boats aren't incredibly special, of course – particularly your *La Mari*. She might have changed name, but for me, your father's spirit is always there on her. And by God, I'm going to go back and tell him what a truly wonderful – if a little headstrong – young lady his little Marinita has grown into!'

Marina put a hand to her face, her eyes stinging with tears, and managed a thank you.

'*Ay...* I didn't want to upset you!' he added, coming round the table and kissing the top of her head. 'I'll see you two later.'

So, then it was just the three of them, which would make it slightly easier to talk about the photograph and have an awkward discussion, but she'd been rather blown sideways by the thought of Diego talking to her father through *La Mari*, just like she'd talked to him through his pale blue T-shirt... Also, sitting back on the comfy sofas with coffees, she asked herself if she could bear to risk spoiling her new friendship with Mati's adorable aunt and uncle. And possibly, whatever it was she had with Mati. She could just leave it, maybe; after all, she'd coped without knowing who that woman was and why she was there for twenty years.

Francisca was remembering how Marina's father used to call her Marinita, or sometimes Marina-Fish.

'You *remember* that?' Marina asked in surprise.

'Of course.'

'In the *office?*' Marina asked.

'We were friends, Marina. My first husband Fernando and I used to meet up with your parents.'

'Oh yes, I think I've come across a photo of you in a

restaurant with them,' Marina said – and immediately regretted it.

'In fact,' Mati said, 'she's brought along a photo of you that you might remember! Looking very glamorous.'

That was it. She could say, no, I forgot to bring it, or she had to get it out right now. She said nothing. Mati – smiling and enjoying this, because she hadn't explained how much this meant, when she really should have done – picked up her bag and passed it to her.

She opened it up. Dug around, her heart beating hard. So hard, it was going to be impossible to speak. She could either shrug her shoulders, implying she'd forgotten it, or make her trembly fingers get it out of the envelope and pass it to Francisca opposite her. But Mati had made sure she remembered to put it in there; she had no choice.

She pulled it out of the envelope – but even as she did so, there was an intake of breath from Francisca. A hesitation. Marina's heart thudded. *It was her.*

Francisca was staring at the photo, forcing a smile. No, not forcing, just smiling sadly, for some reason. 'So, you found this among his photos, here? In that cupboard?'

'Yes. Although in its own envelope, not with the others.'

Francisca continued to stare down at the photo, no longer smiling.

'Perhaps because he'd been *given* it. It's not from the same Polaroid camera as the other ones.'

She was aware of Mati looking at her and then his aunt and back again.

'Yes, I gave it to him. It's a very special beach,' Francisca managed.

Mati reached over and took the photo from his aunt. 'And the beach Marina nearly killed herself trying to reach yesterday.'

Francisca turned to Marina. 'What? Is this true? Because—'

Marina's heart thudded hard. 'I wanted to read the initials of the two lovers on the rock. I... want to know if you're the woman who was in the other boat!' she blurted out.

'What *other* boat?' Mati asked.

Francisca was breathing hard, but she put a hand on Marina's arm. 'Yes, my dear, I was there. Your father and I saw each other as I was coming along in my boat, and I stopped to chat to him. And if I hadn't, he would never have fallen in when going back to his boat, and would be with us today. Or... if I'd realised how bad his injury was, ignored him telling me he was completely fine, I could have taken him to hospital and maybe he would have survived. There, now you know. I don't know if you can—'

'But—' Mati tried to interrupt.

'No.' Marina's heart was tapping away; it was *her*, the woman she'd blamed all these years, but who had clearly also blamed herself.

'You mustn't think that. You couldn't have saved him. He died *minutes* after you'd gone – and maybe... he liked having those last minutes with just me.'

Francisca was reaching for a handkerchief, wiping her eyes.

'And... he told me not to tell anybody about you being there.'

Francisca nodded slowly again, not surprised by this.

Mati had put his arm round Marina.

'Because... you were in love with him,' Marina said, trying to keep her voice steady.

'Theo wouldn't have said that.'

'Maybe not, but why else...' She needed to hear Francisca admit it.

'Okay, I'm going to have tell you everything, my dear. Something I probably should have done a long time ago,' Francisca said, then sighed and took a big breath. 'I loved your father – but no more than everyone did. The whole village. We were friends... close ones, for a short while, because we shared a secret – and pain. And this is what we were sharing when he came aboard my boat that day. The initials on the rock... wait.' She got up and went inside, they could hear a drawer opening, and then another. The drawers being shoved closed. She came back out on to the terrace and sat down next to Marina again with a photo. 'This is in slightly better condition. You can see the initials more clearly. I imagine you thought they were your father's and mine. But as you can see, they are FC and AM. Fernando Caballero, my first husband, and... your mother. I'm so sorry, I'm sure you don't want to hear this.'

'*Mum?* With your...' She felt furious on Dad's behalf. 'She didn't even speak Spanish! Poor Dad – how could she do that to him? And to you?'

'Fernando spoke some English. Used it in the rental agency. And to be fair to her, she wasn't the first to be charmed by his looks and intensity. I remember Theo telling me she'd struggled with the change in her life that his new career had brought about. Don't be too hard on her, Marina. People make mistakes. In fact, she was already realising that, we felt, so we'd decided to not say anything, let it pass. I was already considering a divorce anyway.'

'Which… is why he told me not to say anything, because…'

'Well, I suppose if you'd said he'd gone aboard my boat to talk to me, your mother might have thought we'd found out about her. Typical of your father – even as he was dying, he was thinking of other people's feelings.' She handed her a tissue.

Marina nodded. 'I've never told anyone, not even Polly, until now.'

Mati drew her close. 'That's amazing, Marina.'

She wiped her eyes and thought of her mother – all those years of guilt and wondering if Daddy knew. She breathed out heavily. 'I won't tell Mum that I know. Dad wouldn't want that. It would hurt her dreadfully. And it wouldn't turn back time to stop the accident happening.'

'Ah, that's Theo's Marinita!' Francisca said.

Mati squeezed her. 'So much her father's daughter!' She sank into his hug, her head against the pale blue T-shirt, and somehow heard her father singing along with 'You're My Number One', the way she did when she was dancing about after they set off… and then the tears came. 'I've waited so long to understand. Thought I might never…'

Francisca took her arm. 'And I'm so happy we've done this – because of course, that's why I wanted you to come over today. It was time. Look, how about you and I enjoy some of that coconut ice cream neither of us could quite manage earlier? Maybe with a shot of brandy to go with it?'

Marina nodded wordlessly, stroking Blanquita, who for once had bypassed Mati and come to her.

'And for me too,' Mati said. 'I knew there was something wrong. God, how terrible for you both,' Mati said.

'And poor Diego, having to leave before I got the courage to say anything,' Francisca said. 'Right. Ice cream and brandy coming up.'

21

'Another one of us on *La Mari*, and... here he is on the terrace,' Marina said, passing the photos to Mati. They were sitting on her bedroom's terrace after breakfast, while the other two had gone down to the beach for a swim.

'*Ay*... the house in its best days!' He held up one of her father in a sun lounger, smiling as he kept still for a butterfly that had landed on his chest. 'You look so alike, it's uncanny.'

'Mostly I've been avoiding looking at him or talking about him. There was always this doubt about whether he was actually the person I thought he was.'

'It must be such a relief – even if you now know about what your mother was doing. You were closer to your father, weren't you?'

'Oh yes. I adored him.'

'And now you can adore his memory, and apart from your poor old shoulder, start to heal.'

'Yes. Polly and my mum have been trying to persuade me to see a counsellor for years – but all I needed was the truth.' She looked at her watch. 'Speaking of healing, what time are we setting off to visit my turtle?'

'As soon as they get back – and we've done the breakfast things. Come on.'

Mati washed up the plates, and Marina dried them and put things away.

'I'm so impressed with the way your father made such a bold decision to change his life – even though it would, initially anyway, disappoint his parents.'

'Yes. It certainly didn't disappoint me and Ted – we saw so much more of him, once he was working at the lifeboat station just minutes from our house, and he was suddenly so much more… lively. Smiley and fun. Perhaps we should all live our lives as if we only have a few more years left in the world.'

Mati nodded his head slowly. 'Yes. We should.' He stopped and dried his hands. 'Look, I've got a couple of emails I need to send off, if the Wi-Fi's behaving itself. Can I leave you to finish this?'

They turned off the Almería coastal road into a low-key seaside village on a pebble-and-sand beach. For late morning in August, it was very quiet; apart from a couple of what looked like bed-and-breakfast places, tourism seemed to have passed this place by.

'The centre is here?' Marina asked.

'Yes!' Mati said, reaching the end of the seafront road and pulling into a wide gravelled drive in front of a freshly painted pale blue one-storey building. It seemed to have been extended to one side with a windowless aircraft hangar type building, on which the rescue team's turtle design logo smiled down at them.

'Wow, looks fabulous now,' Yasiel said. 'Last time we came, it wasn't much more than a converted failed hotel with a covered water tank!'

Juanjo behind her tapped her shoulder. 'You're very privileged. Mati seldom brings visitors!'

Mati jumped as his phone pinged loudly. 'Oh. Wait a minute.' He took it out of his pocket and looked at it with a frown.

'Problem?' Marina asked.

'Ha. Yes, and... *no*.'

Another ping.

'Uh. I bet it's work,' Yasiel said. 'Tell them to sod off. You're on holiday, for heaven's sake.'

'Yes,' Juanjo joined in. 'We've got an important turtle to visit; surely these veterinary researcher bods can understand that?'

Mati half-smiled and tapped out a reply. 'Right, let's go and see her.'

It was like any little hospital, with a receptionist and aproned staff, except their uniform was a blue T-shirt with the turtle logo – and the beds, when they went through to the large 'ward', were a couple of large tanks and several smaller ones.

'Where is she? Where is she?' Marina asked, excitedly.

Mati's phone rang, but he silenced it, took her arm and led her over to one of the two big tanks. There she was, with 'Mari' as well as a number written on her back. Swimming strongly just under the water, with *both* wing-like flippers, round the pool.

'Oh!' Marina exclaimed.

She seemed to see Mati and swim over to him. Then she

raised her head out of the water, fixed him with her wide-apart googly eyes, and let out an impressively loud and long burp.

They all burst out laughing, along with the volunteer woman observing little turtles in a tank nearby.

'Not very ladylike!' Yasiel said.

Mati was scratching Mari's shelled back.

'Can she feel that, then?' Marina asked.

'Yes, like you can feel through your nails. They like it.'

Then Mari poked her head out of the water right by Marina, as if checking her out. 'Oh, how beautiful you are!' Marina said. 'And like a little wise old woman.'

'She's exactly that – sea turtles are one of the oldest creatures on earth,' Mati said. 'They haven't changed much in 110 million years.'

'So they were around when there were dinosaurs?' Juanjo asked. 'Wow. They must be doing something right!'

'It's humans not doing things right,' Mati said. 'They've put six of the seven species of these wonderful creatures on either the endangered or threatened lists.'

'Stay away from fishing lines, Mari, okay?' Marina said to the turtle.

'She's lucky. Another turtle with a strangulated flipper like hers had to have it amputated – and now lives in the Roquetas aquarium.'

'But you should go and see her, Mati. She seems very happy there!' said the volunteer woman – Sara, according to her badge – as she threw small fish into the next tank and watched its occupants.

'I know, I keep meaning to,' Mati said.

'Is it far? Maybe we could go today,' Yasiel suggested.

'About half an hour?'

Marina and Juanjo said they were up for it too.

Marina managed to tear her gaze away from Mari and looked into the next tank. 'Babies! Where did they come from?' she asked Sara.

'They hatched on a beach in Mojácar, about an hour up the coast. We're expecting more soon! We'll return them there when they're bigger, to give them the best chance of survival.'

Marina watched with delight as the five little turtles swam around. 'Could Mari have babies one day?'

Sara smiled and nodded.

'She's young, so yes, maybe!' Mati said and put an arm round Marina and squeezed her.

After visiting the turtles in the other tanks and hearing their stories – one who'd had tumours removed, one who'd been hit by a boat, two who'd mistaken floating plastic for jellyfish – Mati had a chat with Sara about Mari's release arrangements while Marina, Juanjo and Yasiel went off to find the donations box and then waited for Mati by the car.

Stopping to answer his phone as he came out, Mati clicked his key to open the car doors for them. Marina, standing nearest to him, could hear a loud but measured woman's voice on the phone. Whoever it was, she didn't seem to be giving Mati much of a chance to answer. Perhaps it was a co-worker about his research. Perhaps it was his ex-girlfriend, the beautifully named Sofía Suárez Alonso she'd seen on one of the research papers, alongside Mati's and his father's names. Her heart sank at the thought the call might not be entirely work-related... but maybe Sofía was just annoyed that he was extending his stay here, not getting back in time for a meeting or something. Or maybe it wasn't her at all.

Mati finally got into the car, looking a little shaken.

Marina wanted to ask again if everything was okay, but not if these messages were something personal between him and his ex. She felt a knot in her stomach and imagined how much worse she would feel if she was having a romantic relationship with him. Although, even though they hadn't made love, it suddenly occurred to her that they somehow *were* having that, whether she'd decided to or not.

'Are you still up for the aquarium, or d'you have to get back to sort out work?' Juanjo asked. Yasiel pointed out they could always promise themselves to go next year.

'*No*,' Mati said, rather emphatically. 'I'm up for some fishes.' He drove off, and they were soon back on the Almería road, driving along the seafront, passing the port, and then diving into the mountain tunnel that Marina had gone through to reach Aguadulce. They came out the other side, and after a few minutes she could see the big marina beneath them as the road clung to the mountain.

'Aguadulce! How appalled the instructor would be if he knew about my Guardia Civil rescue, second time out with the boat,' she said.

'It's like horse riding; we need to get you back in the saddle, so you don't lose your nerve,' Mati said. 'Just pay attention to the weather—'

'I know, I know. Don't worry, I'll now not be taking a boat out for a while unless the sea is totally *flat*.'

Juanjo behind her patted her shoulder. 'Come on now, stop giving yourself a bad time about that. Put some music on, Marina.'

'Okay.' She connected her phone to the music player. 'What do we want?'

'Play us your favourite song of all time,' Mati said, rather seriously.

'Oh God, I don't know...' She flicked through the songs on her phone. 'Ah yes. What d'you all think of this? Don't ask me what the words mean, I don't understand, even in English. Just seems to be about... having the courage to go with the flow.'

On came the Tedeschi Trucks Band's bluesy 'Midnight in Harlem', with the soulful female singer and her husband's soaring guitar solo.

The three other listened in silence and then demanded three more plays, they loved it so much.

'Okay, I've completely got the courage to go with the flow now, *for life!*' Yasiel said. 'Wow, what a song.'

They turned inland and let the satnav take them to a large modern building with 'Aquarium' written in huge turquoise letters under a logo suggesting a shark.

They parked and went in, Yasiel excited about sharks, Juanjo hoping for a good look at a lionfish. It wasn't busy in the aquarium, perhaps because most people were underwater themselves looking at fish, or enjoying eating them for lunch. Mati was strangely quiet, and so distracted that he didn't complain when Marina bought his ticket.

They wandered through the tanks, Juanjo delighted with the beautiful but lethally spiny lionfish, and Yasiel videoing the dangerous bull shark and reassuring Marina that she wouldn't see one in the Mediterranean. Next, she and Juanjo were taken with a ray pressing its angel-faced underbelly right up against the glass. Marina turned to see

Mati's reaction, but he'd wandered off to a dark corner, head bent over his phone again.

'Mati? We'll see you at the turtle tank,' Yasiel said.

'Juanita' the one-flippered turtle seemed in good form, swimming around happily in a large tank with lots of big fish for company.

'But... shouldn't she be with her own type?' Marina said. 'Dreadful that an accident like that has led to a solitary life.'

'Presumably she wouldn't survive in the sea. Anyway, it says here that they're solitary creatures,' Juanjo said. 'It's always difficult to not see things from a human point of view.' He took out his phone and filmed Juanita's face coming up to the glass, accompanied by rapturous greetings from Marina, and seemed to send it off to someone.

'Let me guess, you're sending that to May,' Yasiel said.

May, the lovely half-Thai girl they'd met on Cala Turquesa – apparently she'd been on the San José beach yesterday when the two boys went canoeing.

'Might be!' Juanjo said.

'Where's Mati? This is ridiculous,' Yasiel said. 'Ah, here he comes.'

Mati appeared from the gloom, and put a hand on the glass and smiled, watching Juanita for a few minutes without saying anything. In this low lighting, it was hard to judge his mood, but he was certainly not his usual chatty and dominant self. What on earth was going on?

Eventually he turned and said something about how he should get the two boys back swimming again on their last day. They made their way to the exit, looking at tanks they'd enjoyed, or fish they might have missed.

'Ooh, it's Dory from *Finding Nemo!*' Marina said, as they walked past a tank full of luminously bright blue and yellow surgeonfish. 'Lovely, and... are these kissing gourami?' She was looking at two fish with pronounced lips locked together.

'Yes. But they're not kissing, they're actually having an aggressive battle.' Mati's serious voice, behind her.

Good grief, could he not lighten up? She turned to catch his expression, possibly now ask him what the hell the matter was, but something in her own expression seemed to soften his face into a smile... and make him put his arm round her and briefly kiss her cheek.

'Have you enjoyed it?' he asked.

She nodded and smiled. She would have enjoyed it more if he'd been able to do so properly.

They walked out into the shock of the blazing sun, grabbing sunglasses from pockets. In the car, they discussed where to eat, eventually stopping at a seaside *chiringuito* beach restaurant in Almería. Masses of seafood was ordered – the ravenous Yasiel and Juanjo insisting on treating Mati and Marina, thanking them for driving them around and sharing a house respectively, but their guests seemed to be struggling to eat.

On the way back in the car, and particularly in the boat, Yasiel and Juanjo were talking about where they would snorkel for the last time that year. Mati joined in the discussion and seemed to be planning to go with them. Walking up from the boat, Juanjo asked Marina if she was coming too, but just as she was considering this – feeling weary with tension – Mati received yet another call and told the caller he would do a Zoom chat in twenty minutes. Then he surprised her by saying she looked like she needed a siesta.

The boys changed into their trunks, exchanged some words with Mati on the terrace that made them give him a congratulatory slap on the back, then went off down to the beach. After a drink and seeing Mati take yet another call, Marina went to her bed and lay down to try and take the suggested siesta. But all she could do was lie there completely still, trying to overhear – and understand – Mati's rapid and alternately irritated and patient Spanish. Then she heard him say the name Sofi, as if pleading with her about something. Sofi. Sofía. Sofía Suárez Alonso. So maybe she was the woman who called at the aquarium too. In fact, all the messages or emails pinging his phone might have been from her. Her heart thudded with misery.

Then something else occurred to her. Maybe he'd suggested the siesta to keep her up here so he could talk to her, tell her that he was sorry, in case she was thinking of changing her mind about being more than friends with him, because he was now getting back with his girlfriend. She listened some more – and although she couldn't make out what he was saying, the tone of his voice now sounded calm and warm... Then there was silence. She waited for him to come through, but he seemed to have stopped in the living room, where he sounded like he was moving things around. He dropped something and swore. Scraped a chair on the tiles. There was the twanging fanfare of his Mac starting up. Of course, he had the Zoom call to make. Probably doing it in the living room rather than his bedroom for a better chance with the Wi-Fi.

The Zoom started – with Mati and the other two people

all talking at once. A low but more gravelly male voice then spoke in measured terms, followed by an older woman saying something about listening to his father. *His parents.* Perhaps encouraging him to get back with Sofía – she thought she heard Mati mention her name to them…

Marina didn't want to hear it. This wasn't her business. She put the pillow over her head and stuck a finger in her ear. A tear pooled in her eye and ran down her cheek into the pillow. And another. After some minutes, she took her finger out, heard the conversation sounding calmer, and put it back in again. Maybe she should have put some music on, to assure him that she wasn't eavesdropping, but what would she have chosen? Her jolly reggae playlist, as if everything was cool with her; or a random selection, that was just sure to come out with 'Me Maten', as if what was going on was killing her, or worse, a now overconfident 'Leave the Door Open' or 'Kiss Me More'?

She un-pressed her ear. The call had stopped. He sounded like he was going back to his room… but was now opening the fridge and closing it with a whump. She put the pillow back over her face.

'Marina?'

Oh God. 'Mm?' she said, trying to sound sleepy.

He came in. 'What? You can't have slept through all that!' He was smiling. Well, why shouldn't he be? He wasn't cross with her, just needed to let her down gently from… something she'd said she didn't want. He came over and sat down on the bed, a hand going through the mad hair. 'I've got some news.'

She put the pillow behind her, pushed back the sheet and hitched herself up to hear it, her heart tapping.

'I'm sorry I've been such a pain this afternoon, but it's taken a bit of sorting out. Or at least, the reactions have.'

'What's going on?' she asked.

'I've handed in my notice at the university. I've decided to live down here, find work as a vet, get involved with the loggerhead sea turtle research they're doing at Almería university, even if only as a volunteer, and of course join the turtle rescue team.'

Marina felt fit to burst with relief. 'Mati! That's amazing! Good for you!' She leant forward and patted him on the back.

'Unfortunately, not everyone shares your enthusiasm for the idea. My parents are shocked and angry – and earlier today decided to set Sofía on me like a Rottweiler, thinking she could win me round. They also rang Francisca and gave her a bad time, as if she'd kidnapped me! Anyway, hopefully I've calmed everyone down – for the time being at least. And I'm giving six rather than the usual three months' notice; neither the students nor my current research project will suffer. But my parents… uh, I don't know how long it will take them to forgive this. You know what? I keep thinking of your father. I can almost hear him saying "stick with it, it's your life"!'

'Yes! That's exactly what he'd say! He never regretted it, and I'm sure you won't either. I know Yasiel and Juanjo will be so pleased for you; they've both said they didn't think you were happy, despite all your success there. Apparently you need regular injections of San José to keep you going.'

'Exactly! But now I'll *live* here,' he said, beaming. 'And…' He put a hand to his face, then put it down again. 'If you're wanting to visit San José during the year, and I'm here…

well, us being together wouldn't be a holiday romance, would it? That would be... the milk.'

'The *what?* Oh!' The Spanish phrase for 'icing on the cake'. 'Mati! In the end... I've realised today that... I haven't been able to *choose*. I already feel like your girlfriend, I can't help it!'

His mouth opened in shock.

'Oh...' Her heart thudded. 'I thought that's what you meant by—'

'Well of *course* it is!' he said, laughing and moving up the bed. 'It's just I wasn't sure you...' He put his arms round her – rather awkwardly, because at the same moment, she'd swung her legs to the floor to move towards him. They bumped heads and laughed.

The boys came into the house, chatting and calling out 'hello!'

Marina and Mati hugged and came out of the bedroom.

'Oh...' Yasiel said, putting a hand to his mouth. 'Hope we haven't interrupted anything!'

'No, but we should tell you...' Marina couldn't think how to say it in Spanish. 'We're now a thing! We're going to be a thing!'

'A thing, a thing, best thing ever!' Mati said laughing, while the boys whooped, and cheered.

'And thank you, Marina, for finally helping us persuade Mati to leave the uni and come and live down here!' Yasiel said.

'What?' She realised Mati must have told them just before they went down to the beach. 'I didn't say anything, just told him my father's story!' Marina said.

'Exactly, and then he spent all that time helping both

you and your turtle with your trauma and arm injuries and falling for you both!' Juanjo said.

'It's true, I must admit,' Mati said. 'They were the final push I needed.'

Marina shook her head in disbelief. 'So what about this last night for you two then? What shall we do?'

'Well, with so much to celebrate, there's only one thing…' Yasiel said.

'Music!' Juanjo rapped out a rhythm on his *cajón* drum. 'Then pizzas from the beach.'

'With that film you brought with you that we didn't get round to?' Marina asked. She liked the idea of cuddling up with Mati on the sofa with what sounded like a heart-warming animated film about music.

They all agreed, opened a bottle of wine and fetched their instruments. They worked out a version of Marina's 'Midnight in Harlem', then took it in turn to choose their favourites, Marina having to sing both Doja Cat's and Zsa's vocals when Mati chose 'Kiss Me More'. They ended with '10 Years', as next summer was going to be the tenth year of the three friends coming here together – and they were sure it was going to be wonderful, wherever they ended up staying.

22

She must have fallen asleep in Mati's arms during the final credits of the film; she vaguely remembered him helping her to bed, kissing her cheek and leaving. Not the passionate first night he might have expected! But there seemed to be an unspoken understanding that they would wait until they were alone together, rather than creep about trying not to wake Yasiel and Juanjo.

Today, they *would* be alone together, she thought, with a mixture of nerves and longing. After a big brunch, she and Mati would take the boys to the airport, and come back here, just the two of them – until everyone arrived for Mari's release early this evening.

Showered and in her short tasselled turquoise dress with her bikini underneath, she went through to the kitchen. The usual argument about whose mother's recipe made the best tortilla had today been won by Juanjo, busy preparing one, while Yasiel and Mati put slices of fine ham, avocados and the delicious local tomatoes onto plates. She started toasting the baguettes.

Ewan arrived, bringing almond and apricot pastries and homemade *chirimoya* custard apple ice cream he'd traded with Nina.

'G'morning, Ewan. My God, what a feast!' Marina said.

He gave Marina a kiss on each cheek. 'I gather you and Mati are finally together – about time! I'm afraid the whole cove probably knows by now, after Yasiel and Juanjo's early swim and coffee with Vivi and Edu in the bar!'

'Ha! Most of them already knew – even before we did!' Mati said, squeezing Marina and giving her a kiss.

'I'm leaving you to tell Polly yourself,' Ewan said, 'although make it soon, as I'm hopeless with secrets!'

'Okay!'

The five of them sat down to their huge breakfast and reminisced about Marina and Polly's awkward first arrival, the boys' surprise to find that the girls they'd thought a bit uptight turned out to be such assets for their little band, and Ewan and Polly's first encounter on the beach.

Then it was time for the boys to go, and even though Marina was looking forward to time alone with Mati, she was sad to be helping Yasiel and Juanjo check the house for forgotten belongings and to be going to have to say goodbye to them. 'Maybe don't leave it a whole year this time,' she suggested.

'Absolutely,' Juanjo said. 'Maybe we'll come out for a long weekend once Mati's settled here.'

'We'll probably see him *more*; he was always too busy at the university!' Yasiel said.

Mati nodded his head. 'It's true.'

They went off down to the boat, Ewan and most of the *turquitos* waving goodbye.

The sea was calm and crystal blue, and there was hardly a breath of wind; it was the cruellest day to go.

'Oh... I don't want to leave the sea,' Yasiel said, as they got off the boat in San José. 'Maybe Almería needs an extra accountant.'

'You're lucky,' Juanjo said, 'not much chance of them needing an extra psychologist here, when the quality of life is so good!'

'You two say this every year,' Mati said. 'Just come down more often!'

Mati and Marina were sitting in a café on the way back from the airport so Mati could answer some more 'aftershock' emails.

'How are your parents this morning?' she asked.

'Apologetic. But that doesn't mean they aren't going to carry on trying to dissuade me, after a lull in the storm.'

'Oh no. And what about your head of department?'

'Ah. I don't think I properly explained: my father *is* my head of department.'

'*Jesus*, Mati. No, I didn't realise. Okay, you tap away, and I'll chat with Polly on here,' Marina said, getting out her phone.

After a few minutes, he put his phone away. 'Okay. That's it. There's nothing more to be said to any of these people now, so I've put Out of Office on!' He put his hand on hers.

His phone pinged again, but this time he looked at it and smiled as he tapped out a quick reply.

She looked at him quizzically.

'Little surprise.'

'What?'

'You'll see.'

They set off again, Marina trying to think what it could be.

When they arrived at the port, Carla was waiting for them. 'All yours, you two! But she's back to work at ten tomorrow, I'm afraid.'

'*La Mari!*' Marina exclaimed, admiring the boat, gleaming in the sunshine. 'But aren't you coming to the Turtle Release, Carla?'

'Of course, that's why I blocked out the seven o'clock tour!' Carla replied. 'But I'm going with some friends, don't worry.'

'Oh... thank you so much!' Marina said, giving her Spanish kisses.

'Here you are, Mati, and no – put your wallet away!' She handed him a zipped carrier bag.

'What's that?' Marina said.

'A-ha!' he said.

Mati kissed Carla goodbye and they got on board and set off.

'What do we do with the bag?' Marina persisted, thinking it was something for this evening's turtle party.

'Use what is in it!' he said, going into English. 'Carla has put some towels and bought some drinks, so we don't have to go to the house before our little *excursión!*' Mati said. 'Put the drinks in the cooler, *cariño.*'

She opened the bag. 'There's a bit more than that – bread, crisps, grapes, biscuits... What's this... ooh yum, carrot cake! That's lunch, I'd say. Ha – and some sun cream. How kind of her!'

'Oh, she is fantastic. Before about six we need to help

Ewan and the others tidy the beach and get ready for Mari's release. But until then, we live on *La Mari!*'

'Brilliant! So where shall we go? We haven't yet gone round the point the other side of Cala Turquesa.'

'I know – we must do that. You can choose one of the little beaches for a swim.'

'Okay!'

'Come here,' he said, pulling her up from her seat and putting an arm round her. 'My Marinita! D'you want to drive?'

'Maybe on the way back,' she said, enjoying the closeness.

They were crossing Cala Turquesa now, waving back to Ewan and his friend Lala at the jewellery stall, Dani in the floaty cloth shop, and Nina and Bernardo in the sea. The other side of the cove had a cliff with rocks around the bottom, but round the point there seemed to be a row of tiny sand and pebble beaches, divided by smooth lunar rocks.

'Ooh, different again.'

'Which one do you like?'

'Er... that one... no, another couple are enjoying it... This narrow one! Cosy, very private. It's perfect.'

'And the hardest mooring! Never mind, we can anchor out a bit and swim in.' He turned the boat, switched off the engine, and threw the anchor, dealt with the rope – all in that fluid way he had of handling the boat as if it were part of him.

Then he came back to her, looked her up and down and felt her shoulders. 'Hot. Where's that sun cream?'

She went down into the cabin, where she'd seen him take the bag. It was different to last time. The V of the two single beds had been converted to make a double bed for Carla's seasick sailors – or newly together friends who might…

Mati came down the steps, taking off his T-shirt to swim. 'What are you… Ah.' He looked at the bed, scratched his chin and looked over at her with a smile.

'It used to be quite comfy,' Marina said, getting on to the bed, flopping down on it and sitting up again. 'And still is.'

He got on next to her. 'Aren't you baking in this?' he said. He helped her take off her little dress.

She was wearing her bright blue bikini with white flamenco spots, he was in his bright blue trunks with the white cord. 'Oh look, we match,' she whispered, feeling a bit awkward.

'Of course,' he said with a smile, then cupped her face in his hands and kissed her. He helped her lie down again and moved those sensitive hands down the contours of her body, melting away any nerves, and it was soon easy, delicious and beautiful to give in to the passion they felt for each other, making love with an openness and intensity she'd never known before.

They dropped into the sea and he cuddled her in the water, both looking back up at *La Mari*.

'We had to have the first time in *La Mari*,' Mati said. 'There will be new memories in her now!'

'First *several* times, you mean!'

'But you would never know it. What a perfect – how you say before? – "thing" we have,' he said, laughing.

'Don't tease me; *you* try talking about this in another language!'

'Yes, okay, let me think… What a perfect mating pair we are!'

'Er…' Marina laughed. 'Sounds a bit veterinary! But also kind of… *yes*,' she said, pressing herself against him.

'I never think of *mating* before,' he said, still in English. 'Is what you do to me.'

They looked at each other.

'Maybe one day…' she said quietly.

'I'm *sure* one day, I feel it.'

'God, what are we saying?' she said, laughing, even though she'd had a few daydreams about a big-eyed toddler with a mop of dark curls.

They swam to the tiny sand beach and sat on it, letting the gentle waves break over their legs. 'This is such heaven. We must do this again,' she said.

'Although we won't usually have *La Mari*. So we'd have to…' He looked over. 'Make love behind that rock, look!'

'Ha! Perfect.' They kissed and both soon glanced back at the little private sandy space. 'But I think next time I'd pass out!' Marina said, whirling a finger round near her head in case he didn't understand.

'We forgot the picnic!' he said. 'Come on.'

They swam back to the boat, ravenously hungry all of a sudden, and finished the entire bag. Then they pulled up anchor and made their way back to Cala Turquesa to get ready for Mari's return to the sea.

Marina put a hand above her eyes and peered out at the flotilla of boats coming into the cove. 'My God, it's like the…'

'Armada?' Mati said with a laugh. 'They are invading our beach! But only because they love turtles – and the rescue team needs lots of *donaciones*.'

'I know, I'll do my best!' she said, swinging her blue EQUIPO TRM bucket.

They looked over the cove. They were standing in the cordoned-off part near the end of the beach, where the shelving into the water was steeper and best for Mari's entry. The rest of the beach was temporarily transformed by the expansion of Vivi and Edu's bar-café to three times the size by adding extra tables and shade; an impressive display of turtle jewellery by Ewan and Lala; a bakery stand put up by Barnardo, with Nina's delicious cakes and pastries; and a turtle theme going on in the floaty cloth shop – all of them donating fifty per cent of their sales to the turtle rescue organisation. Then there was the Equipo RTM tent with its turtle books, postcards, fridge magnets and cuddly toys, as well as information leaflets. Marina looked at her watch. 'About three-quarters of an hour until the arrival of the star of the show!'

'Isn't that a boat of the English coming in now?'

They kissed, clunked buckets and set off – Mati towards a large RIB skippered by his uncle delivering his aunt and what looked like an entire boat of their friends, Marina towards the two fishing boats of English people she'd met at the bar and their families. Fishermen Raúl and Ramón – who hopefully hadn't decided to recount her irresponsible boating accident – gave her a big smile and congratulations on 'her' turtle.

Shefali translated for a curious little Zara.

'She's *your* turtle?' Zara asked, wide-eyed.

'No! I just found her. But the turtle rescue team did name her after me – how cool is that?'

'Oh wow! I can't wait to see her!'

'The *tortugas* are a miracle... but we won't see her for long; she will want her sea home,' said a Spanish boy next to her in remarkably good English. Then he translated what he'd said to a cherub-like little Spanish girl next to him.

'You'll have to tell us the best place to stand. These three are so excited. Well, as are we!' Shefali said, indicating her husband and a smiling petite blonde friend patting the little boy's back. 'This is my old pal Andie, by the way – without whom we'd never have discovered San José!'

'Hi!' Andie said. '*Love* your turquoise turtle top! Where? Where can I get one?' she asked, laughing.

'The floaty cloth shop over there. Have fun! And yes, Shefali, best place would be that end of the cordon,' she said, pointing.

'Aha, we'll put ourselves there then,' Mónica said, as she and her artist boyfriend were taking photos for the local paper.

'See you all later! Oh... sorry, been told to shake this bucket at everyone!'

They laughed and all put money in.

Vivi and Edu's place started filling the air with the CD of 'Mari release' songs Marina and Mati had put together. First up was Marina's proud contribution of Elvis Costello's 'She' – which even had mention of being inside a shell! Marina couldn't help singing along and imagined Polly there joining in, maybe offering a turtle-saving yoga class... Somebody else was joining in, though. She turned and saw it was the Spanish-looking expat Juliana.

'I adore this song!' Juliana said. 'How perfect – will it be played as Mari walks into the sea? It would be like a film!'

'Well, that's the idea, if our friends in the bar can get the timing right!'

'Hi, Marina!' English teacher Kim said, holding her little boy, who already had one of the cuddly turtles under his arm. She lowered her voice and patted Marina's arm. 'Ewan just told me about you and Mati!'

'Yes. God, it's only been a day, and news travels fast, for an isolated cove!'

'Bring him along to the expat group. Spanish boyfriends have honorary membership!' Jen said.

'*If* you can get them to come,' Andie said, with a laugh.

'Well, exactly. I'm not hopeful, to be honest, but you never know!' Marina said. 'Right, better mingle with my bucket.'

More money clunked in.

'Are there are any more buckets? We could help,' said Ben the gardener, with the smiling red-haired girlfriend again.

'I don't think so. But you could become members,' Marina said, pointing him towards the rescue team's tent.

She walked on down the beach, smiling hopefully at everyone and, filling her bucket well, made her way to the tent to empty it. Mati was there talking to Edu, maybe reminding him about the 'She' song, but also, she now saw, he was chatting with Francisca, her assistant at the agency, Carla and – of all people – Agustín.

She went over to them and kissed everybody hello.

'Diego's gone off to get another boat load; anyone licensed to drive a boat is in demand right now!' Francisca said. 'Never seen such a crowd! So, are you proud of your turtle?'

'Well of course! And we have lovely music for her send-off… just hope she doesn't ruin the magic by doing one of her big burps in the middle of it!' Marina said.

They all laughed.

'Didn't know you were a turtle fan, Agustín!' Marina said.

'What? Who isn't? I've just been telling Mati and a couple of his rescue team friends about the turtle-friendly external lighting the new houses will have. Long wavelength, shielded and low in height – so as not to distract any hatchlings Mari or another turtle might want to come back and give us.'

'Oh yes, I remember you said you were looking into that. *Brilliant.*'

'Volver', about returning, had just finished, and another suggestion of hers was now playing: 'You'll be in My Heart' from the *Tarzan* film. She now rather regretted it, as it reminded her of the boat CD she and her father had had – but then, the song would now have a new memory attached to it, so maybe it wasn't a bad thing. She looked over at *La Mari*, anchored quite far out to allow room for all the other boats, and had a feeling her father was enjoying the song and everything about the evening.

'She's coming!' one of the volunteer girls in the tent called out. They looked out and saw the large RIB with what looked like four or five people in the team's T-shirts surrounding the star of the show.

Mati took her arm. 'Come on, let's get over there!'

They made their way to the cordoned-off area, Mati

putting Marina right by the water for the best view, and then crossing into the area with a couple of volunteers to help with the boat. Soon everybody was crowded round behind the cordons, and the boat came right up to the beach. It took the four people on board, as well as Mati and three others on the beach, to lift Mari in her stretcher onto the sand, a few metres from the water – much to the delight of the crowd. They untied the protective restraints and all stood back.

Mari stood there a moment, stunned. The volunteers were talking to her. Then just as 'She' started playing, she lifted up her head and started lumbering with four limbs in turn towards the sea, the crowd cheering and clapping. Mati and the others followed her into the water – where she suddenly became a strong, beautiful swimmer and then, with one last poking up of her head above the water, swam off out of sight.

With perfect timing, the sweet 'Remember Me' duet from the film they'd watched last night came on and was maybe too much for Sara and the other volunteers – and Mati and Marina – who were already teary-eyed.

The happy crowd stood staring out to sea or made their way to the refreshments or the stalls to celebrate.

Marina got through the barrier to join Mati.

'Tell me she'll be all right and won't hurt herself again!' Marina said, as he took her in his arms.

He smiled and nodded. 'Isn't she wonderful? So healthy and strong now, couldn't wait to get out there and live her next adventure. Yes, I think she'll be fine!'

23

Five years later

Mum opened the door and gave her a hug. 'Marina! Come in, come in.'

Marina looked around the beautiful Victorian Brighton seafront flat – which looked twice the size, now Mum and Guido had bought the flat above the gallery to use for art storage and Mum's studio. 'Oh wow, it's like a new apartment!'

'And look at the spare bedroom,' Guido said, coming through from the Italian-cooking-smelling kitchen with his apron on. He opened a door to a room that now had a double bed, a little sofa with a couple of teddies, and a wooden train set on the table – not a wrapped-up picture or a painting pot in sight. 'Yours whenever you like.'

'It's *lovely*. What did Ted and Hannah think?'

'They thoroughly approved, and Georgie loved his little sofa bed. Come and sit down.'

She followed Mum through to the living room and sank

down into a new sofa, Guido putting a sparkling apple juice in front of her and disappearing back to the kitchen.

Mum put a hand on hers. 'How are you doing, darling?'

Marina nodded slowly. 'I'm... over the worst, I think.'

'Oh good. Thank heavens for that.' She shook her head and then smiled. 'Especially as it would be good to have your appetite back today. Guido has made his new ricotta and pear ravioli, with his usual amazing tomato sauce of course... and your best blue birthday cake ever.'

'Oh... bless him, especially when you're so busy. Yup, I think I'll manage both of those!'

'And how's it going with Polly and Ewan in Shoreham... and their little Ruby?'

'Wonderful,' Marina said. 'So... have you bought your flights yet?'

Mum bit her lip. Marina waited for her to say she'd changed her mind, they didn't have time, they needed to visit Guido's family in Tuscany... but she nodded. 'We have.'

Marina leant over and gave her a hug. 'Oh fantastic! *The 15th of September?*'

'The 15th of September.'

'Two weeks?'

'Two weeks.'

Finally. After twenty-five years. Marina had to hold back tears. 'You're going to *love* it, Mum. I'm sure you'll find Cala Turquesa more beautiful than ever – and a lot more comfortable and convenient!'

'I'm sure. But... well, you know... it's difficult. Even now.'

She took her mum's hand. 'It doesn't have to be. And Dad will... would love the thought of you coming back.'

'So you've said. But...' She hesitated, looking down

at the rug. 'There are things you... probably wouldn't understand.'

'No, Mum. I *do* understand. And I'm telling you... it's really all okay.'

Mum looked up at her, eyes wide.

Marina nodded slowly and smiled.

Guido called out from the kitchen. 'Okay, I need my salad chef!'

Mum gave Marina a watery smile and went through to help him.

How did that just happen? It seemed she'd somehow just reassured Mum without breaking her promise to Daddy – something she'd never thought possible.

Marina found Ewan and Ruby playing with a Playmobil boat and camping site set by the paddling pool. The two of them looked up as she came in, with identical slightly toothy smiles and fair hair. Ruby's surprisingly English colouring was an unexpected delight for anglophile Polly – in addition to the little girl seeming to have inherited her father's arty sensitivity.

'Can you *be* the boat in my game, Marina?' Ruby asked. 'It needs packing... with yellow things,' she said, her little fingers picking out a life jacket and some tiny camping cups and putting them in Marina's hand. 'But Daddy says we need to pack the *boat* in the suitcase.'

'Well, I tell you what, how about me being the boat but we let Daddy go and pack everything else, first?'

After some thought, Ruby agreed to this, and Ewan hauled his long limbs up and went inside.

After several packings and unpacking of Ruby's boat, Polly could be heard coming back from her yoga class, shouting '*Olé!* Holiday time! Marina?' She came out and found them. 'Hello, you two!' she said, giving Ruby a squeeze. 'How did it go?' she asked Marina.

'They've bought their flights!'

'*Dios mío, finalmente!* That's *great*. Wow.'

'I know.'

'And how are you today?' Polly asked, looking at her carefully.

'Not too bad. Oh, and there's some pieces of blue birthday cake in the fridge.'

'Oh well done. Might have a piece now and then finish my packing, if you're okay getting some boating practice in! Then one of us'll come down and let you get on with your own packing.'

Juanjo was waiting for them in a car just outside the entrance to the airport. 'Hello! Hello!' He gave them all a kiss and helped them get their bags inside. 'Warm enough for you?'

Polly was fanning her face. '*Madre mía*, get us to that turquoise sea, quick!'

They took the coastal road, the blue of the sea always a renewed shock after the grey-green English Channel in Shoreham. Marina was weary, leaving the others to talk about the new young *turquitos* living in Ewan's old cave-hut, Polly's yoga, and the fishing trip Ewan was going to come on with Juanjo and Yasiel.

'Are you okay, Marina?' Juanjo asked.

'Yes, I'm fine,' she said, smiling into the rear-view mirror. 'And congratulations! So happy for you.' After years of platonic friendship with May, which kept looking like it might become something more, May had fallen in love with her new yoga teacher, and set up a blind date for Juanjo with her culinary genius sister Chariya. Both couples were now getting married in the autumn.

They came into San José, and then along what always felt like a miraculously repaired mountain road to the top of the cove. She looked down on the four new houses sitting snug among their *palmitos*, bougainvillea and rocks, with just the odd glint of glass in the sunlight. They were beautiful, and a couple of years of their calm presiding over Cala Turquesa had already nearly erased the memory of the unavoidable disruption of the building work on the *turquitos'* quiet way of life, and her anxiety about whether she'd done the right thing.

Juanjo parked up at Casa Agave, just a short way up from the new Casa Palmito. Polly, Ewan and Ruby got out, saying they'd be over soon. Yasiel and his wife Isa had probably already unpacked at their house and made their way to Casa Palmito, which, from force of habit after too many years, even though barely recognisable as the same place, was always where the friends hung out.

Yasiel, Isa and Juanjo's fiancée Chariya were having an early evening drink on the terrace and got up to give Marina a kiss, Yasiel holding her by the shoulders and telling her she looked good and would be fine. Juanjo fetched her a drink.

'Oh it's lovely to be here!' Marina said. 'But where's—'

Her phone rang. 'Marina! Where are you?'

'Casa Palmito! Where are *you*?'

'I'm sorry, I had a call for a small turtle on Mónsul beach, took him to the centre, and then when I was coming back to San José I suddenly wanted to arrive at Cala Turquesa by boat, like the old days!' he said, in excited Spanish. 'Just leaving home now. Yasiel already picked up our beach stuff. I've got some clothes for you – oh, and I've not forgotten your mini keyboard!'

She smiled. Mati with his usual turtle, sea and music priorities – not that she wasn't the same. 'Great! Enjoy the ride – sea looks gorgeous. Love you.'

'Love you too, my Marinita. It's been a long week without you. See you soon!'

Polly, Ewan and little Ruby had turned up and joined them at the table. None of them were surprised when she told them what Mati was doing. Yasiel said they'd just heard that, as well as the two campsite gigs, they were going to have a spot in a concert in the amphitheatre up the hill on the far side of San José.

'Ooh, that's a lovely place!' Marina said.

'And, Polly, I've already fixed up babysitting by Nina and Bernardo for Ruby,' Yasiel said.

'Good!' Little Ruby said, maybe remembering Nina's baking from last year.

Marina's phone rang again. Mati, whispering her name.

'You all right?' she asked him.

'Get down here quick, all of you!' Mati said, sounding breathless. 'The turtles are hatching! The eggs we'd given up on! But remember, turn out all the lights, no phones, quiet, and keep low, join me behind Edu's boat.'

'Oh my God! Okay!'

'You're not going to believe this!' She told the others

what he'd said. They walked quickly and quietly – even little Ruby – to the beach, then crouched down low to reach the boat. Mati was there, wide-eyed with excitement, wearing the old pale blue T-shirt.

They exchanged a wave and a tap on the heart with Lala, Vivi, Edu and the new *turquito* couple hiding behind the floaty cloth place. There, in the pinkish fading light, were the little turtles, eight of them, flipping their little limbs along the sand to get to the sea. One had them worried for a few minutes, seeming to go off to one side... but no, the setting sun over the water drew him seawards, and he followed the others.

They all felt like they were holding their breath. Ruby whispered that she wanted one but seemed to understand Mati's explanation of the pull of their sea world. All eight turtles finally entered the water and, following Mati's lead, they moved slowly towards the sea to get their last sight of them. Marina was happy but watery-eyed, just like when Mari had launched herself into the unknown.

'Could they be Mari's?' she whispered to Mati.

'It's possible.' He put an arm round her and a hand on her tummy. 'And how's our little hatchling? Has he stopped throwing your breakfast out yet?'

The others were tearfully thanking Mati for getting them down here. Then they started moving back up the beach, leaving Mati and Marina alone, knowing they'd missed each other.

'Almost. He's now doing more swimming practice.'

'Ha – his father's and grandfather's boy! Look, I know we were going to wait until he arrived to decide, but... now we know he's a boy, there's only one name to give him.'

She looked at him. She'd thought the same. 'Theo... but it's Teodoro in Spanish, isn't it?'

'Yes. So... Teo. Sometimes Teito!'

Both still looking out to sea, they spotted a wave of a little flipper, as if the name had been approved.

Locations In *The Spanish Cove*

Cala Turquesa and its *turquitos* are fictional, but they were very much inspired by the cove and free-living inhabitants of Cala San Pedro near Las Negras, half an hour up the coast from the village of San José where I live.

'San Rafael', as anyone who's been to the Cabo de Gata-Níjar Natural Park in Almería will quickly realise, is the old gold mining village of Rodalquilar. I changed the name for this series so that I could add a few amenities for Juliana's convenience in *The Spanish House*, and also because I couldn't bear the thought of the name, so beautiful in Spanish, being read as 'Roddle-quiller'!

All the other villages and towns exist as described in the story. Come and see for yourself!

About the Author

CHERRY RADFORD was a piano teacher at the Royal Ballet Junior School, a keyboard player in a band, and a research optometrist at London's Moorfields Eye Hospital before finally becoming an author. She writes uplifting novels about identity, renewal and romance, and, having been raised by a half-Spanish mother, her love of Spain and Spanish culture comes through in all her novels. *The Spanish House*, *The Spanish Garden* and *The Spanish Cove* are three novels set in the starkly beautiful Cabo de Gata Natural Park region of coastal Andalusia, where she now lives.

Book Club Discussion Questions –

The Spanish Cove

1. Marina

Marina starts the story as a young woman damaged by her father's death, afraid of deep water, *'not in a hurry for Faithless Number Five'*, and really just seeking peace and quiet. And yet, soon after returning to where her father died, she feels she can hear his voice saying *'you loved an adventure. You were never a wimp.'* Can you think of other characters in films or novels who were healed by revisiting somewhere they experienced trauma? How does her learning the truth about her father's last day affect her feelings about entering into a relationship with Mati?

2. The House

'"You think I don't have any feelings about the house?" Marina said. "All my best childhood memories are here." But also, all my worst ones.'

Marina has conflicting feelings about the house, but knows she needs to sell it; for Mati the house is a uniquely restorative annual retreat with his friends that he doesn't want to lose; Agustín sees an exciting environment-friendly development opportunity. How much did you sympathise with each of their differing viewpoints?

3. La Mari, the Boat
'There she was, that same cheeky 'nose', the stripe that Marina used to think of as like a hairband, the boxy little cabin, the little waves clapping around her as if she couldn't wait to get out.'

After all these years, and what happened aboard, Marina is still in love with *La Mari*. Can you understand this feeling? Perhaps she associates the boat with the happy times she shared with her father, or because this is where she feels her father's spirit. Can you think of other examples, in fiction or in real life, where an inanimate object becomes so important to someone? (One comes to me: the episode of Modern Love Season 2, where Minnie Driver's character can't let go of her deceased lover's troublesome old Triumph Stag convertible).

4. Mati
'For Mati, this place is his sanctuary. The place where he remembers who he is, draws energy.'

It takes a while for Marina to get to know the stubborn but kind Mati. Would you have liked to have had his point of view in the story?

5. San José: Living in the Novel Setting
I live in this area, with the cove on which Cala Turquesa and its *'turquitos'* is based just half an hour or so away. Did

you feel immersed in this unusual setting, and how much did you feel it contributed to the story?

6. More or Less?
Who – or what – would you like to have seen more (or less) of in the novel?

7. The Ending
Were you happy with the ending? If not, what would you have liked to have happened?

8. Spotify Music Playlist
'The opening drums of S Club 7's You're my Number One fill the air. "Yes!" She's up and dancing to it, soon singing at the top of her voice. This song is about Daddy, La Mari the boat, this hottest lowest edge of Spain, everything'.

Music is so important in my stories. I enjoy putting a Spotify list together so that readers can listen to the tracks during the chapters in which they occur. Do you think all novels should have one?

9. Who Would Play the Film Roles?
If *The Spanish Cove* became a film, who could you imagine playing the roles? Perhaps Jude Law would take a cameo role as Marina's tragic father, Theo?

10. Return for More!
Which minor characters from *The Spanish House* and/ or *The Spanish Garden* did you enjoy seeing again? Who would you like to see appearing in future novels set in this unspoilt corner of Almería? Sign up to the website for news!

Acknowledgements

The idea for The Spanish Cove came to me after a rocky cove clambering adventure with my wonderful next-door neighbours María José Martín and Paulino Espigares – and a re-visit of Cala San Pedro further up the coast. This paradise of white sand, turquoise water and (unusual in semi-desert Almería) green vegetation is home to the last hippie settlement in Spain. My first thanks has to go to this self-sufficient peaceful community, who tolerate boatloads of beach lovers during the Summer – last year often including an inquisitive novelist.

Research also included getting myself at the helm of a boat, so I also want to thank José, my Federación Andaluza de Motonáutica instructor, for his patience with all my Spanish sorry-could-you-say-that-agains during my navigation licence course.

A big thank you to my wonderful editor Martina Arzu, cover designer Leah Jacobs-Gordon, copyeditor Helena Newton and all the team at Aria Fiction (Head of Zeus) for turning my story into a beautiful book.

Many, many thanks as always to my super awesome literary agent / guardian angel Kiran Kataria (Keane Kataria

Literary Agency), for her invaluable input and patient guidance.

Thank you to the fellow writers who have so generously supported me, and the friends and family who've cheered and generally put up with it all – including my sons Jack and Robin, who have finally started reading my novels! As ever, a special thanks to Phil for all the encouragement and sound-boarding.

Last but not least, I can't forget my half-Spanish mother's part in the inspiration for these stories. She would have loved them.

Website and blog:	www.cherryradford.com
Twitter:	@CherryRad
Instagram:	@cherry_radford
Facebook:	www.facebook.com/cherry.radford